Paradox
Larry LaVoie

Paradox

Disclaimer

This book is a work of fiction. Names, characters, places, events and incidents are products of the author's imagination, or are used fictionally. Any resemblance to actual events or locales or persons living or dead is entirely coincidental.

Acknowledgments

This book could not have happened without the help of my wife Anna who is the first to read my work and for her encouragement, inspiration and critique of the manuscript. I am truly grateful for my editor Sharon Shafa, a continuous believer in my work, and for her constructive suggestions and attention to detail.

Useful Terms

Geosynchronous orbit: An area of space approximately 22,500 miles above the earth's surface where communication satellites orbit at the same rate of speed as a given point on the earth's surface giving them a fixed position above the earth.

Low earth orbit or LEO: An area of space commonly occupied by most satellites approximately 200 to 350 miles above the earth's surface. It is the area where the International Space Station orbits, along with thousands of scientific and spy satellites and the area where most space weapons would be deployed.

High Altitude: An area in the upper atmosphere of the earth approximately 15 miles above the earth's surface.

High Altitude Platform or HAP: A lighter than air device that performs the same function as a satellite, but at a much lower altitude.

Deep Space: Any area well beyond the atmosphere of earth and beyond the typical orbits of manmade objects.

Chapter 1

US Air Force Academy, Colorado Springs

It wasn't the first time General Cramer had addressed the graduates from the Air Force Academy, but this time he was apprehensive, uncertain of his message. He studied the sea of young faces seated in front of him, wondering if they would be up for the challenge unwinding before them like a ball of rubber bands, each thin strand ready to snap back and change the course of history.

The graduates were a special breed, highly trained to fight a battle, not in the conventional sense, but in front of a computer screen using weapons not even imagined a decade before. To them war mimicked a computer game, not the reality of shock and awe he had witnessed not long after his graduation.

He remembered how young and naive he had been on that day, and now twenty-five years later, he must tell them something to prepare them for what they were about to face. He had written a speech, but it didn't seem appropriate to fill the young minds with hope, when the future looked so bleak. He needed to tell them the truth.

"*All war is based on deception,*" General Cramer began. He looked into the eyes of a disinterested young woman sitting in the front row and imagined she just wanted this to be over. He cleared his throat and took a sip of water.

"*All war is based on deception,*" he repeated. "Those words were uttered by Sun Tzu, a fifth-century BC Chinese general. His words are as true today as they were twenty-five hundred years ago. He also said, 'The greatest victory is the one that requires no battle.'

"I'm sure you would be more comfortable if I told you how great you are and that you have a big world out there and you need to take advantage of the opportunities it offers, but there are plenty of others who will build you up, if that is what you seek. I am going to tell you the truth. You will likely be going to war.

"The next war will not be fought with guns and bullets. It will not be fought with tanks, warships, jet fighters or bombers. It will not be fought on the ground or the sea... it will be fought in space and using cyber weapons, satellites, and deception. To be more precise, there will likely be battles where lives are lost and planes and ships and missiles are the method of destruction. Sadly, this is true, but right now the greatest threat to our Nation is circling above us in space." He looked up at the clear blue sky as a cool breeze ruffled his hair.

"Today's world extends twenty-two-thousand miles beyond earth where nations of the world operate in a vast wilderness where there are no boundaries, and only thin sheets of paper in the form of treaties prevent any nation from deploying weapons.

"At this moment, we are engaged in another Cold War of sorts, each nation threatened by the mutual destruction of the other should any of them be foolish enough to orbit weapons in space. The first nation to do so would be a threat to all other nations."

He glanced at the young woman again. She appeared to be paying attention. *Good.* Her Country would be depending on her.

"You, our fighters for freedom, are charged with the enormous challenge of keeping the world safe, here on the ground, and in the heaven above. It is a grave responsibility, but one I believe you are prepared for." He stared off in the distance thinking; *soon you will know what I have told you is only half true. A war in space is not only likely, but inevitable.*

His eyes fixed on the young faces again. "Congratulations to each and every one of you. Keep us safe."

*****

Waldport, Oregon, June

Scott Tanner gazed out over the Pacific Ocean from his home office window. It had been an unusually rainy winter, even for Oregon, and he smiled at the reflection of the morning sun on the wet beach, promising a beautiful late-spring day. He spread a maritime map on a table and considered where he might begin the hunt for a Japanese submarine thought to have been sunk in the early days of WWII. His cell phone buzzed and danced on the edge of his desk. He considered not answering it. He had promised his crew a new underwater site to explore by the first of June and he had still not pinpointed a location to search. The phone continued to ring. He checked the caller ID and answered.

"Hi, Mom, I'm surprised you're up this early." He heard nothing. "Mom, are you okay?"

"Your father is dead."

"Mom, where are you? I'll be right there. What happened?"

"Scott, this is Susan." Susan, Scott's younger sister by three years on his mom's phone hammered home the reality of his mom's statement.

"Susan, thank God you're with her. What happened?" Scott grabbed a jacket and headed out the door. He climbed into his Jeep holding his phone to his ear. The drive to Hillsboro, a small town outside of Portland, normally took three hours.

"I don't know much," Susan said. "I talked to his boss and he said it was a heart attack. He went into work early. Mom said he was fine when he left."

"Stay with Mom. It's going to take me about three hours. I'll get there as fast as I can."

Scott's training had given him the ability to compartmentalize stressful events, but he couldn't escape the winding road through the Oregon Coast Range, and it threatened his patience. Foul weather settled in the passes in the form of a heavy fog accompanied by an off and on again drizzle.

There were few places to pass, and he cursed as traffic backed up behind a truck. He pounded the wheel as he approached one of the few straight stretches where he might pass, but seven cars in front of him told him an attempt would be suicidal. He took a deep breath and tried to relax. About ten miles behind he had lost cell contact with his sister. Through the mountains, maintaining a continuous phone conversation was impossible, but he considered trying to call back. He decided to wait.

A heart attack, he thought. His father at 62 had always been in good shape. A heart attack was the last thing he thought his father would die from, although he couldn't remember considering his death. His own death had come up a number of times in his service as a Navy SEAL, but his father's? Never.

Deep inside Scott hoped the news wasn't true, that his father's death had been a terrible mistake like it had been two years earlier. They didn't find out he survived until after the funeral. At that time they had been so grateful with the news he was alive that they didn't question how North Star Industries could have screwed up and misidentified him. But he also knew they wouldn't make such a colossal mistake again.

Just last week he had asked his father about retirement, but as Chief Engineer for North Star Industries, he had promised the company he would complete the latest project, and that would take another three years.

He remembered last Thanksgiving; his father had completed a physical and proudly announced to the family that the doctor had given him a clean bill of health and a thousand dollar bill for the examination.

How could he die without warning? He tried to think. His grandfather on his father's side still lived independently on a farm in Illinois. He had to be in his upper-eighties. *I wonder if Susan called him,* he thought. He had three uncles all older than his father and all were in excellent health. Heart attacks had never been part of the family history.

As he drove through farm country, vineyards blanketed the rolling hills with vibrant green of new spring growth reminding him how much the country had changed. His parents had moved from the country right after he entered Annapolis. Hillsboro was their home, not his.

Finally, the modern two story house in an upper-middle class neighborhood came into view. *So different from the tiny ranch style home I knew as a child,* he thought.

Cars lined the street and filled the driveway. He parked on the street nearly a block away. As he entered through the front door he saw many faces he didn't recognize. He spotted his mother across the room. Her puffy eyes and red nose told him she had been crying. She looked as if she had aged ten years since he had seen her the week before. "Mom, are you sure you want all these people here?" Scott asked, approaching her.

"They were friends of your father's." Her lips curled. "I needed a distraction." The response wasn't like his mother. She had been the quiet reserved supporting wife. He knew she would rather be with family than surrounded by his father's golfing buddies. *What's going on?* he thought, trying to understand.

He hugged his mother and whispered in her ear. "If you want, I'll send these people home."

She sniffled. "I don't know many of them. Your father was always the outgoing one in the family. They wanted to pay their respects."

"This isn't the time for it," Scott said.

"Scott, promise me you won't make a scene. They will be gone soon enough."

"I promise. I'm going to talk to Susan. Can I get you anything?"

"Go find Susan. I'll be fine."

Scott approached Susan in the center of a small group of men who introduced themselves as co-workers of their father. "Nice to meet you," Scott said, grabbing his sister's arm. "I hope you don't mind, but I need to speak with my sister." She followed him into the kitchen.

"I can't wrap my head around this. Dad dies and on the same day the house is packed with well-wishers? What's up with that?"

"Dad had a lot of friends. I called them and they just started dropping by. I wasn't going to send them away."

"I'm sorry. It's not your fault, but I would like to have some quiet time with you and Mom." He got a glass from the cupboard and filled it with water. "Maybe it's too early to talk about this, but we have to make funeral arrangements. I'm not sure Mom is up for that."

"His boss told us not to worry about it; he said North Star would handle everything. That's him over there." She pointed to a tall man in an expensive suit hovering close to their mother.

"I'm going to talk to him," Scott said. "Do you know his name?"

"He said he was VP of Research. Roger Wilkes, I think."

"What else can you tell me about what happened?"

Susan looked at him and whimpered, "I don't know anything. He's gone."

He held her until she stopped crying. "Okay, I'm going to find out what Wilkes can tell me."

Wilkes had a fading hairline with more gray than brown hair and was the same height as Scott. From his gestures, Scott didn't like the man. He appeared overly aggressive in his mannerisms. Even though the weather was cloudy, he was wearing sunglasses; the wire rimmed kind that were dark enough you couldn't see his eyes. *I'll bet you're not crying. What are you hiding?* Scott thought as he interrupted the man in midsentence. "Mom, may I interrupt. Mr. Wilkes. I'm Scott Tanner, Ty's son." They shook hands. "Could we talk for a minute… alone?"

"Sure," Wilkes said to Scott before turning back to Mrs. Tanner. "Again, if there is anything I can do …"

Scott directed Wilkes to the patio through a pair of sliding glass doors. It was a large cement slab covered by a deck that extended from a room on an upper level.

"My sister said you were with my father when he died."

Wilkes cleared his throat. "No, I got there shortly after he collapsed. One of the employees who knew CPR was with him, but by the time the ambulance arrived he had passed."

"What was he working on?" Scott asked.

"I'm sure Ty told you everything we do at North Star is Defense related and classified."

"Yeah, he told me that. I was just wondering if he was under a lot of stress. He had just had a physical and the doctor said he was in good health."

"I'm afraid I can't help you, there," Wilkes said. "Your father and I were not that close."

"Really? I understand you offered to handle the funeral arrangements."

"I thought it was the least we could do. Your father had worked for us for fifteen years and was a key employee."

"Where is his body?" Scott asked.

"Mason's Funeral Home. He will be cremated on Friday."

"Cremated?" Scott narrowed his eyes. "I'm pretty sure Dad would have wanted a conventional burial."

"Oh, there will be a casket and burial."

"Then why cremate him?"

"It was a request he made on his company insurance policy."

Scott thought that was odd. Why would a vice president at his dad's firm know what he had requested on an insurance policy, even if it was a company policy? He let it slide for now. There might be a good explanation. He decided to set his doubt aside and ask his mom when they were alone. "I'm assuming there will be an autopsy. He was a healthy man and died suddenly."

"Autopsy?" Wilkes shook his head. "The medical examiner said it was pretty clear what happened. He didn't see any need for an autopsy. I brought it up with your mother and she agreed not to have an autopsy performed."

The hair on the back of his Scott's neck stood on end as it sometimes did when he sensed something was wrong. He remembered his mother's request, not to make a scene and bit his tongue.

"Thanks, Mr. Wilkes." Scott shook his hand again and walked back in the house. From the corner of his eye he saw

Wilkes answer his cell phone and stop outside the door. Scott was already in the house and didn't catch if Wilkes had dialed a number or just answered a call. Either way, Wilkes appeared upset. Scott stood and waited until Wilkes came back through the sliding doors.

"I'm sorry," he said to Scott. "Something's come up and I have to leave. Can you express my sincere apologies and heartfelt sympathy to your mother?"

"Sure," Scott said. "Mr. Wilkes, before you go. Did my father have any personal items at the company? I'd be glad to come by and pick them up."

"We'll be taking care of that. I'll have one of your Ty's engineers clean out his desk and drop off any of his personal items." He turned toward the front door. "I'm sorry, I really do have to go."

Scott stood watching Wilkes climb into a shiny red Mercedes SLK sports car. He turned when he heard his sister come up beside him.

"What was that all about?" Susan asked. "He seemed upset."

"I don't trust him," Scott said. "Did you know Dad requested to be cremated?"

"No way," Susan said. "Dad told me he was going to be buried on the family plot next to mother."

"Family plot?"

"You know. Being a devout Catholic, he and mom bought a plot at Our Lady of Sorrows Hillside Cemetery in Forest Grove."

Scott had forgotten his parents both had bought plots shortly after his grandmother had passed away. "I'm going to ask Mom if she agreed to cremation. Also, there isn't going to be an autopsy. Why would she agree to that? Without one, we will never know what really killed him."

"Scott, don't get so worked up. I was here when Mr. Wilkes brought up an autopsy. I'm sure mother didn't want them to cut him up."

"You were here? I can't believe you agreed to that."

"Autopsies are gruesome. I didn't want them to mutilate Dad's body."

"But it's okay to burn him up? I don't follow the logic. Still, wouldn't you like to know for sure what killed him? I would like to know if there is a chance we will suffer the same fate in twenty or thirty years. Dad was in pretty good shape and there isn't a history of heart attacks in the family."

"I didn't think of that."

"How did the subject come up, anyway? Did Wilkes bring it up?"

"He just said there was no need for one. Mom and I agreed."

"Well, I don't agree."

"Please give Mom some time to process this before you ask her if you can cut up Dad's body." Both of them turned back to the front door as it opened. Patricia Westland, Scott's fiancée entered. She dabbed a Kleenex to her reddened eyes.

Patricia wrapped her arms around Scott and hugged him. "Scott, I got here as soon as I could." She hugged Susan. "You poor dear. I can't imagine how hard this is." She turned back to Scott and took his hand. "Do you mind coming with me when I talk to June. I never know what to say in these situations. I'm sure she's devastated."

That evening Scott and Patricia made an excuse to get away. They left his mother with Susan, her husband Jim, and seven-year-old daughter Jenifer. They drove to The Rally, a local sports bar. The Oregon Ducks were playing baseball on one of the overhead screens.

"I'm beat," Scott said. "None of this makes sense. I feel like I'm in the middle of a nightmare."

"I know," Patricia said, "but you can't control everything in life. Some things you just have to accept."

"This advice coming from a reporter who can't walk away from a story even if it could get her killed. You remember the time you were kidnapped by terrorists while covering the Crater Lake disaster."

She gave him a smirk. "I have to get back to the station tonight. I'm sorry I don't have a lot of time."

Scott knew when it came to work, almost everything else took a back seat for Patricia. Covering the news was a brutal business. He hoped someday she would give it up, leave the big city, and join him for a more laid-back life on the Oregon Coast. She wouldn't admit it, but it was one of the reasons they had delayed the wedding.

He ordered a side of chicken wings and a Scotch on the rocks. Even with all the donated food he hadn't thought to eat, and now he was famished. Patricia ordered a glass of White Zinfandel. They sat in a corner of the bar away from a rowdy crowd cheering another baseball game, this one between the Cubs and Yankees.

"What do you know about North Star Industries?" Scott asked, unable to put his doubts about Roger Wilkes aside.

Patricia was a news reporter for KPDX, a Portland based TV station. He was sure she had access to a lot of information that wasn't generally in the public domain.

"It's a huge company and makes all of its money from various branches of the military. It's privately owned, so there are no public records on their finances. It's rumored their projects are all "black", meaning highly classified. Why?"

"I'm not sure," Scott said. "My dad's boss seemed awfully anxious to control everything about my father's death and his things."

"What do you mean?"

Scott took a sip of his drink and swirled the ice around in the glass with his finger.

"He said Dad wanted to be cremated. The company is making all the funeral arrangements. Don't you think that's kind of odd?"

"Well, he did die at work. Maybe they thought it was the right thing to do."

"Mom and Susan say they don't want an autopsy. Wilkes doesn't want one either. I think there is a reason for that."

"Scott." Patricia put her hand in Scott's. His hands were cold. "Your mother told me the medical examiner listed it as a heart attack. Maybe you should let it go."

"I know," Scott said, downing the rest of his drink. "She asked me to go to the funeral home and sign off on the identity of the body. I would like to have an autopsy done. Do you think I can do that if Mom doesn't want one?"

"Probably not. Scott, if there wasn't any suspicion of foul play, why would you want an autopsy? Why don't you leave it? Right now your mother is pretty upset. She doesn't need any more grief."

"That's what Susan said. I don't want to go behind Mom's back. I've got to bring it up with her."

"Scott, I know how you can be when you set your mind to something. Please be sensitive to her wishes."

Scott changed the subject. "Can you do a little digging and see if you can find out what my dad was working on at North Star? I asked Roger Wilkes and he told me it was classified."

"There isn't much I can do. It's a private company and none of their records are public."

"You must have news accounts of things that have happened at North Star through the years. Nothing is that secret these days? I don't know what I'm expecting to find. I just feel uneasy. Something about this doesn't feel right."

Patricia agreed to search the archives and see if there was anything at North Star that had made the news. She dropped Scott off at his mother's house and drove back to Portland. She would barely make the studio in time to air the eleven o'clock news.

"Breakfast is ready," Susan said knocking on Scott's bedroom door. Scott rolled over and checked the clock next to the bed. It was 0800 hours. He couldn't remember the last time he had slept in that late. From his time at Annapolis, he had always been an early riser.

"Be right down," he yelled.

"Pancakes, your favorite," Susan said, putting a plate with a stack of four in front of him.

"That was when I was twelve," Scott said. "I'm more into low carb, now. Does Mom have any sugar-free syrup?"

"I pity Patricia when you get married," Susan said, searching the refrigerator for the syrup. She plopped a bottle in front of him. "Don't get too used to being waited on. I need to go back home."

"How are you feeling this morning, Mom?" he asked turning to his mother. In spite of the way she had looked the day before, today she had returned to the woman he remembered. His mother had aged well. In her late fifties, her face was wrinkle free and her skin clear. The bags under her eyes from the day before had disappeared. He imagined it was due to her rigorous workout routine in their home gymnasium. She had her natural blond hair pulled back and held in place with a sweat band. She looked much younger than her age in the red sweatshirt and matching pants and sneakers.

"I'm still numb," she said. "I don't think it's hit me yet." Her lower lip started to quiver.

Scott poured sugar-free syrup on his pancakes and set the bottle back on the table. "You look like you already got your workout in," Scott said.

"An hour ago, Sleepyhead."

"You should have woken me. I would have joined you."

"I peeked in and you were snoring. I didn't want to disturb you. You must have needed the sleep."

Scott looked at Susan, who was sitting across from him. "Mom, when you agreed not to have an autopsy performed on Dad, weren't you concerned that something unusual could have caused his death?"

"Unusual, like what?'

"Oh, I don't know, maybe a congenital condition no one knew about. Murder?"

"Murder? Scott, don't talk like that. So many things happened yesterday. I can't even remember the subject of an autopsy came up."

"Mom, I would like to know for certain how he died," Scott said. "Suppose there was some kind of a hidden problem and Susan and I are genetically predisposed. Autopsies are important for a number of reasons."

"When Mr. Wilkes said he would handle everything, I might have left it up to him," she admitted. "Your father died of a heart attack. That's what I was told. Susan was there." She looked at her daughter.

"I guess we both went along with Mr. Wilkes. Neither of us was in any condition to be making those kinds of decisions so soon after finding—"

"Do you mind if I ask the coroner to do an autopsy?" Scott interrupted. "I just want to be certain it was a heart attack. You know there isn't a history of heart problems in the family. I just want to make certain that was what caused his death."

"Well if it would make you feel better. I guess you can have it done," his mother relented.

"What about cremation?" Scott asked. "Is that what Dad wanted?"

"Heavens, no! I told Mr. Wilkes your father wants to be buried in the Catholic Cemetery. I have a plot there, too. Why would he be cremated if he is going to be buried?"

Scott eyed his sister. "Don't worry, Mom. I'll take care of it."

Scott couldn't take care of it. When he got to the funeral home he was told by the director his father had already been cremated. North Star had already arranged for a casket and a military ceremony at the internment. Scott, feeling helpless, decided to drive into Portland and see if he could take Patricia to lunch. She had called telling him she had some information on North Star Industries.

Chapter 2

They were to meet at Jake's Crawfish House, an old establishment in the heart of downtown Portland, known for its seafood, microbrew beers, and spirits. As Scott waited at the bar for Patricia to show, he ordered Alaskan Pale, one of the many microbrews on tap, and stood at a high table near the rustic bar. Through the window, he observed the people going about their day, all of them seemingly in a hurry. It was not the first time he realized he had no desire to be a part of the hustle and bustle of the city. He had never lived in the big city, never worked for a large corporation, and had never desired to be part of the rat race. The closest he had ever come to the establishment was the Navy. Even there he had been selected for SEAL training and had become part of a small elite group of misfits who didn't seem to see the world like everybody else.

"I hope you haven't been waiting long," Patricia said, coming up to him from behind.

He hadn't seen her enter. Scott lifted his beer showing the glass still two-thirds full.

"Just got here. Every time I come to Portland, I'm reminded how much I enjoy the laid- back life at the beach."

"Then you won't like what I am going to ask," Patricia said, tiptoeing and kissing him on the cheek. "Do you mind if we eat in the bar? I've got to get back to work. I'm filling in on the five o'clock news and still doing the eleven o'clock broadcast."

"My point exactly," Scott said. He raised his hand for the waiter. "The pretty lady would like a glass of wine." He looked at Patricia. "And then we would like menus in here."

"Tualatin Vineyard Riesling," Patricia said. After the waiter had left she reached in her purse and pulled out a USB drive. "Before I forget; it's not much, but here's what I could find on North Star Industries." She handed it to him. "How'd it go at the funeral home?"

Scott took the flash drive and slipped it in his pocket. "I got there too late. They didn't waste any time putting the torch to him."

"I'm sorry, you make it sound so dreadful. People are cremated everyday, I don't think it's as bad as you make it sound."

Scott shrugged. "If I would have known they were going to act that quickly, I would have called instead of waiting to go there personally, but I doubt that would have changed anything."

"You sound bitter."

"Maybe… a little. I mean, what gives these people the right to stick their noses in family business?"

"You are referring to…?"

"North Star Industries. Why are they so bent on taking care of my father's burial?"

The waiter brought Patricia's wine and they ordered. "Crab Louis," Patricia said. "You should try it."

"I'll have a bowl of New England clam chowder," Scott said.

Patricia took a sip of wine and watched the waiter leave before turning back to Scott. "You want to tell me what you're so pissed about?" she asked.

"I thought I was. Did you find anything interesting on North Star?" he asked, changing the subject.

"That depends on what you call interesting. Mostly the usual stuff; an employee was killed in their parking lot in a work related dispute a year ago. Three years ago they underwent a huge expansion doubling the size of their plant. Stuff like that. I would say it was pretty routine boilerplate info. Finally I called North Star and their press person said he would leave some information for me with the guard at the gate. I picked it up this morning."

"You should have called. I was a lot closer. I could have picked it up."

"How do you think I found out you were at the funeral home? I wanted to talk to June anyway. She seemed much better today. She's a strong woman."

"Thanks for checking on her. I know how busy you are."

Patricia was busy as the anchor on the late evening news at KPDX. She had the weekends off, but since her promotion, their relationship had suffered. The death of his father had brought them together more than anything they had done in the past month.

"The funeral is on Friday. Eleven-hundred hours." He smiled. He knew she didn't like it when he used military time.

"I know. I've already taken the day off. You need to stay close to your mother. It will be a rough day for her."

"She's tough…probably tougher than I am. She worked out this morning. She'll make it."

Patricia touched his face and looked into his eyes. "You were a big help when my mother died. What can I do to help?"

"Honestly, I'm not sure. I'm just having a hard time accepting he's gone."

Scott returned to his mother's house and found her in his father's office sitting in a chair staring at a wall of books. "Hi, Mom. You're alone; where's Susan?"

"She went to the store for me. She'll be back shortly."

"I got to the funeral home too late. They already had him cremated. There will still be a casket, but there will not be a viewing."

"I thought you were supposed to identify him."

Scott shook his head. *It was just a formality. Someone from North Star signed the paper.* He pursed his lips. "What's done is done. We can't do anything about it now. The director told me there was going to be a military graveside service. Dad would have liked that."

His mother started crying.

"He was so young," she said, grabbing a box of Kleenex from the desk. "Look at all of this. He loved to spend time in here."

Scott looked around the room. A wall full of books, pictures of people he worked with, awards and trophies from a few company sponsored golf tournaments. Mostly the office was about his father's life at work. The room said he was an engineer and worked on important stuff without coming right out and verbalizing it. His father loved his work and North Star was his life.

Scott thought of his own office. He knew it would make just as loud a statement about his line of work. He loved the sea and discovering its buried mysteries had become his life.

Scott felt in his pocket and pulled out the flash drive. "Where's dad's computer? I have some information on North Star Patricia picked up for me."

His mother put her hands on the desk. "It has always been right here. Maybe he took it to work with him."

"Did he take it back and forth to work?"

"Never that I recall. I could swear it was here yesterday. I was in the office when Mr. Wilkes came by with the news." She started crying again.

"You were alone when he arrived?"

"Well, yeah. People didn't start arriving until Susan and I started calling."

"But you remember it being here when you called?"

"I used it to get a list of people. You know, email contacts. I didn't think it was right to send them an email." She looked at him curiously. "Scott, honey, what do you think happened to it?"

Susan poked her head in the doorway. She had a plastic bag of groceries in her hand. "Mom, you've been crying again. Come and keep me company while I clean up the kitchen." She looked at her brother. "Scott, you know she shouldn't be in here."

"Dad's laptop is missing. Did you take it?" Scott asked.

"No. I'm sure it was here yesterday. I remember, because I used it to send an email to Jim to let him know I wouldn't be home and he'd have to pick Jenifer up from school. I know he got the message. He called me back."

"Any chance you moved it?" He was looking at his mother.

She wiped her eyes and shook her head.

"Somebody took his computer," Scott said.

"It was right there," Susan said, pointing to the desk.

Scott and his mother sat at the kitchen bar while Susan moved dishes from the dishwasher to the cupboard.

"Do you have your computer with you?" Scott asked Susan, holding up the tiny drive. "Patricia gathered some information on North Star. I want to take a look at it."

"No, I didn't bring my computer. What kind of information?"

"I'm not sure, that's why I need a computer."

The doorbell rang. His mother started to get up. "I'll get it," Scott said.

Scott opened the door. A man about his age was standing there with a box. "I'm Gilbert Thompson," the man said. "I brought the things from Ty's desk. Are you his son?"

"Do you go by Gilbert or Gil?" Scott asked, reaching for the box.

"Gil," he said. "My kids tell me Gilbert sounds like a geek."

Scott took the box. "Come in. We were just having coffee."

"I really have to get back," Gil said, glancing over his shoulder.

"Nonsense," Scott said. "Rush hour has started. Good luck making your way back to Portland this time of day."

Gil glanced over his shoulder again. Scott looked at his car, a late model cherry-red Chrysler 300. The windows were tinted so he couldn't see if anyone was waiting inside. "Do you have someone with you?"

"No, I'm by myself."

"Then you're coming in," Scott said. "If you don't drink coffee, I have something stronger, or Coke or ice tea, if you prefer. I'm not taking no for an answer."

"I guess I could use a drink," Gil said, following Scott.

Scott carried the box into the kitchen.

"Gil, this is my mother, June, and my sister, Susan." He hefted the box. "Gil brought Dad's things from North Star."

"Gil, Ty mentioned you several times," June said. "He was

the one who hired you, if I recall,"

"Yes ma'am. I was devastated to hear what happened. I'm sorry for your loss."

Susan shook Gil's hand. "Can I get you something to drink?"

"Gil would like something stronger than coffee," Scott said. "You like Scotch or Bourbon?"

"Bourbon, will do," Gil said. "On the rocks."

"I think we all could use a good drink," Scott said. "Follow me to the bar."

The bar was a room above the garage that his father had made into a man cave. On the way he dropped the box on the desk in his father's office.

A 72-inch flat-screen TV dominated one wall of the room his dad had referred to as his man cave. Scott walked behind a completely stocked bar and opened a refrigerator filled with several makes of beer. He grabbed a container of ice from the freezer. Playing bartender, he lifted a bottle from a shelf on the wall. "Do you like Jack Daniels?"

"Who doesn't," Gil said. "Put a couple of rocks in it if you would." He took the glass from Scott and walked around the room, looking at several pictures on the wall. Scott poured a Scotch over ice and joined him. His sister opened a bottle of wine and poured a glass for June and another for herself. The women joined Gil and Scott who were looking at photos on the wall. The man cave was more comfortable than his father's office, displaying several pictures of the family when they were much younger.

"This is Dad and me," Scott said. "I was twelve. We were camping on Diamond Lake."

"I never saw your dad that way," Gil said. "I thought Ty was a city guy. He seemed intent on doing his job. A no nonsense boss, but a good one. I learned a lot from him."

"What were you working on?" Scott asked.

"I can't talk about the project," Gil said.

"Sorry," Scott said. "I didn't mean … Dad never talked about work either."

They finished their drinks and Scott poured another round. "Gil," Scott said. "Come down to Dad's office. He had a couple of pictures from work down there and I wonder if you might identify some of the people in them."

"Sure," Gil said. He followed Scott downstairs. He looked around the office and was attracted to the wall of books. Many were engineering related, some on metallurgy, some on aerospace history, and an entire shelf dedicated to patents and patent law. He pulled one of the patent books out and leafed through the pages.

"Your dad was always a visionary. He held several patents in the company name that I know of. Paradox..." He stopped abruptly.

"Paradox," Scott said. "He never mentioned any patents."

Gil looked nervous. "He wouldn't have. They were all classified; Black-box projects. You can't even look them up in the Patent Office."

"Really? I guess there were a lot of things I didn't know about my father."

Gil pursed his lips and nodded. "I really do need to get on the road. Tell your mother thanks for the hospitality. I'll see you at the funeral. Again, I'm sorry for your loss." He walked out the door and down the hall toward the front door.

"Thanks, Gil." Scott called, as Gil walked to his car. After closing the door he saw his mother and Susan coming down the stairs.

"Did he leave?" Susan asked. "He didn't even say goodbye."

"I must have upset him," Scott said. "He didn't finish his drink. He did ask me to say goodbye and he'll be at the funeral."

Later that evening, Scott went back into his father's office and started going through the box Gil had given him. He removed a faded color picture he remembered taking with the family the year he graduated from high school. He chuckled. *Did I ever look that goofy? Must have been a bad hair day.* There were several other photographs. Beneath the pictures, a calendar, a calculator, and several engineering text books, he found a laptop computer.

"Susan," he called. "Could you come in here?"

His mother came to the door. "Susan left ten minutes ago. What are you yelling about?"

"Is this the computer Dad had in his office?"

"It looks like it, but they all look the same to me."

He called Susan on his cell phone.

"Scott," Susan answered. "I'm still in the car, but you're on speaker."

"Was the computer in Dad's office a Mac?"

"Yeah. He had his name etched on the left side of the keyboard."

Scott opened it. He saw his dad's name where she said it would be. "I have his computer."

"Where did you find it?"

"It was in the box of dad's things Gil brought from North Star."

There was a long silence.

"Are you still there?"

"I'm looking for an off-ramp. I'm coming back. There's no way in hell that could be the same computer."

"Susan's coming back," Scott said to his mother.

"Oh dear," his mother said. "Is something wrong?"

"Let me see it," Susan said, entering the house.

"In the office," Scott called from his father's office.

Susan looked at the computer. She opened it and touched the name etched on the keyboard. She plugged in the charger and typed in her father's password when prompted. A screen came up. She remembered it, because it was one of her favorite places at the beach. Her father had used it as a screen saver. She opened the document file where she had saved the email she had sent to her husband. "It's not there! It's the same computer, but my email isn't there."

"Maybe Mom is right. All computers look alike," Scott said, now doubting his sister.

"How did it get in the box Gil brought back from North Star?" Susan asked, ignoring Scott's last comment.

"You tell me," Scott said.

Susan scanned all the document files. "They've been erased."

"How do you know?"

"He had a poem I wrote for him last Father's Day. It's gone with everything he's ever written."

"How do you know it's the same computer? He could have had two of them exactly alike."

"Somehow they got it," she said.

"A good computer nerd can recover the stuff they erased," Scott said. "If you are right, North Star stole it and found something they didn't want us to see."

"They were in a hurry," Susan said. "If I was going to delete files, I would search for the particular files and delete them individually. All the documents are gone." She punched a few keys. "I don't know that much about computers either, but I've watched enough TV to know you are correct, deleting them isn't enough to get rid of them completely."

"My partner is a computer nut," Scott said. "I'll call David and see if he can fly up here and take a look at it."

"I could try and run a recovery program and see if it brings anything back," Susan said, "but that's about the limit of my computer skills."

"Good luck with that," Scott said. "I did a recovery program on one of my computers and none of it came back."

Susan tried to reset the computer to an earlier date, but it kept showing an error message. She finally threw up her hands in frustration. "Whatever they did to it is beyond my expertise."

"I was going to use the computer to check this out," Scott said, holding up the flash drive Patricia had given to him. "Do you have time to look at it with me?"

"I really don't. I promised Jim and Jenifer I'd be home for dinner tonight."

"I'll see you tomorrow?"

"I'm sure it's the same computer," Susan said, as she left.

Scott speed dialed David Stafford. "Hi, Buddy. I need you in Portland."

"Anything wrong?"

"I need your computer skills. Can you fly up here?"

"You know I'm in San Diego."

"You were coming up for the funeral tomorrow, anyway. Why not leave tonight."

"Like right now, you want me up there?"

"I wouldn't ask if it wasn't important. Call me when you get in and I'll pick you up. You can stay in the guest room at my mom's."

"Okay. I'll call you, but I'm warning you, it's going to be late."

"That was it?" his mom asked. "He's going to drop everything and fly up here."

"He has his own jet," Scott said. "We've been through a lot together."

"He must be a good friend," his mother said. "How long have you been in business together and why have you never brought him around?"

"He's a busy man," Scott said. "What else can I say?"

She smiled. "I'll see you in the morning." She kissed him. "Don't stay up too late. You need to speak at the funeral."

Later that night Scott opened the laptop. He inserted the flash drive and clicked on the box that popped up. "Shit," he said. He frantically tapped on the keys, but it was too late. He watched every file with North Star in the title disappear. He was left with a message, 713 files deleted.

"David's going to love this," he said. He finished his drink and went to bed.

*****

The Netherlands, International Court of Justice

The International Court of Justice, commonly referred to as the World Court, resides in the Peace Palace in The Hague, the Netherlands. The fifteen judges elected for nine–year terms are elected by the UN Security Council and no two judges are allowed to sit on the court from the same country. The suit brought before them involved a dispute between the United States and China over the exploding debt accumulated over the past ten years and the failure of the United States to pay it down.

The debt the United States owed China currently stood at 1.3 trillion dollars. Trade with the United States had tapered off when Tindall tightened sanctions on imports from China after China had failed to rein in North Korea and its leader's desire to acquire a missile that could deliver nuclear weapons. While the case before the judges was complex, and had been adjudicated over the past three years, the Court had finally rendered a decision. Of the fifteen judges, the only one with a dissenting opinion happened to be from the United States. The verdict was devastating. The United States would have to repay its debt with accumulated interest. The American people owed the People's Republic of China nearly two trillion American dollars. Knowing that the US Government could just print money to pay the debt; they had been doing that for years, China had convinced the court to provide payment in the form of hard assets. Land, buildings, infrastructure such as bridges and waterways were given as examples of acceptable payment, as well as gold and silver reserves. America had sold her sovereignty for smart phones and microchips and now they had to pay for all that technology.

International Attorney for the United States, Frances Pearce, reading the decision, threatened a counter suit, but it was bluster. China had prevailed. The attorney for China, in an international news conference proclaimed, "It is now time for the United States to put up or shut up!"

*****

Washington DC, the White House

Over his breakfast of a soft boiled egg and a dry piece of whole wheat toast, President Tindall felt his anger rising as he read the *NY Times* headline. *China Defeats US in International Court.* The news made it appear he had created the national debt all by himself. Secretly he admitted he hadn't done enough to rein in the out of control spending, but for the sake of the Country, he had no choice but to fight the decision any way he could. The American people would not tolerate China taking their property and there was no desire to change their lifestyle. Besides, whether China liked it or not, it was dependent on America buying its goods. "I'll break NAFTA," he said to the server, who responded, "You do that, sir."

Tindall grunted, "That will put them in their place. Two can play this game."

His server was used to the President ranting to himself. He smiled.

Chapter 3

Scott was sound asleep when his cell phone rang. He answered and heard a familiar voice.

"Where the hell are you?" David Stafford asked.

Scott looked at the clock, it was 0123 hours.

"David, how close are you?"

"I'm here. You didn't get my text? Of course you didn't. You want me to take a cab?"

"No. I'm only forty minutes out this time of night. Sorry. I fell asleep and didn't get the text."

"Go back to bed. I can rent a car. I'll be there before you wake up. Put on a pot of coffee. I need to talk to you about something anyway."

"Thanks, buddy. I'll see you soon. You have the address?"

"Got it in the message you sent yesterday," David said.

Scott handed David a mug of black coffee as he came through the door and grabbed his suitcase with the other hand. He showed him to the guest room.

"You look pretty fresh for a man who has just flown a thousand miles," Scott said.

"Eleven hundred-seventeen," David corrected, stopping long enough to take a sip of coffee. "How are you holding up?"

"I'm not sure. There are a bunch of things surrounding my Dad's death I'm concerned about. Let me grab a cup of coffee and I'll fill you in."

Scott refilled David's cup and told him his suspicions about his dad's death, North Star, and finally, the automatic deleting of the flash drive.

David sat at the desk and brought up the computer. After a few minutes he said, "I can recover the flash drive, but they scrubbed the computer pretty good. There's nothing left."

"I guess that's something," Scott said. "My dad must have been working on some pretty classified shit at North Star. I guess they wanted to make sure his computer didn't have any company info on it."

"You think?" David said, looking up at him. He had recovered bits and pieces of the missing information. "Look here, it says they were involved in the Star Wars program back in the Eighties."

"How is that important? That was before we were born."

"Technology wasn't where it is today. Reagan's critics called it Star Wars, but its acronym was SDI for Strategic Defense Initiative. It was too advanced for the time, but the technology has caught up with it. They could do it today, except…"

"Except what?"

David paused in thought for a moment. "I was going to say there was a UN Treaty against putting military weapons in space, but the United States didn't sign it."

"Why not?"

"The treaty was proposed jointly by Russia and China. One can only assume they had a way of getting around it when they proposed it."

"Or the United States already had something in its arsenal that was prohibited and didn't want to disclose it," Scott added.

"Here's something interesting," David said, scrolling through the recovered data on the flash drive. "North Star Industries is mentioned in a Congressional Budget hearing as a private research firm promoting the peaceful use of satellite systems."

"Okay, so Dad was working on satellites."

"Their budget is eight billion dollars a year. That's spreading a lot of peace around."

"I agree, but I don't think that's what I'm looking for."

"Which is?" David turned from the screen and peered up at Scott.

"I don't know. Something that would get my father killed. A peaceful satellite system doesn't sound… bad enough to get him killed."

"Killed? That's where you're going with this?"

"Why would they steal his home computer and wipe out his data? Why would they cremate him without getting permission from the family? I'll bet they don't handle the funeral arrangements for everyone who dies on the job, either. This whole thing stinks."

"I'm sorry I can't help you with any of those things. I've scanned the data on the flash drive and there isn't much here, certainly nothing concerning his day to day job, or what he was working on."

"I've got a big day tomorrow," Scott said. "I guess we'd better turn in."

"Sorry, man. Maybe it will make more sense in the morning."

The sun filtered through the translucent green leaves of a huge maple tree as Scott watched the graveside ceremony. He had seen many ceremonies like this one, all of them leaving him wondering why. Why were those who were the best among men taken so early in life? Why did men fight wars in the first place? He had asked the question a hundred times and the answer was always the same. Most of the fighting men were doing their duty, fighting for their Country, but it always came down to the same answer, "because they had to". In war you anticipate death, but his dad wasn't in a war. He had done his duty, fought for his Country and survived. He was working at a job, like an electrician, a carpenter or a plumber. He could have been building houses or automobiles. He was doing a job and somehow it had gotten him killed. Numbly, he watched with his mother, his sister and her husband sitting beside him on one side and Patricia on the other. He looked past the casket at the rolling green grass hills dotted with marble and granite stones, etched with names that would be there long after he was gone. *So this is what it all comes down to,* he thought.

The presenting of the flag while taps were played seemed

to come too soon. He put an arm around his mother as the casket was lowered. He couldn't bring himself to take a handful of dirt and toss it on top. All of the family members had placed a red rose on the casket. That was the last he wanted to remember of this day. He stood for a long time and watched the crowd disperse. He saw David taking pictures. They didn't seem that important now, but he would want them later. At least that is what he told himself. *What was it about funerals that made people want to remember?* Right now, he wanted to forget. He escorted his mother, sister, and Patricia back to the black Lincoln that would take them to the reception at his mother's house. He had ridden to the graveside service with David, while his mother, sister, Patricia, and his brother-in-law Jim, had arrived in the limousine provided by North Star. "I'm going to ride back with David," he said. "I'll see you at the reception."

David's car was parked near the back of the line of at least fifty vehicles. As they walked toward it, he pointed out Roger Wilkes. "That's the man who took my Dad's computer. I'm sure of it," he said.

"Who's that beside him?" David asked.

"Gil Thompson, an engineer who worked for Dad. He was the one who brought the computer back. I think he knows something and is afraid to talk."

As they walked along the line of cars, a girl came up from behind them and called out, "Mr. Tanner?"

Scott and David turned as she approached on a motorcycle. He hadn't seen her at the funeral and though she was dressed in black, he wouldn't have missed her Punk Rock appearance. She parked her bike under a tree and walked toward them. She removed her helmet exposing short, black hair. She had piercings with tiny rings in her eyebrows, nose, lips and ears. What stood out most was a large rose tattoo on the side of her neck. The stem of the rose was covered with thorns and wrapped completely around her neck. He thought she might be out of high school, but just barely.

"Look at her," David said. "Cool."

"I need to talk to you," the girl said, fluffing her black hair, and unzipping a black leather jacket.

"You know *my* name," Scott said. "Who are you?"

"I did some work for Ty," she said. "He owes me two hundred dollars."

"Excuse me if I doubt that," Scott said.

She held out an envelope. "I called the number he gave me. Imagine my surprise when I was told he had died. I had to search the funeral homes in the area to find out he was being buried today."

Scott didn't remember seeing a phone in his dad's things. "You said he owed you money. What for?"

"Two bills, that's what we agreed on. It was tough work, I should have charged more, but seeing he's dead, you can give me the two hundred. And I'll give you the information."

"Just like that, you think I'm going to shell out two hundred dollars. Is this some kind of shakedown? You find a funeral and hit the family up for money. Get lost."

"I did what Ty asked. You give me the money or you don't get the info."

David pulled out his wallet and handed her two bills. "We'll take the data," David said, taking the envelope from her.

"David," Scott protested. The girl had already turned and was on the way back to her motorcycle.

David opened the envelope. He grabbed Scott's sleeve. "I think she's legit. Let's get out of here."

Inside the car, David handed Scott the envelope. "That's an eight gig thumb drive. Now, I'm thinking you're right. Your father could have been involved in something that got him killed. We need to get to my computer."

"What if it's infected with a virus like the one Patricia gave me?"

"The virus wasn't in the thumb drive, it was on the computer. Besides, my guess is she wasn't a North Star employee. There are hundreds of kids like her who make their living by hacking industrial computers. I think she's given you something that could be worth a lot more than two hundred dollars, which you owe me, by the way."

Chapter 4

Roger Wilkes had been with North Star Industries from the beginning. The company had been formed from the bankrupt remains of a company that went down in the late Nineties after President George Herbert Walker Bush defunded the SDI program, claiming it was too futuristic and impractical.

Wilkes was one of three engineers who worked on SDI and pooled their savings to continue space weapons research. They named the start-up North Star Industries.

In what seemed like perfect timing, President Bill Clinton signed an agreement that expanded trade and opened new markets with China. Roger Wilkes was approached by a newly formed venture capital firm that was willing to fund the new company in exchange for half of its stock. The fine print required the company to go public in the future so the partners could make a return on their investment. What Wilkes and his partners didn't know at the time, was the venture capital firm was backed by PRC, the People's Republic of China, money which was funneled through offshore banks in the Cayman Islands.

Wilkes, with the title of Research Director, hired a 47 year old Tyler Tanner to be his Chief Engineer. Tyler Tanner took over one of the darkest programs the CIA had ever funded. Code named Paradox, over the next fifteen years, the satellites were launched under Tyler Tanner's banner.

Like its name implied, Paradox satellites appeared to be something they were not. Launched simply as civilian communication, weather, environmental or GPS satellites, Paradox, like a transformer toy, could morph into something different. In some instances as many as twenty smaller satellites, each having the same capabilities as the larger bird that had hatched them, could break away from its parent. In turn, each of the micro-satellites could be programmed to act in concert or alone to carry out a specific space based mission. Paradox gave the United States unparalleled and complete space superiority. The

Paradox program was responsible for North Star Industries becoming the premier US supplier of space based satellites.

When it became time for the original investors to cash in on the company's success, the information North Star possessed was far more valuable to the investors than the seed money they had provided and any they would receive from a public stock offering.

Wilkes and the other two partners were ready to take the company public, but because the business had only one customer, the United States Government, and the product it created was highly sensitive to national security, the FTC blocked the public offering.

Had the founders of North Star known about the China connection at the time, things would have turned out differently, but it had all been part of a long range strategy on the part of the investors and they were about to collect.

It could have all ended right there, if the partners would have come clean, but they were in too deep. They owed a debt and they had something the debtor was willing to settle for: information.

Roger Wilkes called a meeting with the other two partners. If they were going to continue their lavish lifestyle, they would have to transfer Paradox technology to China. Under the threat of being exposed, the owners agreed to let Wilkes transfer information on Paradox to International Capital knowing full well it would end up in China.

Chapter 5

The guests were gone and the house was a mess. Scott started to clean up the kitchen when his sister walked in.

"I've never been so tired in my life," Susan said. "Why don't you take a break and see how Mom is doing. I've hired a maid service to come in and take care of all this."

"I think she's already gone to bed," Scott said. "You haven't seen David, have you?"

"He's been in Dad's office for several hours with the door closed. I guess he didn't want the guests wandering in. What's he doing, anyway?"

Scott hadn't told his sister about the girl at the funeral. For all he knew the whole thing with the flash drive was a scam. No need to drag his sister into something like that. She would tell their mother and…

"He's trying to get some info from another flash drive. He's probably fallen asleep. I'll go check on him."

David wasn't asleep. The screen was scrolling by with what seemed like millions of lines of code. "What are we looking at?" Scott asked.

"Computer code."

"I can see that," Scott said. "What's it mean?"

"I'm not sure," David said.

"You've been up here for hours and that's all you've got?"

David pushed back in his chair. "Is there still some of that Scotch left in your dad's bar?"

Scott knew if David was asking about Scotch it wasn't because he wanted a drink, it was because he thought Scott would need more than a beer when he told him.

"You want to go to the bar? I'm sure there's a bottle of something worth drinking."

David picked up a small plaque and brought it with

himself. He sat at the bar and Scott reached for a bottle of Glenlivet. He poured a small amount in a short glass for him and asked David what he wanted.

"There was a white wine in the fridge. If it's still there, I'll take a small glass."

Scott poured the wine and joined him on one of the bar stools. "Well, I know you didn't come up here for a drink. Are you going to tell me?" Scott started to laugh and touched his glass to David's. "You bought a bunch of crap and you're going to ask me to reimburse the $200 aren't you?"

David slid the small piece of wood with the brass etching toward Scott.

"What's this," Scott asked, picking it up.

"Did your father ever mention Paradox?" David asked.

"Never." He read the plaque out loud. "Paradox; the illusion of certainty when it is not." He shrugged his shoulders. "Dad always did like puzzles." He took a sip of his drink. "It must mean something to you?"

"There are hundreds of satellites in the sky. What if they are not what they seem?"

"You gotta give me more than that. It's pretty easy to know what a satellite is. I'm sure when you make a telephone call or watch TV you know there's a satellite up there doing its job."

"What if you could turn off that function and make it do something else?"

David took a sip of wine. He was playing with Scott, but it was the kind of game he liked. Scott was a hands-on type of guy, not one to over think anything. Put a hammer in front of him and every problem could be solved by a nail. He grinned and waited.

Scott took a gulp of the single malt Scotch. "You mean stop sending TV signals and broadcast radio instead, or something like that?"

"Come on, Scott. Think outside the box. Remember the toys we used to play with. A car could turn into a robot. What if a satellite was really made up like a rubix cube, each cube functioning as a separate satellite. One of the cubes transmits TV like it's advertised, while the rest of the cubes sit and wait to be given their orders."

"Cool," Scott said. "Like what are you going to tell them to do?"

"First how many cubes are there in a rubix cube?"

"Lots," Scott said. "Each side is made up of nine and then there's the whole thing when it's assembled." He looked at the smirk on David's face. "You already know the answer, or you wouldn't be asking. Tell me."

"The rubix cube we used to play with is made up of twenty-seven small cubes that make up a larger cube, so I guess the correct answer is twenty-eight. If you rearrange the cubes by rotating the faces there are over three billion combinations, many more if you break the cube into its twenty-seven smaller cubes.

"Imagine a satellite that could do the same thing. By changing its faces, it could become a laser weapon to destroy the electronics of another satellite, a frequency jammer to mess with the radio signal of an enemy's satellite, something as simple as a spray gun to paint over the lens of a spy satellite. Imagine if all twenty-seven cubes could break away from the mother cube and float through space and seek out an enemy satellite, cozy up next to it, and blow it apart."

"That's a lot of imagining. Science fiction," Scott said, taking another sip of his Scotch.

"Not science fiction," David said. "Your dad was working on a system that could do all of that and more. There's a reason it was called Paradox. Your dad was working on something that defies the imagination and that might be why he was killed. That file I bought from the girl contains codes that make the Paradox satellites do whatever they are preprogrammed to do."

"You mean our enemies think we have a few hundred satellites peacefully floating around the planet and at any moment we can turn those hundreds into tens of thousands?" He shook his head. "It still sounds like science fiction. How could that information get him killed?"

"I'm not sure if it plays a part in his death, but I'm certain the information shouldn't have been in the hands of a teenager with tattoos and facial piercings. We need to find her and ask her how she got the file and what she was doing with it."

"Good luck with that. She didn't look like she has a listing in the phone book. She probably lives in her parent's basement. We don't even have her name."

*****

Gil Thompson heard Roger Wilkes and another partner arguing in his old boss's office. He raised his eyes from the report on his desk and listened. With the door closed, he couldn't make out the words, but the tone was clearly confrontational. Several of the other engineers in the room were in earshot of the ruckus, but they didn't seem to notice so he kept his head down and listened.

Gil was no fan of Wilkes and didn't like the way Wilkes was handling things after Tyler Tanner's death.

Gil had been the first one on the scene when Ty Tanner had collapsed. Roger Wilkes had said he had called for an ambulance, but later he found out the ambulance driver had been stopped at the gate and had been denied entry. It was a ten minute delay that could have cost his boss's life. Why hadn't Wilkes called the company emergency line? There was an ambulance and an EMT on duty at all times inside the gates. Gil was still pissed about that and now was wondering what the argument was about.

The jangling of Gil's desk phone startled him. He answered and was told Scott Tanner was at the front gate and wanted to speak with him. Just then Wilkes came out of the office.

"Gil, I need to see you," Wilkes said.

"Mr. Wilkes," Gil said, "Scott Tanner is at the front gate and has asked to speak with me."

"I'll handle him," Wilkes said. "You need to get back to work."

Gil didn't like the way Wilkes had answered, but he knew something wasn't right with his boss's death and didn't want to end up in the same place. He would just as soon let Wilkes handle any questions Scott Tanner had.

The guard handed Scott a piece of paper. Scott parked his Jeep in a pull-out space beside the guard house while he waited for Gil to come for him. He read the sheet the guard had given him. For security reasons, visitors were not allowed on the premises without an escort. Your name had to be on a list, and if you made it past that hurdle you would receive a badge, but even with the badge, you had to be escorted at all times while on North Star campus. Even with those precautions, several buildings on the sprawling complex required a higher level of clearance to enter. Many required biometric screening, facial recognition, voice recognition, retina scanning or a combination. In addition, any cell phones, computers, cameras or recording devices were prohibited on the property and were collected and held at the guard station.

"Wow," Scott said, setting the paper aside. He checked his watch, not certain Gil had gotten the message or would come to get him. He had been waiting twelve minutes. It seemed longer. His cellphone rang and he answered.

"I need to meet you in Portland," David said. He gave an address that Scott jotted down. It was on the east side of town in an area Scott wasn't very familiar with, but he knew it was a rough neighborhood. "I can't come right now; I'm waiting for Gil to show." They had agreed to split up to cover more ground, but at the moment, Scott was wondering if it was a good idea.

"I'm outside a tattoo parlor. It looks like a pretty scary place, but I saw a rose tattoo like the one the girl was wearing on this motorcycle chick. I think she's a Gypsy Rover."

"Gypsy Rover? Are you kidding me?"

"No, I don't think so," David said. "I'm pretty sure that's what the back of her leather jacket said. "She pulled into this place and I'm a little nervous about going in. I thought I'd wait here until you joined me."

"Gypsy Rovers are dangerous, man. Don't go in there. In fact, I've got a better idea. Drive to a nearby restaurant and wait for me to call." He saw a guard coming toward him. "I've got to go. I'll call as soon as I'm back on the road." Scott disconnected and rolled down the window.

"Mr. Tanner. Mr. Wilkes is on the phone. He wants to talk to you."

Scott followed the guard to a phone on the outside wall near the entrance to the guard house. "This is Tanner," Scott answered.

"Scott, isn't it? This is Roger Wilkes. We met at your mother's." Wilkes continued without giving Scott a chance to answer. "Gil told me you called. He's not available right now. What can I do for you?"

"When my father's personal effects were returned, there wasn't a cell phone in his things. I was just wondering if he had one on him."

"No one is allowed on the campus with a phone, so I guess the answer is no."

"Thanks," Scott said. He was kicking himself for not figuring that out on his own. It was on the sheet of paper. If his dad had a cellphone on him when he arrived at work, it would be in the guard house. He knocked on the window and motioned to the guard who had spoken to him earlier. The tall, dark-skinned man with short-kinky hair looked to be in his sixties. The guard's badge had Phillips, H. R. engraved on it.

"Mr. Phillips, did you know my father, Tyler Tanner?"

"Oh, yeah. Nice man. Say, I have some of his things here. I was shocked to hear of his passing. He was mighty young to be kickin' the bucket."

"Any chance I can pick them up? They brought back his personal effects, but his cell wasn't with them."

"That's because it's in his briefcase. I saw him put it in there myself."

"Can I get his briefcase?"

"Sure thing. I'll have to check your ID and have you sign for it. No tellin' who might be askin' to see it and I ain't gonna be the one left givin' it to the wrong person."

Scott pulled out his driver's license and handed it to

Phillips. He disappeared into a side room and returned with a battered leather briefcase.

"This here looks like it's been through a couple of world wars."

"That thing is older than dirt," Scott said. "I remember it from when I was a kid."

"Sign right here. Don't forget to take your license. It's clipped at the top of the clipboard."

Scott signed his name and took his license. He checked the briefcase for the phone, found it and turned it on. He didn't know his dad's password, but figured it would be the same as his computer and Susan had known that, or at least figured it out. He used his phone to call Susan and entered the password while he was still on the phone. "That did it, Sis. You're the greatest." He hung up and scrolled through the names on his dad's phone. He found the one he was looking for and called David. The phone rang for a long time. He thought it might go to messaging when David answered.

"David, where are you now?"

"I can't really talk right now," David said. "I'm in a bit of a situation."

Scott could hear noise in the background. It sounded like a male voice and chains rattling. "Are you still at the tattoo parlor?"

"That would be yes."

"Are they bothering you?"

"That would be yes."

"Tell them I'm on my way and they better not hurt you."

"I'm handing the phone back. You tell him."

A male voice came on the phone giving Scott a mental picture of who was talking. Scott figured he dropped out of school before the eighth grade and had spent a good many years doing hard time.

"Who am I speaking with?" Scott asked in a cheery tone.

"Bull."

"Did you just say bull or did you say your name was Bull?"

"Who wants to know?"

"I'm Scott, a friend of the little man you're holding hostage."

"I ain't holdin' nobody. He came here, he's gotta get a tattoo, no ifs, ands, or buts."

"I don't think my friend came for a tattoo, as much as he might like one. We're looking for Rose Thorne. Do you know her?"

"Yeah. Rosy Baby. She's my girl. What do you want with her?"

Scott was racing toward town on the Sunset Highway, trying to decide the fastest way to get to the east side. He had Bull on the speaker phone and figured as long as he could keep Bull engaged, he wouldn't be doing anything unthinkable to David.

"We're not interested in your girl," Scott said. "She did some business with my dad and we need to talk to her."

"Rosy don't date no dudes without my say so."

It took a second for Scott to process the last sentence. "We're not interested in dating her," Scott said. "We want to do business with her."

"You take that back, mister. My Rosy ain't that kind a girl."

Scott edged up to seventy in a fifty-five zone on I-84 looking for the 82nd off ramp. Too late, he missed it forcing him to take the next exit and double back through a neighborhood.

"Listen, Bull," he said, "my friend is a computer nerd, like your daughter." He hoped he was guessing right. He hoped she wasn't a gang member. Bull had to be her dad. How a Gypsy Rover ended up with a computer geek for a child probably said more about the girl than it did about her father or mother.

"That didn't come out right either. My friend, David wants to share some of his computer expertise with your brilliant daughter. You must be very proud of her." Scott had punched in the address on his GPS and hadn't turned it on. He didn't want the voice to be cutting in and out of his phone conversation, but he needed it now and turned it on.

"Bull, can I talk to my friend?"

David's voice came over the speaker. "Scott. I hope you're close. This guy has me picking out tattoos. He wants to do a snake up my arm. I hate snakes."

"I'm a minute away. The girl's name is Rose Thorne. Makes sense now. I'll bet she's Bull's daughter. I've found my dad's cellphone."

The computer generated voice on the GPS said, "Destination two-hundred feet ahead on right." Scott pulled in and parked behind at least ten Harley Davison motorcycles, some tricked out with fancy paint and low rider suspensions. The lights were on inside the building, but through the dirty glass he couldn't see David or anyone else for that matter. He tried the door, but it was locked. He could hear an angry dog growling and barking at a gate near the back of the building. He looked around. At the auto repair shop next door, half a dozen broken and dismantled cars were scattered about, some on blocks others tipped on their side. The only streetlight in the area looked like it had been shot out.

Scott knocked on the front door again, this time banging it with his fist. He peered through the glass and saw a man walking toward the door. He looked like he could play offensive guard for the Green Bay Packers.

The door opened. "You must be Bull," Scott said, holding out his hand.

Bull grunted and ignored Scott's hand. "Follow me. We're in back."

Bull weighed 350 pounds, if he was an ounce, Scott thought, watching the man swagger in front of him. He wondered if he could take him and hoped he would never find out for sure. He wasn't packing, unless you counted the long knife in the scabbard and the chain hanging from his heavy leather belt. He wore a black leather vest with Gypsy Rover on the back. He was bare under the vest, if you discounted the dark hairy arms and chest. Scott could see the man was no dough boy. He had a tattoo around his neck, but it wasn't a rose. It was a woven mass of briars with long thorns, reminiscent of the one Pilot had placed on Jesus before sentencing him to death by crucifixion. He dismissed the image, hoping it wasn't a bad omen.

"Hi, Scott," David said sheepishly as Scott walked in.

David was surrounded by five men who looked just as terrifying as Bull.

"We can clear this up real fast if you'll call Rose," Scott said. "We need a minute with her, which we'll be glad to pay for and then we'll be on our way."

The mention of money seemed to relax the atmosphere a little. Bull made a call and slipped his phone back in his pocket. "She'll be right here."

Until she walked in the room, David hadn't put the girl at the funeral and the girl on 82nd as the same person. The same tattoo should have given it away, but he figured it was a gang thing. Now he knew it was a name badge. She had been upstairs all the while he was being held.

"I gave you everything. What more do you want?" Rosy said, eyeing them suspiciously.

"We have a question and he's willing to pay," Scott said, nodding to David.

"How much?" Rosy asked.

"Don't you want to hear the question first?" Scott asked.

"Last time it was two hundred. The price has gone up," Rosy said.

Now it was David's turn. He was willing to pay about anything. "How much?"

"What's the question?"

"Why did my dad give you the flash drive?" Scott asked.

"He asked me to break some encryption so he could read it. Believe me, I got robbed."

"Do you know where the file came from?"

"That's two questions." She looked at Bull. "Bull, did you check them for a wire? You guys aren't cops, are you?"

Two men immediately had David on his feet and patted him down including ripping open his shirt and checking his ears. One of the men picked David up and turned him upside down and shook him. They patted Scott down.

"They're clean," one of the men said, handing both of their billfolds to Bull, who opened them, checked the driver's licenses and took out all the cash.

"Looks like you boys bought seven-hundred dollars' worth of questions." He grinned at his daughter.

"Same question," Scott said. "Where did my dad get the file?"

"I'm not going to answer that directly. Let's just say the encryption had Chinese characters when I got it. You can assume it wasn't made at North Star."

"You think it was Chinese code?"

"No, it was our code, meaning American military, but somehow it had been in the hands of the Chinese military. I'm not going to say anything else. You've got your money's worth."

"Are we free to go?" Scott asked

Bull handed back their wallets. "Nice doin' business with you fellas. You ever get in trouble, mention my name and they better take note."

"Thanks," David said. He looked at Rose. "Nice work. You're a real pro."

She smiled at him. "You're not such a bad piece of work yourself."

Scott grabbed David's arm. "She's half your age. You take this any farther you'll get us both killed."

"Where are we going from here?" David asked, standing by his car.

"I'm going to check and make sure all of my tires are still on my Jeep and then follow you back to Hertz. We might as well turn in your rental. I don't trust you driving around town alone anymore."

On the way back to Hillsboro, traveling west on the Sunset Highway, David reached over and hit Scott in the shoulder.

"What did you do that for?" Scott asked.

"It's starting to make sense. Your dad was selling North Star satellite code to China. North Star found out and killed him."

"Are you out of your mind?"

"I don't think so. Why else would he have satellite message codes that were accompanied by Chinese characters?"

"The stuff you saw didn't have any Chinese written on it, did it?" Scott said angrily.

"No it had all been translated."

"My dad wasn't a spy. If anything, he found something and was trying to unravel it so he could go to the authorities with it."

"That works, too," David said. "If he was a whistle blower, then the company might not want him to expose something they were doing."

"I think we need to give what we have to the FBI and let them investigate," David said. "You keep giving away my money and we won't be able to get the next model of *Sub Zero* finished."

"He's my dad. I know you're not concerned about the money, but I'll see that you are reimbursed. Now that we know something is going on at North Star, you can return to San Diego whenever you want. I can handle it from here."

"You're going to the FBI, right?"

"Not yet. I don't want my dad's death to be buried at the bottom of a hundred drug cases the FBI may be working on. I'm not going to drop this yet. It could involve national security."

"All the more reason to give it up now," David encouraged.

Chapter 6

North Star Industries

A full moon hovered high in the night sky as Gil Thompson stopped his dirty Toyota at the guard station and handed his badge to the uniformed man. "You're up kind of late, Mr. Thompson," the elderly man said, handing the badge back to him.

It was late, but Gil couldn't do what he was about to do during normal working hours. Most of the nightshift personnel didn't know him and he was hoping to carry out some unauthorized research, an act he knew could get him fired or worse.

Of course there would be a record of his entry to the plant. The guard at the gate had entered his name into a computer that scanned a list to see if he was authorized to be on the premises at that hour. He had entered through the employee entrance that required a full hand fingerprint scan followed by a retina check before entering the main body of the facility. The engineering offices required for him to walk through a device that did a full body scan. Entry into the engineering offices required another retina scan and voice recognition at the same time. He was also aware his picture had been taken and his movements around the office were being digitally collected and sent to a storage device in an area of the North Star complex housed in the basement of the executive offices. There were no secrets at North Star Industries; at least that was the appearance the company wanted to instill in its employees. In fact, there were a lot of secrets; company secrets.

No lights were on in the engineering office and Gil turned on the light as soon as he entered. He sat down at his computer and sent an interoffice memo to plant security asking for a particular video of the assembly area the date and time when his former boss had died. Engineering requests for security tapes of plant areas were not that uncommon. There were numerous valid reasons an engineer might request a tape. The failure of a satellite had once been traced to an employee using an unauthorized permanent marker. The problem was discovered when the security tapes were reviewed. It was determined the mistake had not been intentional, in fact, the marker had come from the company supply room, but the result was a piece of titanium that had been subjected to high temperatures on launch had cracked, preventing the satellite from deploying its solar panels. It was a multi-million dollar error caused by a sixty-nine cent marker. The discovery of the error using security recordings had saved millions of dollars in potential future failures, and engineering was authorized to review assembly tapes any time they wanted after that. He shouldn't be worried about the request, but had come up with an explanation, if he was ever asked about it. He would claim he had no idea it covered the death of Ty Tanner. He was looking for a barcode error that had kicked out a satellite in the final stages of inspection. It was feasible enough since the inspection stations were robotized and a glitch in the computer at the right moment could cause the laser marker to print a partial code or miss a line. It had happened before.

Still, Gil felt apprehensive, as he waited for the video to work its way through the computer system and queue up on his computer screen. He watched it carefully, played it back and over again in slow motion. He was looking for anything unusual. Then he saw his boss in the final moments of his life; Roger Wilkes standing beside him. Wilkes was pointing to one of the new satellites under construction. Half a dozen assembly personnel dressed in white, clean room paper clothing: booties, hairnets, and cotton gloves, hovered around the satellite that, at this point in assembly, looked very much like a giant disco ball from the Seventies.

He stopped the recording and ran it back frame by frame. There it was: Ty Tanner reached for his neck with his right hand, just behind his ear, and swiped at it like a mosquito had buzzed his ear. He didn't grab his chest or his arm like one might suspect if he was having a heart attack, but a simple swipe of his hand as if he'd been bitten. He froze the frame, zoomed in and enhanced the picture. A small red spot appeared behind his ear like it could have been a reaction to a bite from an insect.

Gil leaned back in his chair. They were in a clean room. There were no insects in the plant, let alone the assembly area. All the air in that room passed through H.E.P.A. filters. It was the cleanest air on the planet. Gil carefully reached up and touched his glasses, a casual adjustment of his glasses if anyone was watching, but he captured the image digitally in the SD Chip in the micro camera built into the glasses he was wearing.

Gil leaned back in his chair again. It wasn't enough. He ran the video again. What could have caused Ty to slap his neck as if he'd been bitten by an insect? What were they doing? There was no audio. He played it over and over and finally gave up and recorded the entire sequence on his micro-cam. Now all he had to do was get it back out of the building.

*****

Scott answered the phone almost without thought. He had been shocked out of deep sleep and had reached over on the night stand and picked it up.

"Scott, this is Gil Thompson. It's not much, but I thought you might like a copy of the security tape showing your dad the last few minutes before he died."

"Gil...right. How can I get it?"

"Meet me at Wagon Wheel Park in half an hour. It's on the way out of town on the old highway going toward Portland."

Scott was in a daze. Had he been dreaming? He had his cellphone in his hand but the screen was blank. Either it was the most vivid dream he had ever had, or Gil Thompson had a recording of his dad's death. His heart was pounding in his chest. He checked his phone to make certain he had received a call.

The sun was still below the horizon, just starting to paint a reddish glow in the morning sky as Scott pulled into Wagon Wheel

Park. At a family picnic, he remembered his dad, had told him the park was named after a group of pioneers who had circled the wagons in that spot to ward off hostile Indians. He wasn't expecting hostile Indians, but as his mind cleared, he thought of his dad's computer. Why would North Star provide him with a tape of his father's last minutes when he didn't even know one existed? He was on alert. Could he trust anyone from North Star? Gil Thompson certainly hadn't been a fountain of information in the past.

He saw Gil was already there and wondered if he had been there when he had made the call. This time of the morning no other people were around. Scott pulled up beside Gil who was leaning against his car.

"Your dad was my boss and a friend. I don't know what happened, but you deserve to have the last moments of his life. I wish I had more." Gil handed him the tiny SD Card. It was as tiny as a postage stamp. Gil opened his car door to leave.

"Can't you just answer a few questions?" Scott pleaded.

"Sorry," Gil said. "I need to get to work." He climbed in his car. In seconds he was gone.

That was strange, Scott thought. He looked at the thin piece of plastic between his fingers. *Can this really be what he said it was?*

Still too early to wake David, he went back to his mother's house. He wanted to put the tiny chip into the computer, but he hadn't had much luck with computers and since David had decided to stay another night, he would let him do the honors. He put on a pot of coffee and turned on the morning news.

China and Russia were engaged in joint military exercises off the Korean Peninsula, threatening to interfere with a joint exercise between South Korea and the United States.

Iran had just launched its first communications satellite and North Korea launched a missile 2000 miles out into the Pacific.

The world is on the brink of war, Scott thought, *but hasn't it been for nearly twenty years? Life in the United States continues, seemingly oblivious to what is happening in the rest of the world,* he thought.

"Scotty, you're up early," Scott's mother said, coming into the family room with a cup of coffee.

He hated it when she called him by his boyhood nickname. "Early morning phone call. Couldn't get back to sleep." A lie, but he didn't dare mention he may have a recording of the last few minutes of his father's life.

"I've got to return to California," David anounced, walking into the dining room an hour later.

"I'm sorry to hear that," Scott's mother said. "I've enjoyed having you here."

"Me too," Scott said. "Do you think you can look at something for me before you head out?" He held up the SD Card Gil had given him.

"What's on it?" David asked.

"I'm not sure," Scott said. He waited for his mother to go back into the kitchen. "Gil from North Star gave it to me. He was very mysterious. Called me at oh-five-hundred."

"Let me grab a cup of joe. My computer is still in your dad's office."

"Aren't you boys going to eat breakfast?" June asked, seeing both of them get up.

"Later," Scott said, kissing her on the cheek.

"Gil said this is the last few minutes of my dad's life. It's from the security cameras at North Star."

David took the chip and plugged it into the SD Port on his laptop. They watched as it immediately started playing.

"That's Dad and Mr. Wilkes," Scott said. "They are discussing something."

"Look at that satellite," David said. "I've never seen anything like it. Another one of the Paradox series, I suppose. It must have a thousand Nano-sats in that array."

"Concentrate on my father," Scott said. "Do you see anything strange?"

"Looks like a normal conversation," David said.

Scott took in a sharp breath. "He just crumpled to the

floor."

"Look at Wilkes. He doesn't look too alarmed."

"Wilkes told me he wasn't with my father when he collapsed! Run it back," Scott said.

David put the image in stop frame mode and advanced it slowly like a slide picture show.

"There, freeze it," Scott was tapping the screen.

"I'll zoom in and see if we can get a better look. He appears to be wiping something from his neck."

"Look at Wilkes. He's going for his cell phone. I'd give my right arm to know what he was saying." Scott leaned closer to the screen. "Can you read lips?"

"Not from this angle."

"He was right there and didn't do a thing to help him."

"Maybe he was calling 9-1-1for help," David said.

"Maybe, but it took over ten minutes for help to arrive. Wait, there's Gil. He's applying CPR."

They could see Gil was saying something to Wilkes, but wasn't getting much of a response. David ran the video back and forth.

"I'm sorry, but there isn't much more I can do with this. You have friends in high places; maybe you can pass this along to someone in Washington. They might be able to pull something more from it."

"Thanks," Scott said. "Looks like Gil was right, not much here. You want to have breakfast before I run you to the airport?"

Scott had reached a dead end as far as his father's death was concerned and he needed to get back to work, too. He hated to leave his mother, but his sister had promised to check on her every day.

He left his mother's house knowing that the drive to the coast in the heavily-congested summer traffic would give him plenty of time to decide if he was going to pursue his father's death any further. Getting any more information out of North Star looked to be an uphill battle at best and he really didn't have any evidence they had done anything wrong.

He had just reached one of the most picturesque spots in his drive along the high cliffs that overlooked the Pacific when his cell phone rang. He checked the name on the screen. The display showed an unknown caller, but he was bored and traffic was heavy. He took the call.

"Tanner, here."

"Scott Tanner, this is NSA Assistant to the Director calling." It was a woman's voice.

"Are you certain you have the right number?"

"You know Admiral Nendel, is that correct? He gave me your number."

"Richard Nendel, yeah, is he in some kind of trouble?"

There was a stifled laugh from the woman.. "Admiral Nendel is retiring from the Navy to accept a new assignment. He has been asked by the President to lead the NSA as Director. There will be a small swearing in ceremony at the White House and he would like for you to attend."

"Give me a time and date and I'll be there," Scott said.

"There will be a private plane to pick you up at the North Bend Airfield this coming Tuesday at oh-eight-hundred; that's eight a.m. sharp, Pacific Daylight Time. I'll make the arrangements from this end. You'll need a suit and tie or your military dress uniform. It's a formal occasion. You may bring your wife or significant other. All the information has been sent to your personal e-mail address. If you have any questions, my name is Sandra Fleming. The number I'm calling from is my personal line. Is there anything else, Mr. Tanner?"

"You've given me a lot to chew on," Scott said. "I'll call you back if I can think of anything."

Scott had a hundred questions, but he needed to ask them directly to Nendel.

He wondered if Patricia could get away for a trip to Washington DC, but before he asked her, he had a dozen things he needed to clear from his schedule. First off, he needed to turn over the research on the Japanese submarine to one of his crew. His calendar was already too full for him to help with the search and right now, with the recovery of treasure still being raised from the *Isabella,* another diversion couldn't have come at a worse time.

Washington DC

If you live in the relatively cool summers in the Pacific Northwest, Washington DC in late June is probably not the most comfortable place in the country to be visiting. The day Scott and Patricia arrived it was ninety degrees with humidity to match, but transportation arrangements had been made for them and, thankfully, they didn't have to spend much time outside. They only had enough time to check into their room at Hyatt Place and freshen up before the car picked them up again and brought them to the White House for Richard Nendel's swearing in ceremony. Scott had chosen to wear his Navy dress uniform, it was the first time he had worn it since he was discharged and was pleasantly surprised he still had the lean muscular build that he had when he had worn it in service to his Country.

"It's amazing how well this is orchestrated," Patricia said, as they were escorted to the Rose Garden where a canopy had been set up to shade those attending. As they approached their seats in the second row, Janet Nendel stood and greeted Patricia. They had been close friends from the time Janet's husband was commander of the Coast Guard Base in North Bend Oregon.

The trip to Washington had been an easy sale to her boss, generally a stubborn ass. A White House function always made good news and the appointment of former Coast Guard Commander and Oregon resident Richard Nendel to NSA Director would be a great teaser on her nightly newscast.

Scott, knowing Patricia's desire for a good story, cautioned her about disorderly conduct, but Patricia already had a plan to write a story from the women's point of view. She would interview Janet Nendel, and had already called her and made arrangements.

There was no way Scott was going to keep her from exploiting this opportunity.

"Don't let her ask too many questions," Scott said, kissing Janet on the cheek. "This must be a big deal for you and Richard. Seems like it happened kind of sudden?"

Janet nodded. "We're going to have dinner together tonight and I'll fill you in."

A young man came through the White House doors, tested the microphone and gave those attending a two minute warning of President Tindall's arrival. Richard Nendel and some of his and the President's staff, as well as Secret Service were behind the podium on a makeshift platform.

Scott and Patricia found their seats and waited.

"I didn't know this was such a big deal," Patricia said, excited to be at a White House function. Scott was such an unassuming man, he didn't show any emotion. It seemed to him more of a duty than a privilege, but she knew he was proud of his friend and his accomplishments. It was a route Scott could have taken, but he preferred a quieter life, out of the spotlight and definitely away from politics.

The President walked in and everyone stood.

Patricia raised her camera above the heads of the people in the front row and recorded the short swearing in. "This is great," she whispered, hardly able to contain her enthusiasm. She wondered if she would enjoy the life of a politician. It seemed exciting at the moment.

That evening, what Scott and Patricia had expected to be a formal dinner with many guests, ended up being an intimate dinner for four at the historic Gadsby's Tavern Museum in Alexandria, Virginia.

They listened to Richard Nendel explain the Tavern's history. It dated back to before the birth of the Nation when George Washington used it as a recruiting headquarters for rangers for the campaign of 1754. Mr. and Mrs. Washington were known to frequent Gadsby's and dance in its ballroom.

Scott raised his glass of merlot congratulating his friend on the appointment. "Wishing you the best and many more successes."

"Hear, hear," Patricia said.

"The Country's in trouble," Nendel said, gravely. "It's more a necessity than an honor."

That got a look from the women.

"I probably said that wrong," Nendel said. "It's been all over the news. My predecessor could very well be going to jail for treason, and I'm walking into an organization that's been plagued by scandals and leaks. Frankly, I don't know who I can trust and who I can't. Without having anyone to prepare me, I can't see a sugar coating on this assignment, but there's a saying in Washington, 'when the President asks you to serve, you don't say no.'"

"Putting aside the stupid things we did in our younger years, I'd say they picked the right guy to straighten things out," Scott said, smiling.

Nendel turned to Patricia. "Enough about me. Patricia, I haven't seen you in three years. When are you going to dump this lug and run away with me?"

"I think Janet might have something to say about that," Patricia said, glancing at Janet.

"Hell, you can have him," Janet said. "I never see him anyway."

"Ah, I'm right here," Scott said. "I might have a say in this."

Scott and Patricia both knew the Nendel's well enough to know the banter was friendly. The couple had been married thirty-two years. Janet, a woman in her early fifties, had aged very well and could pass for thirty in most circles. Richard, on the other hand looked much older than his fifty-six years, graying at the temples, wrinkles around his eyes, and a weathered face, attesting to his many years at sea in the Navy, as well as the Coast Guard.

"Scott, I'm sorry I couldn't make the funeral. I didn't know your father, but he raised a hell of a fine son, so I know he was a good man. Was his death expected?"

Scott ignored the compliment. "I can't say it was," he said. "Actually, it was out of the blue. He was about your age, and I thought he was in perfect health."

Nendel gave him a confused look.

"Heart attack, at least that's what his company told us."

"Geez, that's got to be tough. Your mom is still living?" Nendel inquired.

"She's doing all right. I stayed with her most of last week."

"Jesus, that was…I'm sorry. I gave a list of people I wanted here not thinking. I would have understood if you had declined the invitation."

"I was already on my way home when your aide called. I wouldn't have missed this. Heading up a Government bureau, you're now an official part of the political establishment."

"I'll take that as a compliment," Nendel said, laughing.

After dinner, for more catching up and a nightcap, they went to the hotel bar where the Nendel's were staying. Patricia took the opportunity to pull, Janet aside giving Scott a chance to talk to his friend privately.

The subject came around to his father's untimely death again and Scott reached in his pocket. He had carried the North Star information with him along with the SD Card Gil had given him, hoping for an opportunity to ask his friend if he could look at them. He hesitated, not certain he should ask a favor of someone so high up in Government. He pondered the decision for several minutes, all the time clutching the flash drive and SD card in his hand. Finally, he decided to approach the subject through a back door.

"Richard, does Paradox mean anything to you?"

"Where did you hear that?"

Scott knew from Nendel's reaction he had broached a subject that wasn't to be discussed in a public place.

"I take it, it's something you can't discuss here. You think we can talk the girls into taking a walk?"

"Good idea. Better yet, why don't we all go up to our room? It's a suite with a living room and a fully stocked bar. One of the perks of being a public servant." He grinned and motioned to the bartender for the tab.

Scott and Richard stood at a window looking out over the city. The Washington Monument, White House, several National Museums, and many buildings Scott couldn't identify, complimented the view.

Clearly nervous about the conversation he was about to engage in with Scott, Nendel turned on a radio and found some background music. "Let's move away from the window, no telling who is listening in in this city," he said. "Patricia, do you mind if Scott and I change places with you girls?"

Patricia could see it wasn't a request. "Of course not." She stood up with her drink and set it on the table by the window. "The view is amazing over here."

Janet joined her, apologizing for her husband's rudeness. "I never know what to expect from him anymore. Sometimes I wish we were back in Oregon. But Washington DC is a small sacrifice to pay for his added income in retirement."

"You make it sound like a chore," Patricia said. "I would think you would find it exciting."

"Don't get me wrong," Janet said. "There's never a dull moment in DC, but my gosh there are a lot of scandals. Everyone is at each other's throats. You would think we're from different countries... " She hesitated, reached out and touched Patricia's arm. "There has been a lot of talk about war lately."

Sitting on the couch with a low coffee table in front of them, Richard picked up his glass and took a sip of Scotch. "Where did you hear about Paradox?" he asked.

"It was the program my dad was working on when he died. He was chief engineer for North Star Industries. From what I have learned, they work on Black Programs."

"Your father told you this?"

"No, my dad never talked about his work. I had Patricia do a little digging and while going through my dad's things, the name popped up."

"You still have your clearance, don't you?"

"Passed a lie detector test six months ago. David and I are still working on a classified DARPA program. I take it Paradox is top secret?"

"I'm not telling you anything, understand?"

"Okay… " Scott drew out the word, not sure what to make of his friends reaction.

"It's not your fault. You found out about something that isn't supposed to be in the public domain, not even those at the top."

Scott took a sip of Scotch and swirled the ice in his glass. He looked at Patricia and Janet engaged in a lively discussion. "I'll be sure not to mention it to Patricia. She's like a bulldog with a mailman when she gets wind of something, especially if it's not meant to be in the public domain." He took another drink. "Richard, I need a favor." He set the two pieces of plastic on the coffee table. "Don't feel obligated, but I suspect my father was caught up in something that got him killed. If you take a look at these, I think they might have something to do with my dad's death."

"I thought you said it was a heart attack."

"I said the company, North Star, said it was a heart attack. There is a lot of suspicious stuff going on at North Star. They disposed of his body before we could ask for an autopsy and one of the VPs showed up at dad's house, took his computer and scrubbed it clean. Not just deleting information, but making certain the computer was useless for anything else."

"Jesus," Nendel said, trying to take it in. He held up the tiny drives, one the size and thickness of a dime and the other the size and shape of the cap on a ballpoint pen. "What are these?"

"One is a zillion numbers that my partner says are satellite codes that were once encrypted with Chinese characters."

"Chinese satellite codes?" Nendel asked. "Where did you get them?"

"No, he said they were our codes. My father had someone break the Chinese encryption, but died before he got it back."

Nendel leaned back on the couch. "If I didn't know you, I'd report you to the FBI. You're not supposed to have any of this stuff. What were you planning on doing with it?"

Scott was taken back by his friend's response. "Right now I'm giving it to you. I didn't think this stuff should have been out there either, but it was. I considered giving it to the FBI, but I figured it would just disappear at the bottom of some agent's pile of crap and I'd never hear from them again. When I heard you were going to be the new NSA Director, well, you know the rest."

Nendel picked up the smaller SD Card. "What's on this one?"

"A recording of the last two minutes of my father's life."

"How'd you get it?"

"A guy who worked for my father gave it to me. It's from security cameras in North Star."

"Okay, I can't promise anything. The next two weeks I'll be learning where the nearest restroom is and how to find my office. Once I find out who the right person is, I'll get it in their hands. Frankly I'm a little concerned having this in my possession."

"I can help you there," Scott said. "Go to the top floor and pick out the room with the view. That should be your office or someone you can trust."

Nendel laughed and stood up. "I think we should call it a night. I'll get back to you."

They shook hands and the women made their goodbyes. "I'll have a car take you to your hotel," Richard said.

"It's three blocks. We'll walk. It's a beautiful night."

"You sure? The streets in this city aren't exactly safe at night."

"Positive," Scott said. He saw the look on Patricia's face and said, "On second thought. If you have a car at your disposal we'll take it."

"One of the perks," Nendel said. He called down on his cell phone and a driver showed up at his door two minutes later.

Chapter 7

July 5, NSA headquarters, Ft. Mead, Maryland

Admiral Nendel received the news in his daily briefing. He needed to see it for himself and called his aide to queue up the recording from USSTRATCOM, the United States Strategic Command Center. He was in the Situation Room and summoned the rest of his staff in for the briefing.

With all parties present Nendel nodded and the image came up on the wall-sized screen. Air Force Lieutenant First Class Bonnie Woods, the liaison from Global Operations Center, GOC, explained what they were watching. She stood nearly six feet in her low heels. Her hair was pulled back in a short pony tail. She adjusted thick-rimmed glasses before starting.

"Exactly thirty-two-minutes ago China placed a satellite into a geosynchronous orbit twenty-two thousand miles in space. Beijing didn't try to hide the launch and advertised it as a peaceful Area Positioning Satellite, or APS similar to our GPS. My agency tracks every satellite in orbit and thousands of pieces of low earth orbit space junk, so until now, the mission was exactly as China said, but then this happened."

She forwarded the recording to a point where they saw a dozen micro satellites called cubes float away from the main body of the APS. As they drifted away, each cube deployed solar cell wings, making them look much like a flock of birds.

"A few minutes after fixing its orbit, this happened," Lieutenant Woods said, advancing several frames.

Collectively the room held its breath as one of the cubes glided up to within a few feet of a large satellite and exploded, causing the larger satellite to break apart, sending a cloud of debris out in all directions.

"The satellite it destroyed," Woods continued, "was a

defunct communication satellite owned by China, but it could just as well have been one of ours." She waited a few seconds while the information was absorbed.

"Until now, we didn't believe China had this capability. Just as disconcerting, the satellite China launched appears to be an exact copy of our latest Paradox satellite." She was just the messenger, but she expected to take some heat for the disclosure. In her short term on the job, she had seen it happen several times. She delivers bad news that catches those who are supposed to be protecting us by surprise, and they act as if it was her fault. She was just a grunt, for God's sake. Why did they pick on her? She was pleasantly surprised when Nendel responded.

"Thank you, Lieutenant Woods. I would like for you to stay for questions my staff will undoubtedly have." He pulled out a chair next to his.

*****

It had been two weeks since Scott Tanner handed Nendel the information from North Star. Nendel had used the information to start an investigation of North Star Industries. Already a team of FBI agents from the Portland office were checking where the information had come from. They had interviewed Scott Tanner and had placed three undercover personnel in the North Star plant with the cooperation of North Star President Charles Stone, who had agreed to keep the presence of the agents a secret, even from the other officers in the company. The FBI agents had gone through the normal security clearance and were acting undercover as a consulting firm hired to enhance intra-office communications. They had access to all personnel and all computers in the plant.

To date, the FBI had narrowed its investigation down to the two people Scott Tanner had mentioned to Nendel, Gilbert Thompson and Roger Wilkes.

Two plain clothed agents pulled up in an unmarked car to Gilbert Thompson's home in Tigard, Oregon, knocked on the front door, and showed their badges. "I'm Special Agent Gordon and this is Special Agent Reese," Gordon said. Thompson didn't seem surprised and invited them inside.

"This is about the death of Ty Tanner, isn't it?" Gil said, offering the agents a seat at the kitchen table.

Not ready to play their hand, Gordon, the senior agent, a man in his fifties, looking more like an accountant than a cop asked, "What can you tell me about Ty Tanner?" He adjusted his heavy framed glasses.

"Ty Tanner was Chief Engineer and a wonderful boss. Have you spoken to his son? He's pretty certain Ty was murdered."

"Murdered?" Gordon glanced at Reese. This was the first time they had heard about a murder.

"About the murder," Reese said, taking advantage of Gilbert Thompson's lead, "have you got any idea who killed him?"

"I thought you might have reviewed the security tape and formed your own conclusion. I like my job. I'm not going to jeopardize that."

"You're talking about the security tapes..." Reese purposefully stopped mid-sentence.

"From the North Star assembly room. That's where Ty collapsed," Gilbert finished her sentence. "I'm not trying to get anyone in trouble, but someone got to my boss and I was hoping the tapes might reveal something."

Gordon rose to his feet. "That's all we have for you right now, Mr. Thompson. Please don't mention our chat to anyone. You know the drill. It's an active investigation." He headed toward the front door.

Reese was taken by surprise at the sudden halt to the interview. She caught up with Gordon at the door.

"If it's okay, we may have other questions," Gordon said to Gilbert.

"Sure. Anything I can do. He was a good boss."

Reese buckled her seatbelt and started the engine of the late model black Ford Explorer. "What the hell was that? We're supposed to be investigating espionage, and he's talking about blowing the whistle on a murder."

"He's doesn't know anything about the missing data," Gordon said.

"And you could tell that without asking him a single question."

"Aren't you just a wee bit interested in Tyson Tanner's death?" Gordon asked.

"That's not why we're here."

"Tyler Tanner was Chief Engineer on the Paradox Program. If he was murdered, that should be a concern."

Reese wasn't buying it. "It's only normal for a family member to think there is something suspicious about someone dying before their time. People die from unexpected heart attacks every day."

"Gilbert Thompson isn't family. We need to talk to Scott Tanner again. I've got a feeling we weren't told everything," Gordon insisted.

"Now you're sounding like a real conspiracy nut," Reese said. She put the car in gear, "Where to?"

"Let's take a trip to the beach."

As Nendel had feared, when Scott handed him the USB drive with the satellite information, the investigation had centered on espionage, and ignored the death of Scott's father. He had to disclose Scott as the source of the information, and the FBI immediately started investigating Tyler Tanner, suspecting he was a spy.

Even before discovering China had Paradox technology, the FBI investigation of North Star was underway. Anyone connected to Scott's father was being investigated. Nendel knew it was not the type of investigation Scott had envisioned, but he had no choice. The NSA gathered information, the FBI investigated, the Justice Department prosecuted. They had to consider the bigger picture; highly classified information had ended up in the hands of China.

After first reviewing the information, Nendel assumed Scott's father had been involved in espionage, and Scott was completely unaware. Why else would he have given him the information? He couldn't compromise an investigation by contacting Scott and had remained silent, not taking any of Scott's calls. He didn't have the heart to tell Scott that his father was a prime suspect in an international conspiracy. His father's death could have been China's insurance policy. When an asset is of no further value, destroy it to make certain it doesn't turn on you later. Now murder didn't seem out of the question, but for reasons Scott might not have thought of.

"Nice house," Reese said, pulling the car to a stop in Scott Tanner's driveway. "Why is it everyone we investigate lives in houses better than ours?"

Gordon ignored her. He was used to Reese asking rhetorical questions. Before the trip to Waldport, Special Agent Gordon had collected a digital folder on Scott Tanner. He knew his background, right down to his eating habits and his connection to the new NSA Director, Richard Nendel. They knew he was engaged to Patricia Westland, a TV news reporter, and that she had recently done an extensive search on North Star Industries. Gordon had a lot of information and wanted to connect some dots. He knocked on the door.

Scott opened the door and when he saw their badges invited them in. "You're here about my father?" Scott asked. "Let's go out on the deck. We can talk out there. Can I offer either of you something to drink?" He grabbed a cup of coffee from the counter as they walked onto the deck.

Gordon and Reese declined drinks.

Waves crashing on rocks, seagulls in the salty air, and a fishing boat on the horizon made a beautiful picture. Agent Reese leaned on the rail and took it in. "I love the smell of the ocean. Your place is gorgeous. Did you build it?"

"I had it built for my fiancée. We haven't tied the knot yet, but…" he shrugged. "You didn't come here to talk about my house, or my love life, I hope."

"You're right, we didn't," Gordon said, taking the lead. "Gilbert Thompson gave you some information on a thumb drive."

"A micro disc," Scott corrected, "sometimes called an SD Card. It showed the last two minutes of my father's life. Were you able to find out anything from it?"

"Only the SD card?" Gordon asked, ignoring Scott's question.

"The USB drive was given to me by a girl who said she removed some Chinese encryption. It had something to do with a program he was working on at North Star. Did you find a connection to my father's death?"

"We're early in the investigation. What can you tell us?"

"Really? I feel like I'm running around in circles. My father was murdered and I thought you would have figured it out by now. You haven't done anything, have you?"

"Why are you certain he was murdered?" Reese asked.

"You saw the recording, didn't you? It was pretty evident something happened to him. It didn't look like a heart attack to me."

"I'm going to ask you the same question I asked Gilbert Thompson," Gordon said. "Who do you think killed your father?"

"Jesus Christ, are you kidding me? I haven't got a clue. I thought you guys would be able to tell something from the recording. Don't any of you alphabet soup organizations talk to each other? My dad was working on a highly classified project. His death alone should have caused some suspicion. I can't believe we're having this conversation!"

Gordon ignored Scott's rant. "What's your relationship to NSA Director Nendel?"

Scott took a deep breath. "I don't know what the hell is going on. I'm going to assume it's going to get back to my dad's death. I'll answer your questions, but frankly, I'm at a loss as to how Richard figures into this. I gave him the information because I trusted him and I thought he would do the right thing. If that's why you're here, then... okay...

"Richard Nendel and I go back a long way. I served under him years ago in the Navy. Later he transferred from the Navy to the Coast Guard, was a Commander stationed here on the Oregon Coast. I guess you could say we were close friends. That's why I was at his swearing in ceremony and why I gave him the information. You already know all this."

"You had Patricia Westland do a search on North Star. What was that about?"

"Same thing," Scott said. "I couldn't believe my dad had a heart attack. When one of their VPs took my dad's computer from his house and wiped it clean, I thought they were hiding something."

"Anything else?" Reese asked.

"They had my father's body cremated against the family wishes. Roger Wilkes, my father's boss, said it was my father's request. It wasn't. You should look into Roger Wilkes."

"Roger Wilkes, the vice president of North Star," Reese said.

"If you looked at the SD Card, you know he was with my father when he died, even though he told me he wasn't with him. Why did he tell me that if he didn't have something to hide?"

"What do you know about Paradox?" Gordon asked.

"I never heard of it until I got my dad's things from the company. He had a plaque that had the word on it."

"That's it?"

"Well, yeah. It must have meant something to my father."

"Thank you for your time and cooperation, Mr. Tanner," Gordon said, rising.

Agent Reese stood and leaned out toward the ocean and let the cool breeze ruffle her hair. She took in a deep breath. "You work at home, Mr. Tanner?"

"When I'm not on the ocean," Scott said. "Why?"

"Lucky man."

Chapter 8

Scott heard the phone ring and checked his watch. He had been looking at side scanning radar images taken by his crew. They had covered several miles of ocean off Newport, Oregon looking for any sign of a Japanese submarine reported to have been sunk in World War II. So far there was no proof the reports were correct. He picked up his phone and a picture of Patricia smiled back at him.

"Hi, honey. How's your day been?" Scott answered.

"The FBI just left my apartment," Patricia said. "Are you in some kind of trouble?"

"No, they were here, too. They're looking into Dad's death."

"It sounded to me like they were investigating espionage activities at North Star. Why they think I know anything is beyond me. They sure asked a lot of questions."

"I wouldn't worry about it. That's their job."

"Still, I didn't want to say something that could get you in trouble."

"Hey, I've got nothing to hide. I'm trying to get them to investigate dad's death. It's part of the process."

"You know me. My reporter instincts try to make something bigger out of it."

"Are we still getting together this weekend?" Scott asked.

"If you promise not to work."

"Not a chance. I plan on kicking back and getting in some serious down time. I've got my crew doing all the hard stuff."

"Put a bottle of white zin on ice and I'll see you Friday night. I love you."

Scott stared at the phone as it went blank. "I love you, too." he said.

FBI Field Office, Portland, Oregon

"Anything interesting?" Agent Gordon asked one of the surveillance officers. A room filled with electronics buzzed with activity as four technicians hovered over keyboards in front of oversized flat screen monitors.

He and Reese had obtained warrants and five people associated with North Star Industries were having their cell phone and home phone conversations being listened in on and recorded.

"I have something," a young woman said. "It's from the private cell phone of Roger Wilkes and a burner phone we're still trying to track." She handed him an earpiece and played back the recording.

"Gil Thompson knows something. Get rid of him."

"That's Roger Wilkes speaking," the woman interjected.

"You don't think that would look suspicious?"

"Who's that?" Gordon asked. He motioned for Reese to come over and listen in.

"We're not sure. We're working on it."

Wilkes: *"Make it an accident."*

Unknown: *"How about a disappearance?"*

Wilkes: *"No body. I like it."*

Unknown: *"When?"*

Wilkes: *"Yesterday. The FBI is nosing around."*

Unknown: *"FBI, you're certain."* There was an audible sigh.

Wilkes: *"Trust me."*

Unknown: *"Consider it done."* The phone went dead.

"Who's he put a hit on?" Reese asked.

"Gilbert Thompson. This is big," Gordon said. "I need to get hold of the Attorney General."

"Are you sure?" Reese asked.

"There is only one way Roger Wilkes could have gotten the information we were investigating. We need to get a warrant to tap Charles Stone's phone. In fact, we need to get access to all of

North Star Industries files including their security tapes."

"Are you sure about this?" Reese asked again. "Maybe Thompson or Tanner talked to Wilkes."

"It's possible, but not likely. They both think Wilkes is behind Tanner's death." He nodded his head in affirmation. "Get everything we need to raid North Star Industries and make sure Gilbert Thompson has twenty-four hour protection."

"On it," Reese said.

*****

NSA Director Nendel had already received a request for every call Charles Stone, Roger Wilkes, Ty Tanner, Scott Tanner, David Stafford, and Gilbert Thompson had made in the past year. Technicians were piecing together a mosaic of people, places and activities that involved any interactions the parties had had. He reviewed the information, before handing it over to the Attorney General.

At the same time, the SD Card that had been provided to Nendel from Scott Tanner made its way back to the FBI in Portland to be analyzed.

"To prevent any possibility of contamination and compromising a satellite's mission," Gordon said, "the Defense Department requires the security in the assembly area to be the tightest in the plant. Only a handful of the three-thousand employees at North Star are allowed access to the room." He smiled and shook his head, "Kind of amazing, they guard this room this tightly and still Gil Thompson was able to beat the system, and get a recording out of the plant. Who would have thought the security tapes themselves would bring them down?"

"This is the spot we want," Reese said. She started going through the images frame-by-frame. "There," she said. "This is the moment before he went down." She enlarged the frame and zoomed in on Ty Tanner as his hand swiped his neck. "I can't see anything," she said, looking up at Gordon who was hovering over her shoulder.

Gordon had been the one who had found the piece of information that broke the case. He smiled.

"Maybe we're looking in the wrong place," Gordon said. "Try looking at the satellite."

"What am I looking for?"

"It looks like a thousand mirrors put together in a ball," Gordon said. "There's a reflection that speaks volumes."

Reese panned in on the ball. From a distance it looked like a giant ball made up of tiny mirrors, but up close each of the mirrors was at a different angle with its own reflection of the room. Most of what she could see was badly distorted or unintelligible. She scanned each individual square, blowing it up to the size of her screen. "I'll be," she said. "Is this it?"

Gordon leaned in. "Enhance it."

"I can see it pretty clear," she said. She zoomed in on a hand and then on a finger. The tip of the finger was covered with something that appeared to be a thimble, but the thimble had a sharp point about the size of a thorn extending from its tip.

"Whose hand is that?" she asked.

"Wilkes," Gordon said. "You have to remember the image is reversed."

"I'll zoom back out and concentrate on Wilkes and what he's doing with that hand," she spoke as she did it.

They watched as Gordon narrated. "Wilkes turns to Tanner and says something. He brushes off Tanner's neck. Tanner swats his neck and a second later he goes down. Tanner was right, his father was murdered. Why? If Wilkes thought he was spying for China, he wouldn't kill him. All he had to do was turn him in." He pursed his lips and shook his head. "It looks like Wilkes murdered him. We need to find out how."

"And why," Reese added. "Scott Tanner gave the NSA a code he said was his father's. It had Chinese characters on it so there has to be a connection."

Karen Knott, one of the computer analysts across the room, interrupted them. "Agent Gordon, we have something on Wilkes."

The file from North Star security showed Roger Wilkes and

North Star President Charles Stone arguing.

"I was able to use our lip reading translator to pick up the gist of the conversation. It's highlighted on the screen," Knott said. "In a nutshell, Stone is upset because he found out Wilkes killed Ty Tanner. Wilkes said he didn't have a choice, he was about to expose their connection to International Capital."

"That's good," Gordon said. "See what you can find on International Capital."

Knott hit a few keys and International Capital LLC came up on the screen. She did her magic and was able to dig a little deeper. "All of International Capital funds are coming through a Cayman Island Bank. The president of International Capital is Chang Yi. He's a Chinese National living in Washington DC. He appears to be legal. International Capital is headquartered in Washington DC."

"This has all the markings of an undercover shell corp. We need to expand our search. See if we can find any recorded information on Chang Yi," Gordon ordered.

"I can do that," Karen Knott said. She tapped into the NSA data base and did a name search for all the phone conversations Roger Wilkes had made that included Chang Yi. "Thirteen calls in the past year." She looked at Agent Gordon and grinned. "You want to hear them?"

The White House, Oval Office

President Tindall continued to pace the room as Randy Biggs, his National Security Advisor, briefed him in on the latest developments regarding the Chinese satellite.

"The micro-satellites have migrated several hundred miles from the original mother satellite. A few of them have approached our communication satellites and have taken up positions beside them. One of the micro-satellites maneuvered too close to one of our defense satellites and was zapped by an electrical charge much like a stun gun. The high voltage is meant to scramble the electronics and render attacking satellites useless, but not all of our satellites were equipped with defensive capability. The trouble is we don't know if the micro-sats are being guided from the ground or are preprogrammed to do a job," Biggs said. "Our only defense is to activate Paradox, but we know how that will end."

"And you think we shouldn't say anything to China? This kind of hostile activity could start a war," Tindall said.

"We don't want to play our hand yet," Biggs said. "If China knows we have the capability of watching everything they do twenty-two thousand miles up in space, then they might change their tactics. We need more time to figure out what they are up to and determine if we need to counterattack."

"And what would that look like?" the President asked.

"We're not certain. Right now China has beaten us at our own game. Our latest Paradox satellite USS-221 isn't due to be launched for another week."

"And what will happen then?" President Tindall had skipped many of his daily briefings throughout most of his two terms, deciding to scan the reports rather than meet with his staff. Let the experts do the job they were hired to do, but now he was regretting his lack of involvement. He felt like he knew almost nothing about Paradox and what it was supposed to accomplish. Now, he was totally reliant on his advisors. He could sense the Nation was creeping ever closer to war and feared that more than anything.

"Our satellite provider, North Star Industries, has been compromised," Biggs said. "We don't know how deep it goes, but it may be related to the aggressiveness China is showing in space."

"Call a meeting of the Joint Chiefs and make sure Richard Nendel is there. We need to nip this in the bud before we lose everything. I want several scenarios of what could happen and what our response should be. I don't want some stupid reaction from us starting World War III on my watch."

"Yes, sir." Biggs left the room.

The door was still open when Attorney General Juanita

Holmes knocked. "Sir, can I have a minute?"

"If you slipped past Raymond, then it must be important." Raymond Jackson was his new personal aide and was charged with limiting access to the President without an appointment.

"We've got an ongoing investigation you need to know about. It has to do with a breach of National Security."

Tindall walked to a nearby table and poured a cup of coffee and offered it to Juanita. He motioned for her to sit and he sat opposite her at the small table. "Does this have to do with North Star Industries, by any chance?" he asked.

"Maybe I'm giving you old information. North Star is responsible for developing most of our Defense satellites. The company is corrupt, at least through the top layer of management. The FBI just informed me North Star was funded by China through an offshore bank. They've had the company in their pocket since its start over fifteen years ago."

"This is starting to make sense," Tindall said, letting out a long sigh.

"Sir?"

"Biggs just briefed me on the satellite situation. We can't do anything until I meet with the Joint Chiefs. If you bring down North Star management right now, China will know we're on to their game. North Star is critical to our entire military defenses."

"Then we'll stay on top of everything they do until you give the word." She took a sip of coffee and set the cup and saucer on the table. "Sir, if I may say so, we need to act fast. If word gets out that we're investigating North Star the owners could skip the country."

"Revoke their passports, put them on the no fly list, do whatever you have to, but this has to remain out of the press. I don't want anyone from the FBI grandstanding, understand?"

Juanita knew what he was talking about, but he was singing to the choir. The FBI Director didn't seem to care what she said even though he worked for her.

"Mr. President, FBI Director Kerry does what he wants. I can reprimand him, but only you can fire him."

"You're suggesting I speak to Kerry personally?"

"It couldn't hurt."

Tindall stood, indicating the meeting was over.

Waldport, Oregon, Friday

Scott Tanner lit the candles over the fireplace and put on some elevator music hoping it would provide a romantic atmosphere. Truth be told, Scott was terrible at romance. He knew it was a necessary part of courtship, but after a half-dozen failed relationships, he'd come to the conclusion he didn't have a clue. Patricia had been the longest relationship he'd ever had and he felt like it was slipping away.

Patricia and he had not spent the night together for over a month. Tonight he was going to do everything he could think of to turn things around. He had ordered his crew not to call and made certain the few people who liked to drop in unannounced were not welcome this weekend.

The dinner menu consisted of fresh crab cocktails, barbequed fresh salmon with corn on the cob. Nothing fancy, but he had caught the salmon and netted the crabs, giving him bragging rights, besides it seemed like a great meal for the coast.

The latest weather report had promised a dry weekend. It would be a perfect time for the two of them to renew their faltering romance.

He hadn't had a PTSD episode in nearly a year. That was significant. Patricia had used his episodes as a reason to put off the wedding. It was time they made a fresh start and either get on with their engagement, or ...*or what*, he thought. He had been ready for marriage. She was the one holding out. *Or, nothing*, he thought. He wasn't ready to give up, even if this weekend was a bust.

He checked his watch. *She should have arrived by now*, but Friday night traffic was crazy this time of year. It seemed everyone from the big city wanted to get out of town for the weekend, and the beach was a favorite destination.

An hour later, he spotted headlights coming down his driveway. The sun had just set, leaving a red glow over the ocean. He ran out to greet her.

"Crazy traffic," Patricia said, getting out of her car.

He grabbed her and kissed her on the lips. "You can't believe what a great weekend I have planned."

"Well, let's get started. It looks like we're missing the sunset."

Scott grabbed her small suitcase and they walked inside. The weather was warm enough he had all the doors open. He led her out on the upper deck where he had a bottle of Riesling from Willamette Vineyards on ice. He poured two glasses. "Have a seat and relax," he said handing a glass to her.

"I've been sitting almost four hours. If you don't mind, I'll stand and watch what's left of the sunset. I love the smell of the salt sea air."

He stood beside her. The breeze fluttered her long hair. She was a beautiful woman, slender, perfectly proportioned, and had a cute smile. On top of that she was intelligent and a real go-getter, something he admired, though it frustrated him at times. He never tired of looking at her.

"Here's to a quiet weekend away from the crowds," he said.

She touched her glass to his. "This has got to be the most romantic spot on earth. How do you ever get any work done?"

"You know you could say the word and find out for yourself."

She looked out over the ocean, seemingly lost in thought. "With all that's going in the world, how did we become so lucky?"

He gently turned her toward him and kissed her. "I'll bet you're hungry. Enjoy your wine, the barbeque is already hot. I'll have dinner in twenty minutes."

"I love an efficient man," she said.

"You love a man who does the cooking," Scott said. "We can eat out here, if you like."

"Not many summer nights on the coast are this warm, let's

do it."

The music drifting in from the house and the subtle roar of the ocean made for a perfect background for their dinner. Afterwards Scott opened another bottle of wine. At that moment the problems of the past seemed as distant as the ship drifting over the horizon.

By the time dinner was over, the stars were twinkling in a moonless sky. "Let's take a walk on the beach," Patricia said. "I haven't put my bare feet in the surf since I was a teenager."

"I'll grab a blanket and we can build a bonfire," Scott said.

Only a single bonfire could be seen about a mile down the remote beach. Scott built a fire and watched from a distance while Patricia cautiously tested the water with her toes. He knew the water temperature in summer was under 55 degrees. Her toes would turn blue in seconds and she would want to warm them by the fire. He was right. She came running back toward him screaming like she'd been bitten by a shark. He tackled her and they fell to the soft sand, laughing harder than they had in years.

They lay by the fire in each other's arms until the early morning air became damp and forced them inside. It had been the perfect night Scott had been hoping for.

Scott heard birds chirping and the piercing call of an eagle, and sat up in bed. He felt the cool air from the ocean drifting all the way to the bedroom. He rolled over and Patricia was not there. Then he smelled fresh coffee. He found Patricia standing on the deck warming her fingers around a steaming mug of coffee. "I haven't slept that well since I was five," he said, joining her.

"You were so peaceful, I was afraid I might wake you," Patricia said.

"I think you're good for me."

"Really? Maybe we should do this more often."

"You mean like one of those modern couples who have two homes, one in the city and one on the coast."

"There's nothing wrong with that," Patricia said.

Scott nodded. "I can think of a few things, but let's not go there." He set his coffee on the railing, wrapped his arms around her waist from behind, and nuzzled her neck. "I love you," he whispered in her ear.

She turned and kissed him passionately. "You keep that up and I'm going to want to go back to bed."

"You don't give a man much incentive to stop," Scott kidded.

"I didn't tell you to stop."

He swept her up in his arms.

The phone rang and kept ringing. Scott reached over and, not finding his phone, ignored it until it stopped. In a few seconds it started ringing again. Scott checked the bedroom clock. Had they been in bed that long? His phone was on the dresser and he had to get out of bed to answer it.

"Sorry," he said, admiring Patricia's lithe scantily clad figure. He checked to see who was calling. It wasn't a number he recognized, so he sent it to voice mail and headed back to bed, but before he got there, the phone, still in his hand, started ringing again. It was the same number.

"Answer it, Scott. Whoever it is doesn't seem like they're going to give up."

"You're sure? I could throw this thing down the garbage disposal."

"See who it is."

Scott answered. He heard a familiar voice. "Don't you ever answer your phone?"

"Sorry, Richard, I was …indisposed." He looked at Patricia and mouthed, "Nendel."

He heard Nendel laugh. "Tell Patricia I said hi."

"How did…" Scott looked out his window. A Coast Guard Helicopter was hovering just above the waves a few hundred yards off his deck, "tell me that's not you. What the hell, Richard, your new title gives you the right to invade my bedroom?"

Nendel laughed again. "I'm going to have them drop me on the beach. You get some clothes on. We need to talk."

"You heard that?" Scott asked Patricia, setting his phone down and grabbing a pair of jeans. "We've got company."

Patricia slipped into one of Scott's T-shirts that had Seattle Mariners written across the front. It fit her like a too-large dress, reaching all the way down to her knees.

"I'll put on a fresh pot of coffee," she said.

Nendel came up the path from the beach and climbed the steps to the deck. He waved the helicopter off, and watched it as it rose and disappeared to the South.

Scott met Nendel on the deck with a cup of coffee. "This is a little stale. Patricia is making a fresh pot." His face turned a light shade of red. "How long were you out there?"

"Long enough to know you were ignoring my calls." He glanced through the glass doors at Patricia. "I can't say I blame you," he said, raising his eyebrows. "When are you two going to tie the knot?"

"You know how it is. It's complicated, but I bet you didn't come to the West Coast to discuss my love life."

"I hate to break up your weekend, but we need to have a private conversation."

"You want me to ditch Patricia?"

"I didn't say that." Nendel grimaced. "I really need for you to come to Portland with me. It's sensitive." He glanced at Patricia through the glass door.

Scott looked at his friend. He could see he had something important he couldn't discuss in an unsecure setting. "How long will it take? I promised Patricia a special weekend. You don't want to be responsible for screwing it up, do you?"

Nendel pursed his lips and gave him a sideways glance. Scott took it to mean, "stop asking questions and get on with it". He went inside and kissed Patricia. "You know he wouldn't be here if it wasn't something important."

"I get it, Scott. You go with him and I'll close the place up when I leave."

The amazing thing about Patricia was, she did get it. The news business had demanded she drop what she was doing and do whatever news people did when they were working. Scott didn't have to explain it to her. Scott kissed her again. He went into the bedroom and finished dressing, grabbed his go bag and came back out. Nendel was standing in the kitchen sharing a fresh cup with Patricia. She was laughing, so maybe it wasn't going to ruin his chances of setting another wedding date, but it sure as hell was getting in the way of him asking. He had planned on asking her that evening. It didn't look like that was going to happen.

"Good," Nendel said, seeing Scott. "Do you mind if I have a helicopter pick us up in your front yard?"

Chapter 9

The helicopter lifted off. Scott noticed it was like the ones he had seen traveling up and down the beach: painted black with no markings. The crew was dressed in black and wore dark glasses. Sometimes the CIA used unmarked aircraft, but Scott had never seen one up this close and had never flown in one. The interior was upholstered in plush black leather and the walls padded making the cabin reasonably quiet. It was a far cry from the military choppers he was used to.

"We called your partner," Nendel said, through his headset.

"David? Now you've really piqued my curiosity."

"He's going to meet us in Portland. Everything will be explained once we get there."

*****

The six-story home of the FBI field office is located near the Portland International Airport. David had flown his private jet up from California and parked it near the freight warehouses that surrounded one of the taxiways. He had been picked up by an agent and taken to a large conference room that appeared to be outfitted with every kind of electronic communication device known to man. He was checking out several pieces of equipment when Agent Gordon entered and said, "Careful with that."

"Agent Gordon, I wondered if I'd see you here. This is a V-sat broadband receiver," David said. "I was thinking about getting one for our ship. Where's agent Reese?"

"Beats me," Gordon said, taking the device from David and placing it back on the display shelf beside a dozen other radios, sat-phones and tiny dish shaped antennas. "The world can't operate without communications. I guess that's why we're meeting."

"They just told me to be here. Is there a pop machine

around? I could use a drink."

"Stay here and don't break anything," Gordon said. "I'll be right back."

The black helicopter hovered over the building and settled on the roof. Scott and Director Nendel were greeted by an agent who led them to the room where David was waiting.

By the time Agent Gordon returned, Agent Reese, Scott Tanner, Director Nendel and a dozen other FBI personnel were in the room. The National FBI Director was on a satellite link to a large screen at one end of the room.

The Field Office was supervised by Regional Director Sid Grover, a tall, thin man with a white mustache and billiard ball clean head. He introduced himself and addressed the group.

"In two minutes the FBI will serve arrest warrants for the three executive officers of North Star Industries. One lives across the river in Washington and two in Oregon. Other warrants are being served at the same moment around the country to prevent any communication among those arrested. You will receive more details about the arrests later.

"Those of you in this room will be watching the action in real time," Grover looked at the large screen. "I would like to welcome the National FBI Director Dan Kerry, attending by satellite link, and NSA Director Richard Nendel. Also, I'd like to welcome two consultants on the case, Scott Tanner and David Stafford."

Grover shuffled some notes. "Once the raid commences, North Star Industries will be taken over by the Federal Government. Two of the company's top management team, Charles Stone and Roger Wilkes are being arrested for treason under the espionage act of 2017. The other has agreed to cooperate, but is being held until the North Star complex is secure." He turned toward a larger screen showing the locations of the places to be raided.

David looked at Scott. Neither of them had a clue why they were in the meeting. Consultant could mean anything. "Consultant on what?" David asked.

Scott shrugged.

As if sensing their confusion, Nendel leaned toward them and whispered, "Because North Star is critical for National Defense, both of you will be stepping in to run North Star operations." He saw their confusion. "This will make sense once you've been briefed. This has come down so fast, I'm sorry we couldn't have explained it earlier."

Scott tugged David on the shirt sleeve and leaned into him. "If you knew this was happening and didn't give me a heads up, you're in big trouble."

"I was thinking the same thing," David said.

"Heads up everyone," Grover said. "Things are about to get started."

The lights in the room dimmed and the large screen on one wall split into three separate images, each showing a different op.

The larger of the split screens showed the front of North Star Industries. A dozen SWAT vehicles pulled up to the main gate and stopped. The guards were shown identification and escorted from their station and held inside a large black van with tinted windows.

"Station secure," a voice without inflection came over the speakers.

The gate opened and ten vehicles, each containing six agents, rushed through.

In concert with the other raids, on another monitor, three black vehicles pulled silently along a driveway leading up to a large house with a drive-through entry supported by tall pillars. Armed men from each vehicle silently scrambled from the vehicles and covered the perimeter of the house. One team covered the front door and waited for a response to the man pounding the door with his fist. When there was no response two men with a battering ram smashed in the front entry with a single blow. Two of the SWAT team members with automatic weapons at the ready position rushed in. Thirty seconds later they came out with Roger Wilkes in handcuffs.

"Suspect in custody," a disimpassioned voice said.

The third screen was from the home of Chan Yi in the suburbs of Washington DC. He was being escorted to a black unmarked vehicle. No shots had been fired.

On the larger screen, at North Star Industries, the ten vehicles separated into five pairs, each pair covering one of the buildings on campus. Another screen showed the executive offices. There was little activity at North Star on the weekend, but intel had determined Charles Stone was on the premises. He was quickly found and brought out front. One of the teams entered the communication room and shutdown all communication in the facility preventing any calls from leaving the buildings. All the security personnel on duty were located and taken into custody. From the records at the main gate, the rest of the workforce were identified and told to report to the auditorium where they would be detained until the entire facility could be cleared. When all was clear, General Cramer was escorted from one of the black vehicles into the auditorium to address the employees who had been caught up in the raid.

Two of the split screens disappeared, leaving the main screen showing the outside of North Star and the auditorium where General Cramer was about to speak.

"Scott, you and David need to follow me. They are waiting for us," Nendel said.

The black helicopter was waiting on the roof to carry them to North Star. The trip would only take a few minutes.

"Why us?" Scott asked Nendel in the elevator on its way to the roof of the FBI Building. "There are any number of people who could run a company better than us."

"I'll thoroughly brief you when we get to North Star. The situation is such that there are very few people I can trust at the moment."

Chapter 10

North Star Industries

Scott watched from the helicopter as it circled over the rolling green hills surrounding the fifty-acre North Star complex. The helicopter set down on a pad outside the Executive Office building. From the air he had seen that the five main brick and concrete structures were placed at the ends of wide walkways radiating out from a central courtyard like the spokes of a wagon wheel. He had been told each building served a separate function and the large numbers on the upper corner of the buildings needed to be learned or you could easily become disoriented.

The number one building housed North Star Headquarters, Sales, and Executive offices; number two was Research and Development; number three, Employee Services, including a gymnasium, swimming pool, recreation room and cafeteria; number four, Production Engineering and Assembly; number five, Maintenance. Each building was designed so that it could expand in three directions. The complex was supposed to resemble a satellite with the solar panels deployed, but when Scott had first seen it from the air he thought it looked like a giant space station.

From the landing pad near Building One, Scott, David and Nendel were picked up by an electric cart and rushed to an auditorium that was located in Building Three. They entered through a large double door and were taken down a side aisle and up some stairs.

"If I'd known we were going to be on stage, I would have worn a new pair of blue jeans," David said, as they walked out on the stage.

The employees working that day had been directed to the auditorium and were scattered throughout in small groups around the room. Designed to hold 5,000, the auditorium had fewer than

10 percent of that, giving the impression the room was nearly empty.

"Not exactly a sellout crowd," David said under his breath.

Seeing the three enter from the side of the stage, General Cramer leaned into the microphone.

"We can get started now, thank you for your patience. First, I want to apologize for disrupting your day. I am Air Force General Thomas Cramer, Director of the Office of Space Command and currently on special assignment at the request of President Geoffrey Tindall. With me today are NSA Director Admiral Richard Nendel, and two others you will learn about shortly.

"Due to a breach of national security, as of this moment, North Star Industries is under the management of the United States Department of Defense." General Cramer waited as several people moved together and muffled voices rose from the audience.

"As of this moment," he continued, "you are working for the Government of the United States. You are still bound by the nondisclosure agreement you signed as a condition of employment. Word of the change in North Star management is classified. Any mention of this meeting or the things discussed here after you leave this room will be considered a breach of your employment contract, reason for termination, and an act of treason. I say this, not to scare or threaten you, but to remind you that you are under the same obligation to secrecy you have been since your first day of employment at North Star Industries. Your adherence to that agreement is as important now as the day you signed it. That being said, I'll let Director Nendel brief you on a few changes that will be taking place. After that you are free to ask questions."

He turned the microphone over to Nendel.

"I'm sure you are wondering what's going on, and I'm going to tell you as much as national security allows. Unfortunately, that isn't much.

"A few weeks ago we were alerted to a security breach at North Star. The FBI was called in. Their investigation culminated in the arrest of two North Star executives. The two people standing beside me are going to fill in for the senior management for a few weeks, while the damage from the security breach is fully quantified. Nothing in your daily routine at North Star will change. It is our intent to conduct business as usual. You are all aware there are critical deadlines to meet and we don't want to impede that in any way. David Stafford will be the new acting Director of Engineering, including Research and Development." He looked over at David. "Raise your hand, David."

David raised his hand giving the audience a peace sign, or was it "V" for victory? Maybe both.

"Some of you may be familiar with the name Tanner. Tyler Tanner was your Chief Engineer until his unexpected death a few weeks ago. Scott Tanner is Tyler Tanner's son, a former Navy SEAL, and a decorated member of the Armed Forces. He will be stepping in as acting President of North Star until further notice. In this capacity, Scott will be answering to me and I answer directly to President Tindall."

"So much for having a discussion and filling us in," David whispered to Scott.

"Raise your hand, Scott," Nendel said. "Hell, come up here and say something." He turned to Scott and laughed.

Scott gave Nendel the evil eye as he made his way to the podium.

"I was in a lot of tough spots in Iraq and Afghanistan," Scott said, "but none of those situations were as terrifying as this one. I look forward to meeting each and every one of you in the coming weeks. Thank you."

A woman in the front row stood and raised her hand. "I have a question for Director Nendel."

"Sure," Nendel said, removing the wireless microphone from the podium and walking to the front of the stage.

"Since we are now working for the Government, will we be getting a Federal Pension?"

"This is a temporary change. We fully expect North Star will return to the private sector. Nothing in your pay or benefit package will change."

Another young man stood. Nendel pointed a finger. "Yes."

"Can we go back to work? We're getting time and a half today and, while I like the break, I promised my boss I'd finish a job today and he'll keep me here 'til midnight if I'm not done."

"Everyone is free to go. Thank you all for your service." He turned the mike off and turned to Scott. "That went better than I thought."

"I'm hoping you're ready to fill us in," Scott said. "I know as much about running an aerospace company as I do ballet dancing."

"Nonsense," Nendel said. "You'll figure it out. Besides I look forward to seeing you in a tutu." He gave Scott a big grin.

When they reached Scott's new office, several FBI personnel were finishing up a bug search. "This was the last one. The place is clean," the officer in charge said to Nendel.

"Good," Nendel said, "we can go in here."

He sat at a small conference table that had room for eight and motioned for Scott and David to take a seat. "General Cramer will be joining us."

A moment later Cramer entered and shut the door behind him. "How long before this hits the papers," he asked Nendel, taking a seat across from Scott and David.

"We need a month," Nendel said. "If we can get the next version of Paradox in the sky before China finds out, then we have a chance of taking control again."

"A month?" Cramer shook his head. "You can't keep a lid on this for a month. Besides we don't have a month. China already has enough birds in the sky to shut down the Sixth Fleet and most of our bases. Our R-Jams need to be up there now."

"R-Jams?" David said.

"Radio Frequency Jammers," Cramer said. "They search out rogue radio frequencies and jam them."

"We can't do that from the ground?"

"We can, but we can do it without them knowing it if we're in space. Right now we're not certain if that technology has also been compromised. Like us, China is collecting every radio frequency beamed from earth and analyzing it, listening to it, interpreting it, and jamming it if they deem it a threat. R-Jams are space based robotic jamming stations. Once the latest Paradox bird is in place, we will have the capability of blocking all communication on earth, and using our own protected frequency, we'll still be able to direct our planes, ships, and battlefield commanders."

Nendel cut off the General and took control of the conversation. "We can discuss the details of Paradox at another time. We need to have you boys ready to hit the ground running Monday morning. There are going to be thirty-five hundred people showing up for work and we need to be ready for them. David, you and your engineering team need a plan if Paradox has been completely compromised. Now let me catch you up."

He took a bottle of water from a tray on the table, opened, it and took a drink. "Scott, the flash drive your father gave to Rose Thorne was taken from the desk of Roger Wilkes. We know this because the security cams in Wilke's office showed your father removing it and replacing it with, what we believe, was an empty drive. Your father must have known something was up. If that code would have been loaded into the Paradox system, China would have been able to take control of all of our satellites. We think your father found out Wilkes was about to sabotage Paradox; your father found out about it and decided to replace the corrupted code with the original. By doing this, he would have beat Wilkes at his own game."

"Why did he go outside the company? He must have capable code writers working for him?" Scott asked.

"He didn't know who he could trust. We still don't know who provided the Chinese encryption. If it was written inside North Star, we have a huge problem. We're thinking it was given to Wilkes by China and he carried it in with the intention of replacing it for our code."

"How? Security is pretty tight. They don't allow flash drives on campus."

"That may be what tipped your father off. The drive isn't much bigger than a postage stamp. If someone wanted to smuggle it in, they could do it. Gilbert Thompson was able to smuggle out a copy of the security tape of your father."

"You're right," Scott said. "Gil Thompson got it through security."

"He told the FBI how he did it," Nendel said. "Glasses, with built in camera, powered by light, with a memory chip embedded in the stem. You'd be surprised where people hide things, but he told them he normally wears glasses and the security guards didn't question his new frames."

"We're going to have to check everyone coming and going using a full body and cavity search," Scott said sarcastically. "This isn't prison."

Nendel laughed. "Already taken care of. We should already have stress analysis software installed in the security system. Anyone bringing something in or out or doing anything covertly will be caught. We don't need to search everybody, only those suspicious enough to alert the guards."

"So it sounds like you've thought of everything. Why do you need us?" Scott asked.

"I know you'd rather be a team member than the leader," Nendel said, "but I've seen you lead and right now I need the same kind of leadership you showed in the Gulf. We've know each other a long time. I can trust your judgement. As for David," he nodded toward David, who was preoccupied with the safe behind a picture on the wall. "David, we need to know if the latest Paradox system can defeat itself. If China already has our technology we need a way to defeat it."

"When can I start?" David asked.

"There is a full set of prints on the computer in your apartment," Nendel said. "You'll be living on campus while this all unwinds."

The Hotel was set up as a practical way of housing executives when they visited North Star. If they stayed on campus they would only have to go through security once a visit. VIPs from all over the world had used them, but mostly the units had been home to officials from the varying military branches, members of Congress and senators on the Armed Services Committee, Nendel had explained.

David looked around the three-room suite. It had everything he required, including maid service. Because he had been brought in by helicopter, he still had his cell phone. He tried calling his chief engineer at the Sub Zero plant in San Diego, but there was no outbound service.

"This isn't going to work," he said to himself. He switched his phone to Satellite mode and tried again. This time his call went through. He let his engineer know he'd be gone for a few weeks and would not be available.

"No problem," his engineer said. "We already heard you're on special assignment and won't be available."

"For once someone is ahead of me," David said. "If Fay calls, tell her I'll contact her as soon as I can."

"You got it," his engineer said. "Don't worry about anything. I've got it covered."

"I know," David said. "Just wanted to hear a friendly voice."

"Something wrong?"

"No. I just got called away on short notice and wanted to let you all know."

"Okay. You try and have a good time, while I attend to business."

David chuckled. "Bye."

Nendel visited awhile in Scott's apartment. He went over to the bar and poured two glasses of Scotch. "You want ice?"

"A few cubes," Scott said. "You look like you have something on your mind." He took the glass.

"Grab a seat," Nendel said. "I still don't know David well enough to see how he handles stress, so I left out part of the story."

"Believe me, he handles it just fine," Scott said. "I think he needs to know what we're facing."

"We're still assessing the full ramifications of this security breach and I'd like to wait until we have the complete picture, but you know you wouldn't be here today if it wasn't serious."

"I figured that. You want to tell me how serious you think it is?"

"Our entire military is built around electronics and they all depend on satellites. Without satellites we can't defend the Country. Without them we can't even launch a counterattack. If China has the latest version of Paradox and releases it before we can get some kind of counter-measure in place, it will be a worse blow than we suffered at Pearl Harbor."

"But we won that war," Scott said.

"With the atomic bomb," Nendel said. "Without satellites we don't have the ability to deliver a bomb. The latest treaty with Russia made certain all of our conventional ICBMs with nukes have been decommissioned. If China takes out our satellites we're sitting ducks."

"So we're betting the code my father found was not delivered and was the only code they got their hands on," Scott said. "That sounds like wishful thinking."

"Maybe so, but that's what we're banking on."

Scott hadn't touched his drink. "What about a preemptive strike?"

"You mean nuclear?"

"If it's really that bad."

"I think the American sentiment is, they'd rather learn to speak Chinese than initiate what might be the last war the world will ever fight."

"You're saying we couldn't neutralize the threat with a preemptive strike."

"Not with a conventional strike. That's what I'm saying."

Nendel seemed more worried than Scott had ever seen him.

Nendel continued, "We would have to take out all the sites in Russia including their complete nuclear fleet, as well as China's submarines. Right now Russia has submarines two hundred miles off our Eastern coast. We're not shadowing every one of their subs. They have the capability to wipe out every military base and every major city in the US. If we miss even one, it would mean millions of lives. China doesn't have as much capability, but we have to believe Russia would side with China if we attacked first."

"And I take it, talking to China isn't going to resolve this?" Scott asked.

"Even if they don't have the very latest satellite technology, they probably have enough to destroy our birds if they attack first. We think that's why they are unwilling to talk."

"I feel like I'm coming to the game in the bottom of the ninth with two runs down," Scott said. "How did it get this bad?"

"When Tindall put me in this job, I already knew China was becoming a threat. They had teamed up with Russia and proposed a Space Treaty limiting nuclear and conventional arms in space. The treaty was too broad. It limited things we were already doing. The Administration proposed an amendment, but China and Russia refused to sign the amended version.

Every one of our Paradox satellites has the ability to act as a defensive weapon. All we have to do is send the right code. Our intel tells us all the major players have already armed space. The United States has operated on the belief that an attack against us would trigger a like response, but now it's more serious than that. We're absolutely unable to defend ourselves if someone takes out our satellites."

Scott tipped up his glass and downed it in one gulp. "Why doesn't China see it that way?"

Nendel was dead serious. Scott could see he was having difficulty believing the Country he had protected and served, the Country who was the most powerful nation in the world, had gotten into such a predicament.

"They have discovered our weakness. If we don't strike first, China will have the upper hand. By the same logic, they have to strike first or there is no chance they can win a war against us." Nendel looked defeated. "We've brought China into the modern age. We offered an olive branch called free trade and they have used it against us. We thought it would lead to an uprising by the people against the Communist Regime, but the PRC has morphed into a pseudo-capitalistic government. We owe China trillions of dollars and the average person in China thinks things are just fine. China believes they have beaten us at our own game. They could be right."

Scott went to the bar and poured another drink. He brought the bottle over and poured another two shots in Nendel's glass.

"Russia must be watching this and laughing," Scott said.

"You may not be that far off. Some of our strategists say Russia is helping to fuel the fire and holding back just far enough to pick up the pieces if we go to war with China."

"You're saying Russia and China are not the friendliest allies."

Nendel let out a long sigh, finished his drink, and placed the glass on the coffee table. "Sometimes I wish I could go back to my days in the Coast Guard. My biggest problem was a fishing boat in distress, or the occasional interception of a boat trying to smuggle in drugs. We haven't had a serious threat on our coastlines since World War II. Now I have access to conversations from all around the world. NSA's motto is, 'there's no such thing as too much information,'" he quipped. "I think there is, if you don't have the capability to analyze all of it. We think Russia will go along with China to share in the spoils of a war, but I wouldn't be surprised if Russia didn't come out on top."

"No country would want the burden of taking over a nation buried in nuclear waste," Scott said.

"And that's what really has us worried," Nendel said, rising to his feet. "The only way they can win a war is to prevent us from using our nuclear weapons. There is only one way they can do that."

Chapter 11

North Star Industries, Engineering Office

David watched from Tyler Tanner's old office as people arrived on Monday morning. He would have to call a meeting and let them know he was their new boss.

"What's going on?" Gil asked. "Do I need to call security?"

David was dressed in a T-shirt and faded blue jeans. He wore sneakers without socks. Clearly he was under dressed for the occasion. *This isn't a Silicon Valley electronics firm*, David thought. *Maybe it should be.* Many of the engineering staff arrived wearing suits and ties.

He had seen Gilbert Thompson walk in, recognizing him from his employee file picture. He reached out his hand. "You're Gilbert Thompson, and I'm David Stafford, your new boss."

"No one told me they were replacing Ty," Gil said.

"Not Tyler Tanner," David said. "I'm replacing Roger Wilkes. I want you to take this office and Tyler Tanner's job as Chief Engineer."

Gil looked at him with wide eyes. He looked around. "I don't know how you got through security, or how you know my name, but I don't believe you."

"That's okay," David said. "While you're figuring it out, could you let all the Engineering Department know there will be a meeting first thing? Meanwhile clean out your desk and move your things in here. We've got a lot of work to do and I want as few disruptions as possible." He reached out his hand, "Congratulations, Gil, on your promotion."

Gil shook his hand. "Ah…thank you. Where do you want the meeting?"

"The main Engineering office will do. I'll stand on a desk and shout if I have to. How many people are we talking about?"

"Two hundred in this office, but another fifty, if you count R&D."

"Good," David said. "Get Research and Development in here. I'll kill two birds with one stone."

North Star Industries Executive Office Building

Scott brought the executives of North Star into his office and gave them a brief summary of the events that transpired over the weekend. He was short on details and heavy on the need to keep thinks quiet. They in turn were to inform the people working under them. For the most part, there would be no changes to the normal work force. He emphasized how important normal work was not to be disrupted. The people needed to know there had been a change at the top, but not why. As soon as he was free, he jogged over to Engineering. He wanted to meet with David and his team.

When he arrived at the Engineering Building he found David standing on a desk addressing a crowded room of engineers and scientists.

He saw the engineers removing their jackets and ties.

David saw Scott standing in the back of the room. "There's our new President now, Scott Tanner. Scott, do you want to say something?"

Scott made his way through the crowd. He climbed up on the desk next to David. "I want you all to know, other than the relaxed dress code, there won't be any changes in your daily routine. Everyone needs to get back to work."

"You heard him," David shouted. "Everyone is dismissed except for Gil Thompson and Charlene Wilson. I need you two to stay behind for a short meeting. We'll meet in the Gil's new office."

Charlene Wilson was a young woman with a slight build and distinctive Asian features. David had learned she held two doctorates, one in Applied Physics and the other in Nuclear

Engineering. She was the head of R&D, a position of equal status to Chief Engineer, and had worked side by side with Tyler Tanner up until his death. Charlene was married to a medical doctor who was finishing his internship at St. Catherine's Oncology Laboratory.

Gil, on the other hand, had a BS in Mechanical Engineering and a Master's in Computer Science. David had done his research and both were highly qualified individuals. They were about to be tested. He needed to see if they could change directions in midstream.

"We need a new mission for Paradox," David said, locking eyes with Gil and Charlene. "You both know Scott and I wouldn't be here if it was business as usual. We've had a serious breach of security and think the Paradox line of satellites has been compromised." He gave them a shortened version of what China had done. When he was finished he looked at Scott. "Do you have anything else to add?"

"Dr. Wilson, how long did it take to develop Paradox 221?"

"Please call me Charlene." She smiled at David. "We're pretty informal around here."

"Charlene, it is," Scott said.

"All the Paradox satellites are an evolution," she said. "As new technology becomes available we incorporate it into our next model."

"So it's a continuous effort. What would Paradox 222 look like?"

She thought for a minute. "We don't have a model yet. What would you want it to do?"

"I haven't got a clue," Scott said, "but whatever you come up with it has to be able to defeat Paradox 221."

"We think China has the code to 221," David added. "If they use that technology to disable the existing Paradox satellites where would we be?"

She looked like she had seen a ghost. The color drained from her face. Her lips turned down.

"Are you okay?" Scott asked.

She took a deep breath. "This is a nightmare none of us want to see."

"What?" Scott asked.

"Paradox 221 is capable of detecting and intercepting any signals coming from earth that would alter a satellite's ability to function in another mode. For instance, Paradox 220 has the capability to search and destroy. It's a communication sat, but with a signal from Sat-Com it can release a hundred grenade size satellites that can search out and destroy anything within a hundred yards. That's pretty close in space. Once in search and destroy mode, the smaller sats cannot be jammed. They persistently look for something to destroy."

"You mean you can't call them back once you've sent them out."

"That's right. They are suicide bombers on a mission to find a target."

"I'm having a little difficulty following the logic of such a capability," David said.

"Do they distinguish between our satellites and the enemy?" Scott asked.

"Two-twenty-ones were designed to take out all satellite capability. If there are nuclear bombs in space, then they would take them out along with the communication satellites."

Charlene looked off in space like she was searching for something. "We were faced with a dilemma when we were developing it. The scenario we were given was, what if our communication satellites were destroyed and we had no capability of delivering our nuclear weapons? It would be the first action any hostile nation would take against us. It would be a surprise attack. Paradox 220 would automatically be activated in such an event."

"How does that happen?"

"Paradox 220 is activated if our communication satellites stop speaking to it. If it gets the silent treatment, it automatically activates and all satellite capability is destroyed…within the geosync sweet spot, that is. Other LEO sats and deep space non-geosync satellites wouldn't be affected."

"Okay we have Paradox 220 floating around in space so we don't really need to worry about China. Even if they have the same capability, no one is going to wipe out their geosynchronous communication network. It would shut down the world. It sounds like much ado about nothing." Scott said.

"Except," Charlene said.

"Except what?" David asked, scooting up in his chair.

"If you follow me out to the assembly floor. It will be easier to explain it with a Paradox 221 in front of us."

They stopped and looked in windows overlooking the assembly area. They saw an assembly line with a hundred robots picking and placing components barely visible from their vantage point, into an array that resembled a giant ball the size of a small car. The sphear was Paradox 221, the latest version. It was attached to a cart that moved it down the line through a gauntlet of robotic arms.

After they had passed through the security checks and donned clean room clothing, Charlene led Scott, David, and Gil onto the assembly floor.

Scott recognized the room from the two-minute video of his father. He looked around the room and tried to imagine the spot where his father had collapsed.

"Scott," Gil cautioned, "You need to stay behind the yellow line. These robots are smart, but they don't interface with humans very well."

Scott stepped back and followed them down a line the length of a football field. He realized the room was ten times the size he had imagined from the video. "When we talk about Paradox 221, we're not just talking about one satellite, are we?" Scott asked. There were at least a dozen satellites moving down the assembly line as he spoke.

Charlene continued: "Each satellite designation consists of ten production satellites all launched by a single rocket at the same time. They are preprogrammed to seek out their geosynchronous orbit by honing in on a ground signal. They float in orbit until they fix. It's like having a twenty-two thousand mile long invisible string stretching from earth holding it in place. Once it's stabilized then the string is cut."

"What's the string? " David asked. "A radio signal?"

"Laser," Charlene said. "It happens very rapidly and is nearly impossible to jam."

They stopped at a point near the end of the assembly line. A giant disco ball similar to the one Scott had seen in the video was in front of them.

"Each tiny mirror is a separate satellite," Charlene said.

"How many are there?" Scott asked. There were too many for him to count.

"Thirteen thousand," Gil said.

"So what can these little puppies do?" David asked.

"They swarm," Charlene said. "They surround a target and block all communication to it. They can even block a laser by deflecting it."

"So this giant ball is not a satellite, but thirteen thousand satellites," Scott said incredulously. "What does it take to activate them?"

"Nothing," Charlene said. "We saw a flaw in Paradox 220. Neutralizing space, wiping out every satellite, would shut us down too. Everyone needs to communicate. The problem with mutual assured destruction is you have to trust your enemy to do the right thing. If our enemies think they can win a war by bluffing they are mistaken."

"So," David said, "let me propose a scenario."

The robots worked silently in the background. Occasionally a worker would show up but the room was amazingly quiet and free of humans.

"We launch Paradox 221 as it is now and China already has an equivalent satellite in orbit. What happens?"

Charlene said, "That would be up to China. They would probably want to prevent us from having equal capability with them. They could swarm Paradox and prevent it from deploying."

"You mean they would prevent it from sending or receiving any communication."

"That's correct." Charlene seemed to be thinking, looking out into space again.

David gave her a minute to consider the option.

Charlene nodded like she had reached a conclusion. "By China preventing 221 from communicating with our satellites it would automatically deploy Paradox 220. That would be chaos."

"How so?" Scott asked.

"There aren't enough Nano-sats to block all of our Nano-sats. It would be like shooting a shotgun at a beehive. If they block our satellites from communicating with one another it triggers the nuclear option, so to speak. Space would be destroyed by Paradox 220."

"Charlene, you see why we can't send these up," David said. "We have to find a way to give Paradox a new mission and do it fast. As soon as China learns we are at a stalemate, it would be an ideal time to attack."

That evening Scott and David met with Sat-Com Director General Cramer in the North Star Hotel conference room. The General had established permanent residence on the top floor just down the hall from Scott and David. Scott thought it was important to pick Cramer's brain. He was the one who was buying satellites, and Sat-Com, an arm of Space Command, controlled them from a black site deep in the Nevada desert.

General Cramer was a short man with huge brown eyes, probably how he got the nicknamed *Banjo Eyes*. He entered the room, nodded to Scott and David and went straight to the bar. He studied the label on a bottle of bourbon and poured a water glass about half full. "I never drink anything that's younger than my grandson," he said, chuckling. "Every year the whisky gets a little bit better." He laughed again and tipped up the drink. "Now, what's on your mind?"

Chapter 12

Tuesday morning, as the sun rose over the treetops on the North Star campus, Scott talked David into a morning run.

"Hold up," David called to Scott. He was bent over trying to catch his breath. He looked up as Scott ran back to see what was wrong.

"Exercise is for those who can't think," David wheezed. He sat down on a bench. "I never should have let you talk me into this."

"It'll make you a better man," Scott said. He raised his eyebrows. "It will help your love life, too."

"My love life was doing just fine, that is until the spooks showed up and told me they needed me in Oregon. How come you can't operate in the natural world, like the rest of us?"

"Natural world? Look around you, beautiful grassy hills, green trees, no smog. You want to go back to Southern California? No wonder you're winded."

"That's where my love life is. Yours is right next door. Why don't you bring Patricia in for a conjugal visit so I can have some peace."

Scott laughed. "You got up on the wrong side of the bed. You want to take a shower and meet up for breakfast?"

David got up and started walking toward the apartment building. North Star labeled it as a hotel, but the arrangement of the apartments was more like a condominium. "I couldn't sleep last night," David said, trying to match strides with Scott. "Remember when we learned about the space race in grade school?" He went on without giving Scott a chance to answer. "It was all about reaching the moon or Mars or beyond, at least I thought it was. "We've really made a mess of things. I don't see any way to win."

"Sometimes it's not about winning," Scott said. "Right now

a tie would suffice. I'm with you, there doesn't appear to be any way to win. We do something; they do something a little bit better. It hasn't changed since the first cave man hit another over the head with a stick and someone threw a rock back at him. If I knew a way to change that, I would."

"Good luck. You'd have to change the nature of man first."

"When I was in training there was a little guy named Peters. Everyone gave him a hard time because of his size. He barely met the minimum for size and weight to be accepted into the Navy. The little guy was nuts. He would intimidate everybody. One day he started harassing Swenson, the biggest guy in the outfit, for no reason at all, and no one could figure it out.

"Swenson wasn't known for his calm demeanor. He had made the first cut at a pro football draft right out of high school and weighed over twice as much as Peters. One day Peters tells Swenson he's full of shit. We are all standing back wondering what kind of drugs Peters was on that he would make such a foolish move. We knew it was going to end poorly for Peters. Anyway, Swenson picks Peters up with one hand and throws him across the room. Peters hits the wall and slides down in a heap on the floor. It didn't make any sense to any of us, and we all figured Peters had it coming, but a strange thing happened after that. No one kidded Peters about his size anymore, not even Swenson. Last I heard Peters was skipper of an Aircraft Carrier."

"Geez, that was a beautiful story," David said. "I thought there would be a point to it."

"Okay, Smart Ass, my point is you don't always know what someone's motives are. We couldn't figure Peters out. Maybe he wanted everyone to know he could take anything that was thrown at him; whatever it was, it seemed to get the outcome he was looking for."

"So you think China, like Peters, feels like we are pushing them around and they want to tickle the dragon, so to speak, and see what our response is?"

"Something like that. They may want to see how far we are willing to go. Once they know that, they own us."

"For starters, we could knock them back into the Stone Age, but we risk taking the rest of the world with them."

"But are we willing to do that? Worse yet, what if China thinks they can slay the dragon?" Scott asked.

David considered Scott's comment for a moment then added, "We think of China as a Third World nation, but they have been modernizing rapidly over the past forty years. Maybe they think they can defeat us. If that's what is happening, we could pick them up to toss them across the room, but they could have one hand on our balls, so to speak."

"Crudely put, but if that's where we are, I don't see there is much we can do about it."

USSTRATCOM Global Operations Center, Offutt Air Force Base

The two-foot thick reinforced concrete walls make the two-story US Strategic Command Global Operations Center nearly impenetrable. In addition to the reinforced concrete walls, the framework of the structure is designed to withstand the electromagnetic pulse from a nuclear blast. In the event of war, inside the 14, 000 square foot special structure, the commanders and senior staff members of the Armed Forces control the combined battlefields of the United States throughout the world. In the heart of the structure, technicians sit at semi-circular desks, each surrounded by a half-dozen monitors where they receive and relay information to the commanders in the field. The facility is manned 365 days a year, 24 hours a day. In the event of a global war, USSTRATCOM is at the top of the list of targets.

General Cramer made a stop at USSTRATCOM on his way to the Pentagon. He met with General Mitchel, a friend and former member of the SATCOM team. Mitchel was six inches taller than Cramer and, with his thin mustache, looked more British than American. He was never without a pipe in his mouth or hand, even though he had long quit smoking. He hung onto it like a child holds onto a comfort blanket. In times of stress he was known to grab it in one hand and clamp down on the stem until he regained his composure. There had been a lot of stressful days lately.

"We keep having these power interruptions," General Mitchel said, removing the pipe from his mouth. "Before the back-up generator kicks in, the power comes back on. No one has given me a good explanation."

"Have you checked with any of the other GOCs?" Cramer asked.

"First I'm making certain it isn't something we're doing. Our technicians have been installing shielding to protect against a terrorist attack. Yesterday they caught a guy at the front gate with a bomb in his car. It would have made national news had it detonated, but to keep copycats from getting ideas, we kept it quiet."

"Sounds like you've had your hands full," Cramer said, "but what I wanted to see you about was my trip to see the President. Is there anything on the world front other than your electrical problems I should know about?"

"Nothing unusual. We've got eyes on Russia and China. Both seem to be minding their own business, which you could say is unusual. Maybe Russia bit off more than they could chew when they toppled Bashar al-Assad. They're learning the same lesson we learned in Afghanistan. It's a lot harder to get out than to get in."

"It's China I'm worried about," Cramer said. "First we see them doing strange things with their satellites, now we're seeing aggressive moves from Beijing, and our people are having trouble determining how serious they are. We have a President who wants to serve out his term without starting a major war, and China seems to be begging us to engage."

"China." Mitchel nodded his head in thought and tapped his forehead with the bowl of his pipe. "They aren't going to do anything on a whim. There is a reason they have survived as long as they have. Strategic thinkers; if they start something, you can bet they are planning on finishing it. With twelve percent of the world's population, they have a lot of people to keep satisfied."

"Right now every man, woman, and child in American would have to come up with a thousand dollars just to pay off our trade deficit to China," Cramer said. He chuckled and shook his head as if he didn't believe it. "China's Military Chairman proposed just that to President Tindall at the last UN meeting."

Mitchel laughed. "That's never going to happen. China needs us too much. We stop buying junk and they stop feeding their people."

"Did you ever think it was a mistake?" Cramer asked.

"What, opening up free trade with China?" He put his pipe in his mouth and was lost in thought for a few moments, before removing it again. "Our money built a hell of a military power for them; they should love us."

"We both know they don't. I'm concerned they believe we will pay back their debt so they can buy weapons to destroy us." Cramer patted Mitchel on his back. "Before I go, General Mellon asked for me to put together a team of advisors should we get into a space based conflict with China. Do you mind if I recommend you as a member?"

"No problem. Let me know. I'll be glad to help."

"Good seeing you Mitch," Cramer said. "Drop by next time you're on the West Coast. I expect to be out there for a while."

"Sure thing, Tom. Give my best to Bess and the kids."

Chapter 13

Portland, Oregon

Patricia Westland left the KPDX studio in a hurry. She had just finished the 11:00 p.m. live news and hadn't eaten dinner. She was famished and entered the covered parking area checking her watch. It was after midnight. Where was she going to get a bite to eat at this hour? She punched the keyless entry for her vehicle and was about to open the driver side door.

"Miss Westland?" A male voice came out of the shadows. She froze. Who would know her name and what were they doing in the parking garage at this hour? Her first inclination was to run. She turned to see if she could put a face with the voice. "I have a gun," she lied.

"I'm not here to hurt you."

She wasn't convinced but had hesitated too long to make a run for it, besides she was in heels. The person stepped out of the shadows. He was tall, dressed in dark clothes with a baseball cap pulled down over his eyes. He had three days of dark stubble on his face.

"I don't have any money," Patricia said. "Do you want my car?"

The man was standing too close for her to run. *Was he a threat?* Were *his* moves aggressive? She glanced at her car, still ten feet away. *Why hadn't she dashed for it, climbed in and locked the doors?* She looked around for a camera. The only one she spotted was behind the man. "There are cameras watching us."

"No need to be afraid of me," he said. "I have information for you."

"What kind of information?"

"The Government is involved in an undeclared war with

China."

Crap, another conspiracy theorist. They had been coming out of the woodwork like termites thinking we were about to go to war. She turned them away almost daily. "Look Mr.—"

"You can call me Ray. That's not my real name, but it will do for now."

"Okay, Ray. You have my attention. Do you have proof?"

"North Star Industries has been taken over by the Government. That should be proof enough. If you want to hear more, we need to go someplace where we can talk."

North Star Industries, he had her attention. "Do you know any restaurants open this time of night?"

"Joe's Diner, they cater to the after-hour bar crowd."

"Fine I'll meet you there."

"Do you mind giving me a ride? I took the bus here and they aren't running this late."

Patricia had been sizing the man up. He looked to be in his thirties, fit and clean. She looked at his hands as he removed them from his pockets. They were clean, not the hands of a vagrant.

"Remove your cap," she said.

"I'd rather not," Ray said.

"I want to see your eyes."

Ray removed his cap. His hair was close cropped, almost military short. He looked at her and quickly put the cap back on and pulled the bill down.

"Okay," Patricia said. "You need to know my fiancé is a former SEAL. You do anything to me and you're dead meat."

"Scott Tanner," Ray said. "I'll bet you didn't know he's the new President of North Star."

"I don't know who you are or where you're getting your information, but Scott Tanner isn't the President of North Star. You are probably thinking of his father who worked for North Star."

Ray stifled a grin. "I was betting he didn't tell you. Everything at North Star is hush hush right now."

"I've changed my mind," Patricia said. "Let me check a

few things out and I'll get back to you."

"No deal. You hear me out or I go to KGW."

She hadn't spoken to Scott since the day Richard Nendel had appeared outside their window at Scott's house. That was nearly a week ago. Scott hadn't returned any of her calls. Nendel being the new director of the NSA and suddenly appearing at his house was unusual. She had thought it curious, but decided it was something about Scott's father. She knew Scott had asked Nendel to look into his death.

Maybe Ray is telling the truth, she thought.

"Get in," she said. "You better know what you're talking about."

Ray got in the car.

"Is this place any good?" she asked, starting the car.

"If you like bacon and eggs."

*****

It was Saturday morning and Scott had been at North Star for one week. He had learned the names of his chief executives and the major heads of every department at North Star. There had been a constant stream of department heads, supervisors, team leaders, and administrative assistants, funneling in and out of a special room set up for the FBI to vet the employees. The FBI wasn't subtle about interrogating North Star employees either. Everyone was given a drug test, a lie detector test, and a new background check, each a line item on the nondisclosure agreement they had signed as a condition of employment. Some did it willingly, others under duress. A few refused, and were terminated on the spot, and were escorted off the premises.

David had left for a weekend with his girlfriend in Berkley. Scott called Patricia and woke her. "Sorry," he said. "You usually don't sleep in."

"I didn't get in until three," she said.

"Out partying with the girls?"

"No, I was with a man, if you must know. In fact, I was

going to try and call you again. You know you haven't answered your phone for a week."

"I was hoping we could have lunch together. Could you pick me up at FBI Headquarters?" Scott asked.

"Out by the airport?"

"Yeah. I'll be there about eleven."

"Where are you right now?"

"I can't say. I'll see you at eleven, okay?"

Patricia brought sandwiches and they drove along Marine Drive and pulled off in a graveled spot that overlooked the Columbia River. Across the road, behind a chain-link fence, one of the Portland International Airport runways stretched out as far as they could see. Air traffic was slow that time of day, but every so often a jumbo jet would glide over them shaking the car with the massive roar from its engines.

"I told you I was with a man last night," Patricia said.

"A man, should I be jealous?"

Patricia handed him a deli sandwich. "He told me the most preposterous story."

"Really. I'll bet that happens a lot in your business."

"I think this one has some credibility, let me spin it past you."

"Sure, anything I can do to help."

"He said you are the new president of North Star Industries. Of course, I said that could never happen without me knowing it. After all we are engaged. I also told him the last thing you wanted to do was run a company."

Scott felt his throat tighten. He tried to swallow but it felt like he had swallowed a golf ball. "What's his name?" Scott managed, after clearing his throat.

"That's it. You're not denying it. You want to know where it came from!"

Scott looked at her, not saying anything.

She continued: "He said the former president of North Star and the vice president are both under arrest and the military has taken control of the company."

Scott stared at her, holding his sandwich with both hands. He took a bite and chewed it. "Hmmm, turkey club, my favorite."

"He also told me there is a rumor that China has stolen some of our satellite plans."

She offered him a bottle of green tea. "You know it all started to make sense; you asking for information on North Star, Richard Nendel showing up a week ago in a helicopter and whisking you away like you were James Bond."

She looked at him, disappointment on her face. "I thought we were close. My god we should trust one another enough to let each other know if something this big is happening."

"I can explain," Scott said. Of course, he knew he couldn't. At this point anything he said would backfire. Better to say nothing and let her be pissed, than to say something and have her still be pissed. If he told her anything, she would want to know more. She was a reporter. It was her job to check out a lead. She wanted to have him verify the story, then what? No, he needed to end this. If news was going to break from North Star it wasn't going to come from him. "No, I can't explain. I can't talk about it."

"Okay. I understand. You don't have to say anything, just nod. I'll ask the questions."

"Patricia. I cannot comment on anything regarding North Star or what I am doing. Stop asking me questions."

"If you loved me, you wouldn't keep secrets from me."

"If you loved me you would trust me when I say I can't talk!"

Patricia started the car. "I'll take you back. I know I'm not going to drop this and if I push you anymore you'll become angry."

"I'm already angry," Scott said.

"Don't be mad at me," Patricia said. "I'm just doing my job."

"I'm not mad at you. I'm mad that the world works this way."

"Please explain," Patricia said, pulling up in front of the

FBI building.

Scott leaned over and kissed her. He put his sandwich back in the sack. "Thanks for lunch."

"How can I reach you?"

"You can't. You need to drop anything you hear about North Star."

"Scott…"

He shut the door, taking the sack lunch with him. "How am I going to explain this?" he mumbled as he entered the building.

"Hey, Scott," Special Agent Reese said seeing him enter. She was coming out of the elevator. "Gordon and I were just talking about you."

"I know," Scott said. He pointed to his ears. "They're still burning."

"Seriously, if you have a minute, Agent Gordon is still in his office."

Scott followed Reese down the hall to Agent Gordon's office. "Knock, knock," Reese said standing in Gordon's doorway.

Gordon looked up. "Scott, come in. I heard the helicopter drop you off earlier. I'm glad we caught you."

"What's up?" Scott asked.

"We're just about finished clearing the employees. It's remarkable, but so far we haven't found anything deeper than Stone and Wilkes. The other owner, CFO Marten Ramos checked out clean."

"Does that mean I can go back to my business?" Scott asked.

"You'd better ask Nendel about that. We're just involved in the local investigation. Last I heard there's a bigger problem involving national security."

"What can you tell me?" Scott didn't know what could be bigger than our satellite information getting into the hands of China.

Gordon eyed Reese as if checking with her before talking. "I'll probably get my ass reamed for saying anything. Forget I said it."

"For what it's worth, I don't know what you're talking about," Scott said. "While I'm here I might as well disclose my fiancé is on to something at North Star and it didn't come from me. She said someone approached her who seems to know a lot about what's going on. He knew about me and the military takeover. Nendel is going to be concerned the news has gotten out."

"Could have been any of the employees," Gordon said. "We had a few who refused to sign new nondisclosure agreements. We reminded them they were still bound by the old agreement anyway. Funny how easily someone will sign their rights away to get a job and how loudly they'll complain once they are employed. No one failed the polygraph, though. She wouldn't tell you who it was?"

"I didn't ask. I knew she wouldn't give up her source. She wanted me to confirm it, but I grabbed my lunch and left." He held up the bag. "I got one bite out of my sandwich and walked away."

"You didn't tell her anything?"

"I didn't confirm it, but she's not stupid. She was with me when Nendel picked me up at the beach. Someone out of the blue approaches her with a story about me and North Star, she's not going to sit on it."

"We'll take care of it," Gordon said. "Was she headed home?"

"You guys are going to get me in a lot of shit. You talk to her and she's going to know I told you."

"You're right," Reese said. "If we show up it just adds credibility to the story."

"You think she'll run with it?" Gordon asked.

Scott shook his head. "She won't report it unless she has a second source."

"Okay. Don't worry about it. You got a ride coming?"

Scott checked his watch. "He should be arriving any minute."

Scott took the stairs to the helipad on the roof. He sat on a bench and finished his sandwich and washed it down with the green tea.

"What do you think?" Gordon asked Reese.

"Put a tail on her. If she meets with the informer again we'll nab him."

"Do it," Gordon said.

*****

Berkeley, California

David walked across the UC Berkeley campus. He remembered the days he had spent on campus as a student. At the time he didn't know Fay Connor and didn't know she was also a student. *Small world*, he thought. *We are right next to each other and don't meet until we are half a world away.* College was such a distraction. He saw a young woman in ragged jeans and sandals and it reminded him of attending classes in flip-flops and cut-off jeans. Not much had changed. There were only a few students still roaming campus this late in the school year.

He found Fay in her office packing boxes. Finals were over and she had no place she had to be. In years past she would be returning from Antarctica with enough work to keep her busy in the lab through the summer months, but that was behind her.

"David, what a surprise," she said, seeing him in the doorway. She rushed over and kissed him. In her white sneakers, she stood a few inches taller than David.

"I grabbed a few days and thought you might fly with me to San Diego. I remember you said school was out."

"You arrived just in time. I need help packing these boxes out to my car."

David grabbed a box and Fay picked up another one. When they got to her car, he could see she had made several trips before. "Are you working this summer?" he asked.

She shook her head. "I thought I'd take the summer off. Maybe head to Europe on a vacation. You should join me."

"Maybe. Right now I'm in the middle of something."

"You're always in the middle of something. What is it this time?"

"This time I'm in over my head."

"Hop in, we can grab a cup of coffee and you can tell me about it."

David looked inside her Smart car. Boxes were stacked everywhere including the passenger seat. "Why don't I follow you? I have a rental."

She kissed him lightly on the lips and smiled. "You know where I live."

Fay fixed coffee and they took their cups out to the balcony overlooking Lake Merritt. The paved drive around the lake was lined with vintage sports cars. "There's a fifty-five Mercedes 300 SL Gull Wing," Fay said, pointing out a bright red sports car. "My uncle had one of those in his collection. He said it was worth three quarters of a million dollars."

"And some guy is running one in a rally? I'll bet his insurance agent is riding shotgun," David quipped.

Fay laughed. "You're not into cars are you?"

"A little, but I prefer engines. Take that Mercedes, for example. Mercedes designed the inline-six engine to slant at an angle so they could keep the car's low profile. They gave it direct fuel injection, something that was way ahead of its time back then. The body is aluminum, something also unheard of at the time. The gull wing doors made it a classic even while it was still in production and the steering folds, making it easy to get in and out."

"Now you're showing off," Fay said.

They went inside and Fay topped off their coffee. "You said you were into something over your head. Why do I not believe you?"

David pulled up a stool at the kitchen bar. "I can't talk about it, but I'll be tied up for a few more weeks and then I might be able to join you in Europe."

"That's right, you work with the Government. Everything is secret."

"Well this time it's a little different, but that's not why I dropped by. I do have something you may be able to help me with," David said.

"Oh," Fay raised her eyebrows.

"Not that," David felt the warm glow of embarrassment rise to his cheeks. "I've been handed a puzzle that doesn't seem to have a solution. You're a scientist. What do you do when it seems the direction you're going in just isn't working out?"

"You flew all the way up here to ask me that?"

"I flew up here because I missed you. After I arrived, I figured why not get your opinion."

Fay was playing with him. She enjoyed his company, and even though he wouldn't tell her what he was working on, they could talk about it in abstract terms. They had done it before. "When all else fails, I resort to the Vince Lombardi," Fay said.

"Vince who?"

"You never heard of Vince Lombardi?" Fay looked at him disbelieving. "You're kidding me."

"Okay, maybe. He played baseball or some sport didn't he?"

"Oh... my... god. You are a nerd."

"Hey, not everything revolves around sports."

She leaned over and kissed him. "I don't know what you're working on, but you asked what I do if I'm stumped on a problem. I go to Vince Lombardi. My dad was an avid football fan. He told me about Vince Lombardi, probably the greatest football coach ever. Look him up. I guarantee he will help."

"You sound like he was some kind of a god."

Fay sipped her coffee. "He wasn't a god. He would tell you himself that he wasn't brilliant. He believed in winning. All winning, whether it is football or business requires certain basic principles to be put into practice. You're a problem solver, but you've relied on your own wit and creative thinking to solve a problem. You say you're in over your head. When that happens, you have to grow taller or drain some water to get your feet back on solid ground. Lombardi would say you have to get back to the basics."

David stood up. "Fay, I have to go."

"But you just got here."

"I'm sorry," David said. "I have to get back to work. I'll call you. Better yet, I'll join you in Europe. Let me know where you're going to be in a few weeks." He ran down the steps to the parking area and pulled out beside the continuous line of antique sports cars. He mused the rental car he was driving could beat any of them in a rally. Technology had come that far, but nothing beat the story behind the individual car. The magic was the struggle the people went through to produce a Jaguar, MG, Mercedes, Alfa Romeo, or any of the other classic cars lined up along the lake. A few minutes with Fay had given him an idea. He had to fly it by the team at North Star.

If you're in over your head, either grow taller or drain the water. Could it possibly work?

Chapter 14

North Star Industries

Scott was the first one David spoke to about his idea. Paradox 221 was the latest satellite technology and no defense against it had been developed. But launching Paradox 221, knowing China had the capability to prevent it from ever deploying, could start a space war the US couldn't win. Even if they equipped it with AEHF or advanced extremely high frequency communications making it more difficult to jam, it still wasn't a foolproof fix. Since Sputnik first circled the earth in 1957, nations had been striving for space superiority and the US had taken the lead, but now with China holding the latest satellite information, the two nations were on equal footing. Every generation of satellite contained advanced electronics making the one it replaced obsolete. Now they had reached the end of the line. If the present race for space dominance continued, the last frontier was in danger of becoming no man's land. The plan was simple. Stop launching satellites. If you can't win the game, stop playing it.

Scott was silent for a minute while he considered David's words. "But isn't that what China, and Russia for that matter, want? Won't that be giving into them?"

"I have a plan for that," David said.

"Of course you do," Scott said, kicking himself for falling into David's trap again. David never presented a problem without already having a solution.

*****

North Star Industries

General Cramer arrived back at North Star late Monday evening. The sun, low in the western sky, cast dark shadows from the large oak trees across the grassy knolls. He hoped the team at North Star was ready with an upgraded satellite configuration. After visiting three NORAD Global Operation Centers, and a meeting with President Tindall, he was even more concerned than when he had left General Mitchel. Every NORAD base had been the target of hundreds of cyberattacks. What was disconcerting was the attacks seemed to be aimed at the electrical grid powering the stations rather than the computers in the facilities. There had been numerous blackouts, but each time the backup generators were about to kick in, the power came back up. It was no coincidence. He checked by phone with all nine command centers and found the same story. By design, in the event of a power failure, the backup generators waited two minutes to kick in. The NORAD stations were without power for only ninety seconds in each event. Someone knew the NORAD system and was playing with them.

Ninety seconds is a lifetime in cyber warfare. For ninety seconds USSTRATCOM had no control of their satellites. They were without communication. They were blind. *What was happening in those ninety seconds?* He felt ten years older than he had on Friday the week before. He caught up with David Stafford and his team in the executive conference room. He glanced at the digital clock on the wall. It was 10:18 p.m.

"I hope you are all more awake than I am," Cramer said, looking around the room. He saw David Stafford, Gil Thompson and Charlene Wilson. *Had the fate of the country come down to this group of misfits?* "Where are Nendel and Tanner?" Cramer asked gruffly.

"I told them 10:30," David said. "They should be on their way."

David poured a cup of coffee and offered it to General Cramer. "How was your trip, General?"

"I'll wait until the others arrive," Cramer said. He was in

no mood for idle chit-chat.

Washington DC, the White House

For most of his administration, President Tindall had said he would let the generals fight the wars, but now with war seemingly more likely every day, he questioned that strategy. He had a legacy to protect. He now wanted to be in every meeting and in the center of every discussion that might lead to conflict. He sensed his new interest was pissing off his generals, but at this point he didn't give a damn. They could put up with him for the few remaining months of his term and then deal with the new Commander in Chief.

He was in the situation room when they had used a drone to take out a terrorist leader in Iraq and had agreed with the military when they wanted to fire off a non-nuclear ICBM to put Iran on notice that he wouldn't tolerate another nuclear program. Now with China, it seemed, as his second term was nearing an end, world events were forcing him into becoming a hawk rather than the peacemaker he liked to think he was. With China, diplomacy had failed, sanctions had failed; stopping trade had failed. It seemed the only thing that would satisfy China was settlement of the debt the United States owed, and there was no way of doing that without crashing the economy. With less than a hundred days left in office, he woke every morning wondering if his efforts to improve the economy, strengthen education, and rebuild critical infrastructure would be overshadowed by a war. If the Nation went to war, he wasn't going to be the one to start it. *My Joint Chiefs will have to respect that reality.*

Tindall looked up from his desk and greeted his Chairman of the Joint Chiefs. "Sit down General Mellon."

Out of respect for the office, Andrew Mellon, a four star Army General remained standing until Tindall took a seat on the couch. Mellon sat in a chair opposite the President, a low table separating them. An ornately sculptured silver pot of coffee and two cups with saucers sat on the table. The President's aide poured coffee and offered cream and sugar to them. Both declined.

"Raymond, close the door and make sure we are not disturbed," Tindall said to his aide.

"Yes, sir Mr. President," his aide said, leaving the room.

"Every time you ask for a private meeting I get a knot in my stomach," Tindall said. "The last time you were here, North Korea had lobbed a missile two hundred miles off the coast of Japan. What is it this time?"

"Our Global Operation Centers have been under cyberattack for the past week. We think China or Russia or both are behind it. We've lost power in every one of our centers. The first step an enemy will take in the event of war is disrupting communications. The command centers receive critical information from troop and equipment movements, to weather conditions around the world. All of it is communicated through satellites. If we lose communication with these satellites, we lose the ability to communicate with our ships, planes, battlefield commanders, and our military supply chain. In short we, can't fight a war without satellites and our systems are being tested."

"Well, you managed to ruin my day again. What can I do to help?"

"Sir, you need to tell China to knock it off, or else."

"Or else what, General?"

"Or we will strike the building in Beijing where this is coming from."

"You've narrowed it down to a single building in Beijing?"

"Well, to the city block. We've been watching that area for years."

"Can you give me some specifics? I'll need absolute proof, if I put China on notice. I've already personally complained to both Mordashov and Xi Wuhan about their fiddling in our afairs. I already told them we would retaliatein kind, but it doesn't look like that worked. What more are you suggesting I do?"

"With all due respect, the last time we gave you something,

you refused to accept it."

Tindall stood up. His face reddened and a vein on his neck started to show. It was something that few people had seen. Usually, Tindall was a poster boy for keeping his cool. "If you think I'm going to start a nuclear war over a few power blackouts, then you are sorely mistaken."

"With all due respect, sir, they are blacking out our command centers, that's Goddamned close to waging war."

"You need to show me an option that will prevent a war, not start one." Tindall demanded.

General Mellon rose to his feet. "Sir, if China starts a war, they will win. We don't have the high ground anymore. With the compromise of North Star, the playing field has been more than leveled. We are now the underdog."

"General, the threat of a nuclear strike has been overplayed. China knows we aren't going to launch nukes. If that threat had any credibility, they would have stopped building islands in the South China Sea."

"Mr. President if you would have dropped a MOAB on one of those islands before it was completed, they would have stopped construction. Now they not only have completed them, they have set them up as military basses. When we failed to act, we lost all credibility with the Philippines and Malaysia. Even Japan doubts we will protect them. We are losing this war and you are part of the problem."

"General, might I remind you, I can have you removed for insubordination. I have to consider the safety and security of the American people. You seem to think everything needs to be settled by military action."

"What about the Country, Mr. President? How safe and secure are the American people going to be if we let China win the information battle. We have no way of knowing how far they have come. They may already be in our Defense Department computers. We just don't know."

"General," Tindall softened his voice. "We are both fighting for the same thing, but it sounds like you have given up on all the options. A year ago you were going to fight cyberwar with cyberwar, not with nuclear weapons. What happened?" He motioned for the General to sit again and he did the same.

"Mr. President, while we were fighting cyber with cyber, China was stealing our satellite plans. There is no way to minimize the damage they have done. China has taken over our position in space. There is no way of gaining it back except for all-out war."

"And you told me we would lose."

"I said if China strikes first, we will lose. Mr. President, we need to preemptively strike. If we wait, they will knock out our communication satellites and we will be helpless. We won't even be able to launch our ICBMs."

Tindall looked thoroughly defeated. "I'll need to go to Congress with this. Prepare for a joint meeting with the House and Senate Armed Services Committee." He stood up. "General, if you have any rabbits in your hat, now is the time to pull them out. I can guarantee the American people do not have the stomach to go to war."

General Mellon stood. He had accomplished his mission. The President knew the situation. *The last thing he wanted was war, but if it was inevitable, we needed to win.*

North Star Industries

David Stafford shook his head in the negative to a question from General Cramer. In addition to Cramer, NSA Director Nendel, the North Star managers and Scott Tanner were in attendance. David was presenting an alternate plan to the Paradox satellite system. He had only discussed it with Scott before. He proposed the delay of the next generation of Paradox.

"Paradox 221 was our final trick. We can continue to put up new birds, but they are entirely useless if China wants to shut them down. Unless we stop China from launching any more satellites we've reached a standoff in space. Any overt action against China will be met with an equal or stronger reaction. My team believes we have exhausted all the geosynchronous orbit options. From here on out we are spending millions of dollars on every bird and launching nothing but space junk. My team has a different proposal."

David brought up an image on the largest monitor, a screen that spanned the entire width of the conference room. "We are proposing we stop the space race in its tracks and divert all of our resources into a new program. It has been under development for several years and has recently been tested. DARPA has given it the acronym HAP, or high altitude platform. It can do everything a peaceful satellite can do without the high cost to launch. It doesn't have the vulnerability of being compromised by our enemies, and allows us the full use of our defense delivery capability."

General Cramer shook his head. "I've never heard anything so ridiculous in my life. How are a bunch of high altitude balloons going to be better than satellites in space? We already have high altitude platforms. They are called Low Earth Orbiting satellites. I don't think you were even born when we decided it was necessary to launch satellites into geosynchronous orbit twenty-four thousand miles out. Those stations just sit there and do a job for us. You're suggesting we abandon them and launch a bunch of balloons."

"General, can I have a moment with you outside?" Nendel headed for the door not waiting for a response.

"I've had it up to here with civilians running our Defenses," General Cramer said in the hallway.

Nendel wasn't going to let the General bully his main contractor.

"I get it, you're running Space-Com," Nendel said, "but the people who have been supplying the equipment that kept you in business for the past fifteen years are telling you it's time to go in a different direction. Their jobs are on the line, too."

"They need to launch Paradox 221. If China destroys it, then we'll cross that bridge when we come to it."

"You want to call China's bluff. I get that too, but all of my intel says they aren't bluffing. The company that has been supplying your hardware has been in China's pocket. Maybe it didn't start out that way, but it's a fact right now. We're running out of time. We either come up with something novel or wait for China to drop the hammer. Three hundred million Americans without the ability to watch a movie or talk to their families on the telephone isn't an option the President will accept. You should listen to what Stafford and his team are proposing."

"I've heard enough," Cramer said. "General Mellon has asked for my input. I'm going to tell him, we send up the next bird and let China play its hand. If we have to send a few nukes their way to convince them we're not going to be held hostage to their piracy, then I'm for that, too."

Nendel watched as Cramer stomped down the hall.

Inside the room, David, Scott, Gil, and Charlene could hear enough of the shouting to realize they had stirred up a hornet's nest. When only Nendel came back into the room, Scott was concerned.

"Richard," Scott said, "David is just giving his best assessment of the situation he was thrown into. That was what he was asked to do."

Nendel raised his hand and waved him off. "No need to apologize for doing your jobs. I've been asked to fly back to Washington to attend a meeting of the Joint Chiefs of the Armed Forces. I need to be brought up to date. Tell me about High Altitude Platforms and how they will save us. Maybe I can find a sympathetic ear."

Washington DC, White House Situation Room

It was cramped quarters for a meeting with the Joint Chiefs, but for security reasons the President had restricted attendance to General Mellon, the four Chiefs of the Armed Forces, their staffs, his National Security Advisor Biggs, NSA Director Nendel,

General Cramer, and General Mitchel, and one staff member each. The room was packed, but it was the most secure place in the White House and off limits to any press members.

Everyone in attendance knew the meeting involved the growing threat from China. All diplomatic options had been exhausted. It was the first step in preparing a strategy for handling an ever-growing threat.

Chapter 15

Portland, Oregon

Patricia Westland felt her anxiety rise every time she entered the parking garage after her late night news broadcast. She had asked her cameraman to walk her out, but when it came time to leave, he was nowhere to be seen. She stopped at the door to the garage and looked across the dimly lit space. She saw three cars, but no people. She had a straight shot to her car and walked at a quick pace. She climbed behind the wheel and noticed a note on her windshield. She checked her mirror and looked around again before quickly opening the door and grabbing the note from under the wiper blade. She got back in and locked the doors.

Ray, the man who had given her the news about North Star, seemed to have vanished. A week had gone by and she hadn't aired the story because she couldn't get a reliable source to speak on the record. Really, there wasn't enough there unless someone would allow their name to be used as a reliable source.

The public record was nonexistent when it came to any news surrounding North Star Industries: no record of Charles Stone being arrested, no answer at his home. She had driven to his mansion in an upscale neighborhood in Lake Oswego, but the place appeared vacant. She made an unscheduled visit to Roger Wilkes' home the same day. The curtains were drawn and no one answered the door. She left messages, but didn't expect to get a return call. The story was all but dead.

She read the note.

Sellwood Park two a.m. Come alone. You won't be disappointed.

Sellwood Park was a small green area in an old neighborhood close to the river on the East side. She noticed her hands were trembling. She knew from Scott's response to her inquiry, that what she was doing could be a breach of national security. "Damn you, Scott," she said. If he would just tell her something, she wouldn't have to meet with creeps in the middle of the night to break a story. She felt like she was breaking the law, burglarizing a jewelry store or robbing a bank. She grabbed the steering wheel squeezing it tightly. "It's your job and the First Amendment gives you every right to do it," she said, breaking the silence.

Two people in a black SUV at the end of the parking garage raised their heads. "What's she doing?" Agent Reese asked Gordon.

"Just sitting there. I think she took a note from under her windshield wiper. I didn't see anyone put it there."

"Good, maybe we finally have contact."

As Patricia pulled out of the garage, Reese followed her. They had installed a tracking device on her car three days earlier so they could stay a safe distance back. They wanted to know who was leaking information from North Star and put a stop to it.

"Any bets on who her source is?" Gordon asked.

Reese was driving. She could see the taillights from Patricia's Prius a few hundred yards ahead. Traffic was light, so she wasn't concerned with following too close. "She's taking the Milwaukie Expressway," she said, turning on her blinkers to take the exit.

"We've checked out the employees who quit over signing the new agreement. I don't think it's one of them," Gordon said.

"Then it has to be someone who is still working there."

"Not necessarily. The kind of information Wilkes was leaking wasn't going to Chang Yi in Washington directly. There may be a Portland connection."

"And you think they would leak information on their own spy efforts?"

"Maybe, if it would bring down North Star. The office in DC has been closed. China isn't getting any more information from Wilkes. If they can put the pressure on they can shut down North Star. The best way of doing that is a huge scandal that involves the Government, the military, and greed. Turn the public against the company. Make North Star the enemy."

"It's damn hard to argue with your logic. If it is someone on the outside, they could be dangerous."

They followed Patricia down a narrow side street with cars parked on the sides leaving only enough room for one way traffic. A sign announced there was a park at the end of the street. Huge trees provided a canopy making the dark street even darker. No lights were on in the park, but street lights in the distance and a sliver of a moon provided enough light to make out shapes.

"Stay back," Gordon cautioned.

Patricia pulled into the parking area. She looked across a baseball diamond, but couldn't see anyone. She waited. The digital clock in her car radio showed 2:03.

He should be here, she thought. She turned her car off and the headlights went out. She nearly jumped out of her skin when someone started banging on her car.

Bang, bang, bang. The dark figure was pulling on the handle trying to get in. She turned on her dome light. It must be him, who else would it be this time of night.

"It's Ray. Open up and turn off the goddamn light."

She unlocked the door and he slid in next to her. He had grown a scruffy beard and looked older than she had remembered. "I said, kill the damn lights." He reached over and fumbled with the dials on the dash. "I'll do it," Patricia said. She reached down and twisted a knob. They were in the dark.

"Give me your hand." He slapped a flash drive in it and closed her fingers. "You will air this message. We can get to your brother, Billy. He attends Portland State. We have eyes on him."

"What! Who? Billy doesn't have any..."

"North Star is about to start a third world war by launching a satellite designed to destroy all other satellites in the sky. It's aimed at retribution for the debt the US owes the Chinese People's

Republic."

He got out of the car and ran into the shadows.

"Shit!" Gordon said, seeing the scene unfold. It happened so quickly Reese had not yet stopped the car. The figure disappeared so quickly into the darkness, there was no hope of finding him.

"What do we do now?" Reese asked. "Do we play our hand?"

"No. If she knows we are following her, she might panic."

"He was inside her car. Maybe he left fingerprints."

"We can get a team to dust it when she arrives at work tomorrow. Let's call it a night."

Patricia locked the car doors. He had said something about her brother. *How did he know his name and where he went to school? Public records; that wouldn't take much digging. What did he say about North Star and China?* She squeezed her hands together trying to stop them from trembling. She needed to talk to Scott again. *This time he's going to tell me something.*

North Star Industries

Scott Tanner rolled over in bed. In his dream he was hearing an alarm and running towards a fire. People were running. A child fell in front of him. Tiny arms reached out for help. He reached for her. Half of her face was missing. He sat up abruptly. There was a loud knock on the door. He felt sweat trickle down his face. He checked the clock. 3:57 a.m. "Who is it?"

"Grayson, sir. Front gate security."

"Give me a second." He took a deep breath and willed his heart to stop beating so fast. He got up and opened the door. "Grayson, what's going on?"

"There's a woman at the gate. She insists she has to see you. I tried calling, but you didn't answer."

"It's okay. Did she give a name?"

He checked a notebook. "Patricia Westland. She seems distraught."

"Can you bring her here?"

"No sir. She doesn't have clearance. You'll have to meet her outside the gate."

"Let me get dressed and I'll ride with you," Scott said.

Patricia opened the car door as soon as she saw Scott. The morning air was cool and humid. She pulled her sweater around her and waited for him to exit through the gate. She ran to him and wrapped her arms around him. "Thank God, you're here."

"I know you wouldn't be here this time of the morning if it wasn't important." He lifted her chin. She had been crying. He hugged her.

"This man threatened Billy," Patricia said between sobs.

"Start at the beginning. What man and what did he say?"

Patricia told him what had transpired. "I drove straight here."

"You don't know what's on the flash drive?"

"No. He said I have to put it on the air or he'll hurt Billy."

"Did you get a look at him?"

She nodded. "It was the same man who contacted me before. He calls himself Ray, but said it's not his real name. He looked serious."

"Get your things. You're coming inside with me. First, were going to call the FBI." He walked her into the guard house and signed her in. They printed a badge.

"You'll have to leave your phone and any electronic devices here," the guard said. Another guard ran a wand over her. "Ma'am, your hand?"

She had her hand clinched around the flash drive. She looked at Scott.

"I'll take that," Scott said. "Grayson, I'm taking the flash drive. I'll be responsible for it."

"I'm sorry sir, paragraph twelve, section three-point-nine strictly prohibits electronic recording storage or memory devices from entering or leaving the premises without express written permission from the chief executive officer."

Scott pulled Grayson aside and spoke in a low voice, "Just so you know in case we ever meet again," Scott showed him his badge, "I'm the new sheriff in town."

"I'm sorry, sir. I heard we had a new boss, but I work at night."

"It's okay," Scott said, patting him on the shoulder. "If you need to make a note that we brought in this device, I'll sign for it."

"I'm sure it'll be okay," Grayson said. "Where would you like to go? I'll drive you."

Scott turned on the lights in the executive conference room, picked up the phone and woke David.

"I think I'd feel better if he's here when we stick this in a computer," Scott said, looking at Patricia. "I remember the last time you gave me a flash drive."

Patricia smiled, looking at the large desk, the monitor on the wall and the 24-inch globe in the corner. A shelf had a model of every Paradox satellite that had ever been put into orbit. She spun the globe waiting for Scott to get off the phone.

While they waited, Scott opened the tiny refrigerator and got them both a bottle of water. He twisted the cap and handed one to her. "By now you know you're in the middle of something the Government doesn't want made public."

"I didn't start this. That man came to me."

The phone rang. Scott answered, listened for a minute and turned to Patricia. "The FBI is out front. They are going to dust your car for prints."

"Why would they do that?"

"Was the man you met earlier wearing gloves?"

"No."

"Good. Maybe they can identify him."

"What about Billy?"

"They'll want to interview you. They can protect him, too, if necessary."

David walked, still half asleep. "Hey, Patricia, what's up?" he said, yawning.

"That was quick," Scott said. "Grab something out of the fridge." He handed the flash drive to him. "Remember the guy I was telling you about. He gave this to Patricia and wants her to air it."

David plugged the flash drive into the computer. The screen showed a picture of a town being bombarded from space. The voice said, "The United States is sending weapons into space in an effort to rule the world. The demand for payment of debt from nations once friendly to the United States has brought about a hostile response that is threatening a global war. This time the United States will be standing alone. The World Court has spoken. It is time for the richest nation in the world to pay its debt to China. Does it make any sense that some nations have been taking food out of the mouths of their people to subsidize the affluent lifestyle of the average American? Are the American people ready to go to war?

"Recently, after the United States lost a battle in the World Court against China, North Star Industries based in Hillsboro, Oregon launched a satellite capable of destroying China's new peaceful Communication Satellite System. President Tindall believes that he can threaten the Chinese people by launching nuclear weapons into space. China asks the American people to tell their congressmen not to vote for war. Pay China what is owed them and return space to the peaceful place it has historically been. Do not let North Star Industries continue to produce weapons of mass destruction and threaten the Chinese people."

The screen showed a massive military parade in China. Truck after truck loaded with missiles on mobile launchers paraded by. Then the screen panned to a view of a massive submarine firing missiles from the water. The screen showed a satellite view of the United States and mushroom clouds rising from every major city.

"Call your State Representative and members of Congress. Tell President Tindall, war is not an option," the voice said. "The

United States does not have the funds to fight a major war. Tell your congressman to pay off the national debt and keep the world free of war."

"I can't air that," Patricia said. "It isn't true…is it?" She looked at Scott and then at David.

"It's propaganda," Scott said. "If China can convince the American people they can't win a war, then China wins without firing a shot."

"But North Star Industries. You aren't building nuclear weapons and launching them into space."

"You're right about that," David said.

"Then what are they talking about?"

"You tell her or I will," David said. "She needs to know why this has to be kept from the public."

Scott removed one of the Paradox models from the shelf. He handed it to Patricia. "This is a communication satellite." He took it back from her and opened it, peeling back the sides like the pedals of a lotus flower. "This is how the satellite got the code name *Paradox*." He showed her how the tiny satellites could split off from the base. "Now, these tiny satellites can seek out and destroy enemy satellites. For the past few years, China has been stealing Paradox plans from North Star. We found out about it too late. China already has their version of Paradox in orbit, and that's where we are today. Why David and I are here."

"But, you haven't attacked China or destroyed any of its satellites."

"That's correct," David added, "but it doesn't matter. China gained the upper hand when they got their bird into orbit before ours. Now China has space superiority and we are being held hostage."

"From China's perspective, stealing our information has been a plan that started fifteen years ago," Scott said. "They decided to use their leverage against the owners of North Star and caught the U S Government by surprise, until a few weeks ago when it was discovered they had technology they shouldn't have. Now, China can prevent us from putting any more satellites in orbit, and at any time take out the entire network of communication satellites."

Agent Gordon knocked and came through the open door. "Do you guys ever go to bed?" he asked.

"She woke us up," David said.

"Yeah, I confess, it was all my fault," Patricia said.

"Miss Westland, don't worry. We have identified the man and have agents on their way to arrest him." He turned to Scott. "We don't have his motive, yet, but I'll keep you informed."

"He threatened my brother if I don't put this on the air." She pointed to the computer screen.

"We can take that for evidence," Gordon said, pulling an evidence bag out of his pocket.

Patricia removed the thumb drive from the computer and handed it to him.

"It's been a hell of a night," Gordon said, stuffing it into the bag and sealing it.

"I'd like for Nendel to see that when he gets back from Washington." Scott said.

"No problem, send him by the office," Gordon said.

"Are we done?" David asked. "I've got to meet my team for an early morning call from the Pentagon."

"I forgot about that," Scott said. He kissed Patricia and held her close. "Are you going to be okay? I really do need to be on that call." He turned to Gordon. "Can you see she gets back to her car?"

He kissed her again. "Promise you will keep all of this secret? You understand the risk."

"I promise," Patricia said.

Chapter 16

North Star Industries

"Good job you guys," Nendel said, looking at the team from the computer screen in the North Star engineering conference room. "High Altitude Platforms are a go, but you still have a lot of work to do. We're going to launch Paradox 221. In fact we are going to launch ten of them. How soon can you have them ready to go?"

"Admiral," David said. "Will there be any changes to the satellites."

"Negative. We're going to launch them as designed."

"You obviously know something we don't," Scott said.

"I'll explain later. Get those birds ready to fly."

Washington DC, the White House

"Mr. President, Senator Brookman is on the phone," Tindall's secretary said.

"I told you I didn't want any interruptions for the next hour," Tindall growled.

"He says it's important and I couldn't find your COS. The senator says he won't leave a message."

"Put him through."

"Senator Brookman, how are things on the Hill?"

"Turn on your television. We're about to be attacked from within."

Tindall hit the remote and brought up Fox News. "What am I looking at Senator?"

"Riots in every major city across the country," Senator Brookman said. "A video posted on the internet. Now every major news network is airing it like it's real news."

Tindall turned up the volume. "…it appears the crowds started forming at six this morning and have been growing in size. This is Lisa Whitman, reporting from Chicago. Back to you, Jim."

"Thank you Lisa. We now go to Los Angeles where Greg Norman is outside the Federal Court House…it sounds pretty loud there, Greg."

"That's right, Jim. We have an estimated twenty thousand demonstrators here. So far they have been peaceful, but with a crowd this size, tempers sometimes flare."

"Greg, can you ask someone what this is about?"

Greg put his microphone in front of a young woman with short hair and dark makeup.

"Can you tell me why you are here?"

"We are protesting the Imperialistic actions of the United States against China."

"Can you be more specific," Greg asked.

"The United States has put nuclear missiles in space. We're protesting against that and all nuclear war."

"There you have it, Jim. It appears to be an anti-war rally."

Tindall picked up the phone while he watched the live feed go to New York City. "I want to know who organized this size of a rally and why Homeland Security wasn't on top of it."

"I'll see what I can learn. Have you looked out your window?

Tindall didn't have to look outside. The news gave him a better view. Pennsylvania Avenue was a mass of protesters.

"Thanks, Senator." He hung up the phone. "Margaret, I want Randy Biggs in my office, right now."

"He's not in his office, sir."

"Find him!"

*****

North Star Industries

Scott picked up the phone. "Mr. Tanner, this is the front gate. I thought you should know the gatehouse has at least a hundred people outside demanding to be let in. It feels like we are under attack."

"What's the protocol?" Scott asked

"We've never had anything like this happen before."

"Call 9-1-1."

Scott hung up and his phone rang again. This time it was David. "Have you got the television on?"

"What's up?"

"That tape you gave to the FBI is on the internet and every station across the country is broadcasting it nonstop. There are riots all across the country."

"Outside our gates, too," Scott said. "I just got off the phone with the guards."

"We need a plan," David said. "If they get inside the gate, they can do a lot of damage."

"I'll call Nendel and see if he can help."

Nendel was still in Washington DC when he saw the news. He was caught by surprise and immediately called North Star.

Scott had just hung up when his phone rang.

"Scott, this is serious. I've got a call in to the Oregon Governor. She needs to bring in the National Guard. Round up all your people and take them to Building Seven. We need to keep the facility secure."

"Building Seven? Richard, there are only five buildings."

"Shit, I forgot to tell you. Open your safe and get the key to the basement of headquarters. There's a bunker down there that will hold a thousand people. Do it now, I don't have time to talk."

Scott went to the safe. He had preprogrammed it with his own security code, but had not checked the contents. Inside he saw a metal box and pulled it out. In the box was a Beretta Px-4 handgun and two loaded clips. He put the clips in his pocket, made sure the gun had a clip in it, and slipped it under his belt. He removed a plastic card. On it was written, *Building 7*. He shook his head. *I wonder if there is a building Six?* Underneath the card was a folded slip of paper. It was titled, *Emergency Shelter and Evacuation Plan*. The back of it had a drawing of the bunker and showed an evacuation tunnel. "They must have been expecting this could happen," he said under his breath. He gave the card to his secretary.

"Go to the basement and open the door with this key. We're going to evacuate the complex."

Scott got on the company PA system. "This is North Star President Scott Tanner. We have a situation and are going to evacuate the premises using the emergency plan you have all practiced. Secure your work stations and secure the building when you leave. Proceed in an orderly fashion to the Executive Building and make your way to the basement." He was reading from the paper. "You will be given further instructions once you are safely in Building Seven."

Scott turned on his TV and switched to the security channel. He used the remote to thumb through the hundreds of cameras around the grounds. He came to the front gate. The crowd had overrun the armed guards. He could see one of them on the ground, one of the rioters pulling the rifle from him.

Poor bastard, he thought. *He wasn't going to fire on the crowd.* Scott heard a commotion downstairs and looked out over the handrail to the lobby below. People were streaming in through the door. He reached for the hand gun before realizing it was the employees evacuating to Building Seven, actually the basement of the Executive Building. He watched, glancing at the front door, then back at his TV.

It was evident the crowd didn't know what they were doing. They were milling around looking for some direction. Each of the buildings had a large number on the upper right hand corner, but the facility name was in smaller letters over the front door and on small signs posted at the corner of the lot on which they sat. From the front gate most of the buildings were hidden behind gently rolling hills of grass and trees. An organized demonstration would have gone for a certain building. This was chaos. *Maybe it was meant to be*, he thought.

There was a commotion in the lobby, and he watched as a female employee struggled back to her feet after taking a fall. One of the supervisors grabbed her hand and helped her. David waved as he came through the door, but the flow of the crowd took him along with them. The evacuation from the other buildings into Building Seven, took half an hour. When there were no more people, Scott went downstairs, and after taking a last look outside, locked the front doors.

Streams of rioters were heading toward the building. He went down the stairs, closed and locked the basement door behind him.

Down a long hallway employees were gathered in a large room. He entered, looked for his secretary and, getting her attention, motioned her to him. The voices in the gathering sounded like a gaggle of geese, drowning out individual conversations. She handed him the key. "You'll need this," she shouted. "It's the only way to secure the door." She put her hand on a security panel inside the room.

Scott put the key in the slot and an alarm announced the door was closing. There were a few nervous stares as the room began to be sealed off. A thick steel plate rose from the floor and sealed off the room. He made his way to the stage at one end of the room. It looked like a stadium with semicircular seating and an open floor the size of four basketball courts. Off to one side of the room was a kitchen with supplies. Another room had sleeping quarters with triple-high bunks. Restrooms and showers were announced by signs for Men and Women above doorways at the far end of the room. He knew this from looking at the plans and checked the location of each. Finally he looked around for the emergency exit as he made his way to the stage. As Scott climbed the steps, David was waiting for him.

"Cool place," David said.

"Yeah. I'll talk to you in a minute." He turned on the microphone. "Team Leaders and Supervisors, I understand you

143

have been trained for a situation such as this, so you know better than I what to do. I'm going to let you gather your teams and give them instructions. For right now, everyone should know the National Guard has been called in to restore order. As soon as they have the campus secured you will be free to leave. Until then, I'm told there is food and soft drinks in the kitchen. Use the facilities as you wish."

"That was refreshing," David said, "a bunch of kids with guns. I feel safer already."

"I saw what's going on out there and you're going to be glad those kids have been trained to use their weapons," Scott said.

"Let's see if we can find a place to settle in," Scott said. He looked at the diagram. "There are some rooms back here. I'll bet that's for us."

He pushed his way through the crowd and turned down a hallway. At the end were several doors on opposite sides similar to a hotel. Each room had a number. One door had a proximity sensor pad next to it. It was marked control room. He held up the plastic key. "This must be the key to the executive washroom," he said, placing it in on the proximity sensor. There was a click and the door opened.

"Sweet," David said, entering behind Scott. The room had bunks, bathroom facilities, and a full wall of communication equipment: radios, TV monitors, and electronic devices. "Here," Scott said, handing a cell phone to David. "I guess they are okay to use in an emergency."

"Who do you want me to call?"

"Try 9-1-1 for starters. Find out if the police are out there yet."

Portland, Oregon KPDX Studio

Patricia watched the riots outside the studio. She had come in early, only taking time to freshen up after she left North Star.

The video played over and over in her mind and she wanted to talk to her boss about it, not because she thought she should have put it on the air, but because it was news important enough for someone to threaten her family if she didn't play it. She had talked to Billy and the FBI had picked him up and taken him to their headquarters. He had told her they were going to keep him there until they caught the man she had called Ray. She answered her cell phone seeing it was Billy calling.

"Billy, you are still with the FBI?"

"A lot going on out there," Billy said. "Nothing gets college students riled up like the threat of a nuclear attack."

"The clip is fake," she said. "We don't have nukes in space and we aren't going to launch any."

"Says you."

"Yeah, says me," Patricia said. "I saw a copy of that clip before it made the airwaves. It's Chinese propaganda. China is trying to get the public riled up by posting a video full of half-truths."

"They are doing a good job of it," Billy said. "I've been watching news around the world from the communication room at the FBI. Do you know we are the most hated nation in the world?"

"Billy, I'm telling you not to buy into that shit. China has a beef with us and they are doing everything in their power to weaken us as a nation."

"My bet is President Tindall coughs up the cash we owe them," Billy said. "They are rioting in every country in the world."

"Except China and Russia," Patricia said.

"You're wrong. The streets of Beijing are packed with protesters demanding America pay its debt."

"Billy, it's nice to know you're safe, I've got to get back to work."

"Don't hang up. They caught your man."

"Really?"

"Yeah. His Name is Symone Enrico Flores, an international fugitive originally from Mexico City."

"That doesn't sound right," Patricia said. "This man spoke

English without an accent."

"Just telling you what I overheard."

"Bye, Billy. Stay safe."

"She had to prepare for the news. She knew what was going on was not going to stop because she reported it as propaganda. As in most lies, there was enough truth to make the lie believable. The growing debt to China had been reported for years. Now China was using that to undermine the Tindall Administration.

Washington DC, the White House

President Tindall paced around the oval office reading the report from a special committee on the security of the United States. The oath of office he had taken played over and over in his mind. *I do solemnly swear that I will execute the Office of the President of the United States, and will to the best of my ability, preserve, protect and defend the Constitution of the United States.*

Is this the best of my ability? Russia has two Yasen-Class submarines 500 miles off the Atlantic Coast in a joint exercise with China. At the same time there are three Type 094A Chinese subs the same distance off the Pacific Coast. Both classes of submarines had the ability to strike anywhere in the United States or from much farther away.

What am I to think? Are they testing me?

He had no choice but to match the threat with a show of force. He had to let them know if they attacked, we would respond in kind. The location of the nuclear submarines and the joint exercise left him with no other option. He called a meeting with his Secretary of Defense.

*****

North Star Industries

Inside the control room, David brought up the monitors from around the North Star complex. There were enough cameras that everything that was going on outside could be watched in real time. All events were being recorded and stored in the cloud.

Scott pulled up a chair. "Look, there's a guard down," he said, pointing to the screen. "How to zoom in?"

"Use the mouse." David pulled a chair up beside him and zoomed in on the man.

"That's Grayson," Scott said. "We need to get him some help."

"I tried 9-1-1," David said. "The line is busy."

"He's hurt," Scott said. "I've got to help him.'

"How," David asked. "You go out there; you'll end up just like him."

As they were watching, a figure wearing a black mask kicked the guard and struck him with a baseball bat."

"That's it. You hold down the fort. I'm going out."

Scott used his key to open the door. "Stay in here. I'll be right back," he said to a group of employees wanting to follow him out. He closed the steel door and made his way down the hall, up the stairs to the front lobby. He looked outside. The crowd had grown to several hundred, most of them milling around with their cell phones in the air, seemingly recording the event while they urged the more rowdy ones to destroy something. Scott decided leaving through the front door would draw attention to him. Instead, he ran down the hall and stopped at a side door. He cracked it open enough to peek out. *Good, the crowd hasn't made their way around the side.* He slipped out and ran a good hundred feet before turning toward the front gate. As he ran he saw more people streaming toward him. He was like a lone salmon swimming downstream in the middle of spawning season. No one seemed to care that he was headed north when they were headed south.

He reached Grayson just as another masked figure was

kicking him. Scott grabbed the person by the back of the collar, jerked him up, ripped off his mask, and threw him in the air. He landed ten feet away with the wind knocked out of him. He was just a kid. If it would have been someone older than a teen, he might have cold-cocked him. He leaned down and checked Grayson for a pulse. He was unconscious, but alive. Scott picked Grayson up and cradled the man in his arms. He saw the first of the police arriving in patrol cars. He tried to get the attention of one officer dressed in riot gear, but the noise from the crowd made it impossible.

He saw the police were setting up a perimeter down the road stopping any more people from streaming in. The police formed a line, but the crowd was pushing the line of officers and Scott knew things would get worse. One by one the officers put on gas masks. Scott was fifty feet behind the line of riot police. He stood there watching them as they were pushed back toward him. One bumped into him and was startled. He brought up his nightstick. Scott held his ground with the bleeding security guard cradled in his arms. "I'm Scott Tanner. President of North Star and I have a thousand employees trapped underneath the Executive Building.

The officer got on her radio and called for an ambulance. In a few minutes the crowd split and the ambulance emerged.

Tear gas canisters started to explode. The crowd screamed and scattered while the siren from the ambulance added to the chaos. Two EMTs wearing gas masks got out of the ambulance and took Grayson from Scott. "We'll take care of him. Are you hurt?"

"I'm fine."

The officer he had spoken to earlier was tugging on his sleeve. He turned to her. "I'm Sgt. Green," she shouted. "I notified the Chief. She wants to talk to you." She handed Scott her radio.

"Mr. Tanner, I understand you came from one of the buildings"

"That's right. I have about a thousand employees barricaded underground. My guess is about five hundred rioters are storming the buildings," Scott said. "Some have bats. I didn't see any guns."

David, watching Scott on a monitor from inside, made another attempt to get help, gave up and called Nendel. "David Stafford here, in case you didn't hear, we're under attack," David said the second the phone stopped ringing.

"What? The National Guard should have arrived by now," Nendel said.

"Scott went out and cracked some skulls. The police have arrived, but it's all they can do to keep more demonstrators from pouring in."

"David, you stay safe. Keep the people safe. I'll find out what's happening and get back to you. Are the employees calm?"

"They seem to have taken it well. I'm sure their families are concerned."

"There's a footlocker full of cell phones in the security office. Hand them out and let them contact their loved ones. Caution them not to comment on classified material."

David got up on stage and addressed the crowd. "Attention everybody, the police have arrived. The riot should be under control shortly. I've got about a hundred cell phones in the office down the hall. If you want to call your family to let them know you are okay you will have two minutes each. Make the call short and give the phone to the next person. We're all in this together so please share. One more thing, remember you must keep information concerning your work confidential."

Before he had finished, the hallway to the office was jammed with people. He had left Gil and Charlene in the office to hand out the phones. Having foreseen the impossibility of him getting back once the announcement was made, he had stuffed as many of the phones in his pockets as would fit. He started pulling them out.

"Attention everybody, I have a few phones with me." He held one up in the air. The crowd turned and David threw a phone into their midst. There was a mad scramble, but it had eased the pressure on the hallway. He tossed another phone. "Remember, two minutes." When he had only one phone left, he called Scott.

"Are we any closer to getting us out of here?" David asked.

"I'm fine. Thanks for asking," Scott said.

"It's a madhouse in here. There was less panic before I handed out the phones. I called Nendel and he said he would see why the National Guard hasn't showed up."

Scott heard a helicopter and looked up. It was hovering over a low grass covered hill that was near the Assembly Building. "Have you got contact with the National Guard," he asked the sheriff.

The sheriff handed Scott his radio. "The commander is Colonel Haines."

"Colonel Haines, I'm Scott Tanner."

"Tanner, Director Nendel told me to find you. Where are you?"

"Near the front gate. Is that your helicopter that just set down?"

"That's us. A bunch of unruly kids are storming us."

Scott handed the radio back to the sheriff. "Thanks, I've got to meet up with the Colonel."

"You're not armed," the Sheriff called after him. Scott raised his weapon so the sheriff could see it and stuffed it back in his belt.

"We need to give the demonstrators an escape route," the sheriff yelled at several of his deputies. The crowd was now putting pressure on the police, sandwiching them between the ones already on the grounds and those outside the gate. For a moment there was chaos within the police agencies, as well as the crowd, while they tried to figure out how to disperse a crowd that was closing in on them from two directions.

Several more helicopters arrived and hovered over the demonstrators inside the complex. A loud voice filled the air, "This is your only warning. You are on private property and are trespassing. Disperse immediately or you will be physically removed and prosecuted. This is your only warning."

The State Police with the help of the Washington County Sheriff's Department formed a corridor holding the crowd at bay as a mass of demonstrators turned around and ran from the grounds toward the front gate. Several explosions echoed off the buildings causing more panic.

The demonstrators with weapons were taken into custody along with those who had their faces concealed. The bays of three police vans were filled and more vans replaced them as they left for a makeshift jail.

Scott fought his way through the fleeing crowd and stopped when he came upon a line of armed soldiers surrounding Colonel Haines' helicopter. He raised his hands as a soldier raised his weapon. The rotor blades spun down with the decreasing whine of the turbine engine.

"I need to speak with Colonel Haines," Scott said to the first soldier he saw wearing bars.

The lieutenant sized Scott up, lowered his handgun, nodded toward the helicopter and stepped aside so Scott could enter.

In Building Seven, David pushed his way through the jammed hallway back to the control room. Once inside, he grabbed a megaphone. "Attention everybody, get out of the hallway. Go back to the assembly area. You can take the phones with you." He turned to Gil who was sitting in a chair in front of the monitors. He was flipping from camera to camera, like a kid with a remote control.

"What's happening outside?" David asked.

Gil looked up. "The Assembly Building has been broken into."

"If they get to those satellites, we'll be set back months. Any other buildings breached?"

"That's the only one."

"It can't be coincidence," David said. "They know that will

shut down North Star."

"They have to get through three layers of security," Gil said.

"Keep that camera on. I'm calling Scott."

Scott had just climbed aboard the Colonel Haines' helicopter. He answered David's call.

"David, what's up?"

"The Assembly Building has been breached."

Scott hung up. "The assembly building has been breached, Colonel."

"Nendel told me protecting it was our top priority," Colonel Haines said. "Can you get us in?"

Haines got on his radio. Suddenly the helicopter was packed with soldiers again and the whine of the turbine filled the cabin. They all hung onto anything they could as the helicopter lifted off.

"Can we land on top of the Assembly Building?" Haines asked.

"I'm not certain."

"Never mind. We'll drop some troops and go through the roof."

"There's a door on the roof," Scott said, remembering exploring the building one night when he was having trouble sleeping. On the roof were half a dozen antennas and devices used to communicate with satellite testing facilities around the country. It was part of a qualification process that tested the signal frequency and strength required to communicate from the ground to a satellite in space. If the helicopter landed on the roof, it could wipe out the testing system. Also, breaching the roof would destroy the clean environment. The satellites would be lost.

"Colonel, drop me down and I'll open the door and get the troops inside. Landing the helicopter on the roof will destroy critical equipment."

Chapter 17

The normally short trip from her studio on the East Side of Portland, to North Star Industries took Patricia over two hours and still, the news van was a mile back from the front gate, stuck behind a police barricade.

"Find a way around this," Patricia told her driver.

The driver touched the dash screen and brought up a satellite image of their location.

"That's North Star and we're here," the driver said, pointing to the display in the dash of the van. "We're on the only road leading in. "I'll bet they did it on purpose," he driver continued. "Better control of traffic for security."

She looked outside through the tinted windows. "You wait for me here," she said. She grabbed her backpack and a light jacket, opened the sliding door and jumped to the gravel shoulder. She tapped a motorcyclist on the shoulder.

"A hundred dollars if you get me to the perimeter of North Star." She waved the bill in front of the cyclist's dark visor.

The motorcyclist removed the helmet and ran her hand through her hair, fluffing it in the breeze. "Make it two and I'll get you inside the fence."

Patricia dug out another bill and handed it to her.

"You're that lady on the news," the girl said, snatching the bills from her and stuffing them in a zippered pocket inside her black leather jacket.

Patricia noticed the Rose tattoo on her neck and the long stem wrapping around. "Patricia Westland," she said.

"Rose Thorne," the girl said. "Hop on and hang on tight, we're going cross country."

Patricia waved at the van driver and her camera man as Rose turned off the road and went through the ditch. Losing her balance, Patricia quickly brought her arm down and wrapped it around Rose, holding on tightly as they sped through a field of rye grass. She looked at the logo on the girl's jacket. *Shit*, she thought. *What have I gotten myself into?*

They entered a grove of small oak trees and wandered along a game trail, taking them to the other side. Rose stopped on the edge of the grove. They were on a hill overlooking the North Star facility. "We need to go on foot from here," Rose said.

"What were you doing here?" Patricia asked.

"Off the record?"

"Of course it's off the record, I'm not interviewing you."

"I wanted to see if the Russian's could pull it off."

"Russians?"

"You know they are behind the riots and the break in, don't you?"

"How do you know that?"

"I have my sources. I was on my way to warn Scott Tanner when, well you saw it. I was too late."

"You know Scott?"

"You bet. I met Scott Tanner and David Stafford at the funeral and then they came to my dad's place."

The hair stood up on the back of Patricia's neck. She looked at the girl. She couldn't be much older than sixteen: Facial piercings, black lipstick, and dark eyeshadow. How could anyone like her know Scott and David? And what did she know about North Star? She was shaken from her thoughts when Rose pulled a pair of bolt cutters from her bike's saddlebag.

"Come on," Rose said, holding up the heavy-duty cutters. "I have the key to the place."

Patricia heard an explosion in the distance. She could see a plume of smoke rising from somewhere in the North Star complex. *Do I really want to go in there?*

Scott and three National Guard Elite Force were knocked backwards from the explosion. They landed in a pile on the hallway floor in the Assembly Building. The explosion had come from outside and had blown in a doorway they were approaching.

Smoke and debris clouded the air. Scott rose to his feet and dusted off his pants. He could hear voices and they were distinctly Russian. Suddenly he realized this wasn't a bunch of bored students trying to find purpose in life by answering a professor's call for them to carry out their civic duty with a protest march. This was a planned operation, possibly a foreign intrusion.

"Did you hear that," Scott said to the man behind him.

The soldier nodded. Scott flipped off the safety on his handgun. Fine particles of dust danced in the sunlight streaming through the blown doorway He stepped past the opening. Others were converging on the building from outside, but these voices were coming from in front of them. Scott continued down the hall and stopped short of another door that had been breached. A soldier squeezed past him, taking the lead and crouched down in the opening. The voices were louder. A figure emerged and the soldier fired before Scott could get off a round. The intruder fell halfway through the door. "Which way?" the soldier asked.

"Follow me," Scott said, taking back the lead. Behind him one of the soldiers called for a medic. Another explosion rocked the building. This time Scott took off in a sprint toward the direction of the blast. There would only be one more layer of security and they would be in the Assembly Room. If they breached the wall to the cleanroom environment, that act alone would destroy the highly sensitive electronics in the satellites.

Scott jumped through the breached doorway and caught an intruder by surprise. He fired a shot, but it didn't seem to faze the man. He was taller than Scott and outweighed him by twenty pounds. He didn't look happy to see Scott. Scott started to fire again, but the insurgent was lightning fast and kicked the weapon from Scott's hand and threw a fist that caught Scott in the stomach. Scott tackled the man, hoping those behind him could slip past and stop the activity ahead of them. Scott landed a punch on the man's jaw, but the man shook it off like it was nothing. The man said something in Russian that was probably a curse word.

The brawl ended when a soldier crashed the butt of his weapon into the Russian's face knocking him out.

"Thanks," Scott said, getting up and heading toward the final door to Assembly. He was stopped by the Elite soldiers who were staring at two insurgents packing plastic explosive on the hinges to a steel door. The men were so intent on completing their work that they ignored the visitors. "Take them out," Scott said to the squad leader.

"He's not going to blow that standing next to it and we're less than ten feet away in the only path they have to get out," the squad leader whispered. "We can take them alive."

Scott pushed the squad leader aside, went around him and jumped over a soldier who was down on one knee. He charged the two Russians placing the C-4 on the Assembly Room door. They turned, startled by the ruckus, and scrambled for their weapons standing on the wall next to the door. Scott reached the weapons first and shoved the muzzle of an automatic in one of the men's gut while kicking the other weapon away.

Scott held the man at gunpoint, while he grabbed a chunk of C-4 from the hinge on the door and held it in his hand. His captive yelled something in Russian that sounded like profanity although Scott didn't know the language. "He's going for the detonator," a voice behind him shouted, seeing the man reach in his shirt pocket. Scott shoved the explosive down the shirt of the man he was holding. A shot rang out piercing the neck of the Russian going for the detonator. His head snapped back and hung limply to one side as he slumped to the floor.

"Lucky for you," Scott said to his captive, grabbing his hands and wrapping them behind. "I was hoping he would set it off."

"That would kill us all," the man hissed.

The squad leader caught up with Scott. "What the hell was that?"

"I couldn't take a chance he would blow the door. We have fifty-million dollars of technology in that room! It would have become worthless the second that door was breached."

"If you were under my command, I'd have you court-martialed for that stunt."

"Then let's both be glad I'm a civilian. We quite possibly just saved the Country."

The soldier talked into his headset. "This is Alpha One. Assembly Building secure."

David watched the action from several camera angles. When he saw Scott grab the plastic explosive from the door he shouted at the monitor. He turned to Gil and said, "Tell me what happens. I can't watch this."

Finally he turned back to the monitor. "Maybe they'll rescue us next."

*****

Patricia stopped at the fence and put her hand out to stop Rose from using the bolt cutters.

"We don't need to go in," she said. "I have my story." She turned her portable video camera on Rose.

"You can't use my face or name. My dad will kill me," Rose said.

"I won't show your face."

"He'll recognize my voice."

"We have devices that can make you sound like a three-hundred pound Sumo wrestler," Patricia said.

"That might be cool," Rose said. "I had a feeling something big was going down when Ty Tanner ended up dead. When David Stafford didn't hesitate to pay for the work I did and came back for more information, I was sure, of it."

"Where did you learn about the Russian involvement?"

"A better question is how. There's a Russian gang in town that deals in narcotics. They are an arm of the Columbian Cartel. I overheard one of them talking."

"Where did you hear about them?"

"You can't go there," Rose said.

"Okay, just so you feel comfortable with what I'd like to air, I'll make sure you get a chance to see a final draft."

"This isn't going to put my dad back in jail, is it?"

"Your dad? I don't know your dad."
"Let's keep it that way."

*****

David tried calling Scott, but couldn't get him to answer. Several hours had passed and those locked in Building Seven were threatening to riot if they weren't released immediately. Many had called their families and complained. The police told David he would have to calm them down. The FBI would need to interview each of them before they would be allowed to leave. He was angry when he finally talked to the FBI.

"There are a thousand of us in here," David said. "Are you planning on keeping us here for a week?"

After a long silence, Agent Gordon said, "Have everyone line up by the door. We'll get a dozen agents over there to take names and numbers as they leave. We can let them go and talk to them later."

"How soon will you be here?"

"Ten minutes."

"Thank you. I was afraid you were going to find me dead. Everyone in here would be a suspect."

From the stage David called for order and devised a plan to get the crowded assembly to exit in an orderly fashion. He stepped up to the microphone, "Ladies and gentlemen, listen up. I just got off the phone with the FBI. We will be allowed to leave in about ten minutes, but it is necessary we do it in four separate lines and in an orderly manner. This is what we're going to do…"

As the line of employees exited, the FBI had a camera focused on the faces of the individuals as they filed past. Facial recognition was cross checked with North Star employee records and the person was allowed to pass. The matching took less than a second per person. David was the last person out. He saw Agent Gordon, and looking up at the night sky said, "No rest for the wicked. You haven't seen Scott, have you?"

"They set up a temporary Federal holding cell at the Portland Airport. Some of those who raided North Star are being charged with Federal crimes under the Espionage Act of 1917."

"I'm sure he doesn't need to be there for that," David said.

"He's being held. I told them he was one of ours, but one of the National Guard commanders called in to secure North Star filed a complaint charging he interfered with the op, putting his soldiers at risk."

"That's ridiculous," David said. "I watched the whole thing go down. If Scott wouldn't have done what he did, the cleanroom could have been breached. We would have lost everything."

"You're preaching to the choir," Gordon said. "You're going to have to find someone with a higher grade than me to clean it up. He must have really pissed off the Army."

David dialed Nendel's number. "The National Guard is holding Scott. Is there anything you can do about it?"

"I'm in the air on my way out to North Star to assess the damage. Where is he?"

"He's at a temporary Federal prison set up at the airport."

"Meet me there. I'm another hour out."

*****

Portland Airport, Temporary Federal Prison

A light fog hung low over the Columbia River as David pulled up to several National Guardsmen in front of a rolling chain link gate. From his vantage point he could see no markings on the building they were protecting. David stopped his car and a woman in uniform approached with her automatic weapon hanging loosely in front of her. She placed one hand on her weapon and waited while his window rolled down.

"I have a meeting with NSA Director Nendel," David said. *It can't hurt dropping names,* he thought.

"What's your name?"

David answered.

"Just a minute." She talked to a person at the gate controls and walked back to David.

"Park over there and proceed to the gate on foot. No cameras or firearms allowed."

David parked his car in the indicated area. There were no other vehicles. He approached the guard at the gate, was patted down and allowed through where another soldier escorted him to a side door in a concrete walled building. It looked like it might have been an aircraft repair facility, or a manufacturing plant at one time. There were high windows along the top of the walls and large sliding doors on one end.

A small door on the side led to an office where several plain clothe personnel were gathered. They eyed him cautiously and spoke into wrist mikes. An inside door opened and Admiral Nendel appeared.

"David, follow me," Nendel said. They walked along a stretch of chain link fencing that had been arranged into cages looking like a dog kennel. *Perhaps this had been a holding facility for animals clearing customs*, he thought. In each cage, from one to four people were being detained. Many were yelling obscenities.

"These are the people from the North Star riot?" David asked.

"The FBI has been questioning them one by one, trying to find out who was behind the riots."

"Have you talked to Scott yet?"

"Yeah. He really pissed off the commander of the force that secured North Star."

"I have something that might help," David said, holding up a flash drive. "I got the whole thing here from several camera angles."

Nendel smiled. "I was beginning to think it was his word against theirs. This is good news."

They walked a hundred feet and entered through a door that appeared to be a partition through the center of the building. On the other side they were still assembling cages.

"Near as I can tell they are sorting on one side and bringing the leading suspects to this side," Nendel said. "Scott's down at the end."

"Who's running the show?" David asked.

"Homeland Security, the FBI, and CIA Deputy Director Gary Nolan."

"Nolan? I'm surprised he still has a job after what he did in Antarctica."

"It's Washington," Nendel said, as way of an explanation.

"So why is Scott still here?" David asked.

"Nolan's in that office. I'll review the video with him. In the meantime, if you want to talk to Scott, I'll be back for you shortly."

Scott was lying back on a bunk, seemingly not concerned that he was a prisoner.

"Hey inmate," David said. "I never thought I'd be bailing you out."

Scott sat up. "You really know how to ruin a good night's sleep."

"Check your watch. It's morning; time to get you out of here."

"If you're here, that means the facility was secured. They let everyone out of the basement?"

"They agreed to interview everyone later. I can see why. Looks like they have their hands full."

"So, what do I have to do to get out of here?"

"I brought the video from the Assembly Building break in. I think, once they see it, Nendel will get you released."

"Sons-a-bitches wouldn't let me explain," Scott said. "I've been thinking about what went down and I think most of it was a diversion. The protests were a cover up for the break in. Paradox was the real target."

"China probably had a copy of the Paradox codes," David said. "And the video they had all over the internet might also be a diversion."

"This was Russia," Scott said. "China and Russia have to be in this together. The leader spoke with a Russian accent."

"I couldn't tell what he was saying, but you surprised the hell out of him when you stuffed that plastic explosive in his shirt pocket."

Scott laughed. "I was hoping the other guy wouldn't blow up his buddy or the rest of us for that matter."

Chapter 18

Pearl Harbor, Hawaii

President Tindall was vacationing at a friend's estate on Maui; at least that was what the news was reporting. In fact he was watching the launch of the first of several thousand HAP communication stations. After the launch from a clearing on a remote island estate, he gave the order to start *Operation Oracle,* the program he hoped would save the Nation.

The container ship, *NIKI,* skippered by Akito Teramura, a Japanese citizen, accompanied by US Navy Commander Larry Schmitt, CIA Agent Karen Nelson, and their crew of twelve handpicked specialists, left port as it had done a hundred times before. But this time as soon as it hit open ocean it wasn't alone. Beneath the surface, in the shadow of the giant ship were two submarine escorts. The ship sailed in a zig zag pattern at full speed slowing every 500 miles just long enough to launch a HAP.

The Mylar balloon attached to the HAP seemed under inflated as it ascended, but it had enough helium to reach its design ceiling of fifteen miles above sea level. At that altitude the wing of the giant platform was fully inflated and became functional.

Fifteen miles up, the operational altitude for the balloon, was chosen because it is a band of air relatively free of wind and upper atmospheric disturbances, it is well above the flight path of any commercial aircraft. The HAP would remain as a stable base for years, but it would take hundreds of them to replace a single communication satellite.

The inflated wing of the HAP was the size of several football fields. The upper surface was coated with a new type of polymer-based flexible solar cell which provided power. Each high altitude platform serviced a ground area of 500 miles and the overlapping grid-work of platforms provided a minimum of three stations assessable from anywhere below. It was nearly impossible for the enemy to defeat due to the sheer number and location of the platforms that would be launched.

On the same day the container ship *Concordia*, also loaded with High Altitude Platform Stations left Long Beach, California. The *Concordia* had a CIA agent aboard, a US Naval Commander, and a crew of specialists. Like the *NIKI, Concordia* traveled west for 500 miles, slowed, released the device that appeared like a weather balloon, and turned due north. Off the coast of Oregon it released another package, and another off Vancouver Island. It continued its journey releasing a HAP every 500 miles, until it reached Alaska where it turned west again, traveled 500 miles, released a package, and turned due south. At a top speed of 27 knots a HAP was launched every fourteen hours.

Concurrently with the ship deployment of HAPs, in the air over the United States and Canada, B-52 Bombers loaded with ALHAPS, or air Launched High Altitude Platforms, zig-zagged across the sky dropping platforms from 30,000 feet up. The ALHAPS attached to parachutes fell from the planes and glided toward earth until the balloons inflated. The parachutes were jettisoned and the balloons began to rise. At the designated altitude the communication station unfolded into its final shape.

In a similar manner, airplanes all over the globe launched high altitude platforms. It took one week and the United States and her allies had in place the ability to communicate free of the network of geosynchronous satellites they had depended on for decades. Around the globe, television networks and cable stations were connected to the new service. *Operation Oracle* had taken two weeks, but it was a resounding success.

Phase one of the plan was in place.

*****

Portland, Oregon

Three times Patricia had approached her boss and pitched her on why they needed to broadcast the interview with Rose Thorne. She had given Rose the code name Mack Bell. The figure of Rose had been heavily shadowed and the voice altered to sound like a man. Rose had seen the video and reluctantly approved it. She still had concerns that her father would see it and somehow recognize her.

Each time her boss had demanded more information, more sources to back up the story. She had gone to David and Scott and both had told her to back off in kinder words, but with the same effect. "You need to let this go," Scott had said. "You're sticking your toe in a pool filled with sharks."

"It's news," Patricia argued. "If the Russians are behind an attack on American soil, the public deserves to know about it."

"It's a matter of national security," Scott said. "If the news gets out now, it could have a negative impact on our ability to keep the Country safe."

"So you admit there is Russian involvement?"

"Don't put words in my mouth. I don't know what you think you know, but I guarantee you don't have the full story. Drop it."

Scott had been angry and she had backed off, but she knew there was a story and the reporter in her couldn't let it go. She went back to interview Rose Thorne again to see if she could gather a little more info.

"I need to meet the Russian source," Patricia said.

"I heard the FBI captured him," Rose said. "They have him in custody."

Patricia drove out to the FBI building and asked to meet with the director in charge of the field office. "I have information I'm about to air and wanted to give you a heads up," she told Field Office Executive Director Martha Peebles.

Peebles let out a sigh. She'd had enough distractions from reporters lately. The *Oregonian* had quizzed her about the makeshift prison which still housed fifteen rioters, held without access to an attorney. She had denied knowing about it to them but the news was out.

"The prison is under military control," Peebles said. "I don't have anything to do with it."

"Well, I'm going to run with this," Patricia said, holding up a tiny SD Card. "If you let the military handle everything then you shouldn't have objections."

"Let me see what you have," Peebles said.

"I'm not letting go of this," Patricia said.

Peebles shook her head and grimaced. "Follow me."

They climbed the stairs and entered the information room. Patricia inserted the card into a laptop and the interview came up.

Peebles fidgeted as she watched. "Who is she?"

"How do you know it's a she?"

"I've been in the business more than a day. Nobody is going to think you have Deep Throat in your pocket."

"You aren't denying any of it?"

"You need to give up your source. She knows too much to be an innocent party."

"I'm a reporter. My source stays secret."

"We'll see about that. I'd confiscate it if I didn't think you've already had a backup."

"It goes on the air tonight, eleven o'clock news."

"You don't want to do that."

"It's true. The public has a right to it," Patricia argued.

"You'll be meddling in a Federal investigation. I can charge you with obstruction."

Patricia left the SD card in the computer and stood up. "You can have it. You're right I have other copies."

KPDX Broadcast Studio, Portland, Oregon

Patricia put the finishing touches on her makeup. There was

a knock on the door. She thought it was the five minute warning. "I'm ready, be right out."

"Patricia Westland?"

Patricia got up and opened the door. A sheriff deputy handed her a summons.

North Star Industries

David picked up the phone and called Scott. "Have you seen the eleven o'clock news?"

"Just saw it," Scott said. "It has to be Rose Thorne."

"What about the Russians. I didn't see any Russians."

"She's spot on with her information. If Rose's dad figures this out she could be in real trouble. The Gypsy Rovers are not known for family ties."

"Bull doesn't strike me as the type who watches the news," David said. "Maybe he won't see it."

"I'm not going to rely on luck, I've got to call the FBI," Scott said. "I warned Patricia not to go on the air with it."

"Now the Russians have a heads up," David said. "We still have ten satellites to deliver."

"I'll catch you in the morning," Scott said. He called Agent Gordon.

"You saw the broadcast?" Scott asked Gordon.

"She gave us a copy. She wanted to get the FBI on record for neither confirming nor denying an investigation. I'm getting tired of her games."

"I know who the source is," Scott said, "and she might need protection."

Scott told him about Rose Thorne and her father, the head of the Gypsy Rovers.

"She can't be that innocent," Gordon said.

"She's just a kid with the wrong person for a parent. She's trying to do the right thing."

"Then she should voluntarily come forward."

"Would you, if your dad ran a gang of murdering thugs? She could have a hit on her from the Russians as well as the Gypsy Rovers. I'll give you her name, if you promise to keep her somewhere safe until you have everyone in custody."

"Sorry, Scott. The best I can do is put a watch on her. If her father is involved, there's nothing I can do about that."

"Do your best. She's the reason this broke wide open. If she hadn't come forward with the satellite codes, China would still be stealing our data."

*****

The White House, Oval Office

The Washington-Moscow hotline had been installed in 1963. The *red telephone,* as was the public's perception, was never red and the hotline had never been a telephone line at all. Originally, it was set up as a teletype and, today, was a secure computer link. Communications were exchanged by email. But thirty minutes had elapsed and Tindall's message had not been acknowledged. To avoid a potential nuclear disaster, President Tindall wanted to assure Mordashov that the launch of several rockets was for communication satellites and was not an attack on Russia. He was certain Russia would be concerned about the scale of the launches and might perceive it as a threat. Russian President Mordashov finally answered on the other end of President Tindall's call. Tindall had been impatiently waiting for someone in the Kremlin to locate Mordashov. It had been ten minutes, a lifetime in a world crisis situation.

As Mordashov answered, Tindall checked the digital clock on the wall. It was 3:00 a.m. in Moscow. If the situation wasn't so dire, he would have chuckled at the timing. The simultaneous launching of US space satellites was highly unusual, but it was the second step in the plan to take the United States and its allies off the geosynchronous satellite grid. Timing was everything, and things were happening fast.

"We are replacing our satellite communication system," Tindall explained to Mordashov. "It has to be done simultaneously so that we do not interrupt our global network. This is a curtesy call, to avoid any misconceptions."

"It is good of you to call, President Tindall, but if one of those rockets strays off course, I cannot guarantee a peaceful outcome."

"I assure you that will not happen."

Tindall hung up. "The son-of-a-bitch is going to be watching, but I'd rather have him on alert than caught by surprise." He looked at the staff members in the room. "God help us if this doesn't work."

Biggs, his National Security Advisor, handed him his phone. "General Mellon is on the line waiting for your word, Mr. President."

Tindall grabbed the phone. "It's a go, General. Don't screw it up."

Pentagon Air Force Space Command Situation Room

General Mellon, Admiral Nendel, General Cramer and General Mitchel with their staff, were all seated around a huge circular glass-topped table. In the center a slowly rotating holographic display of the earth showed ten launch sites around the globe. Each had a heavy lift delivery system in place with a Paradox payload. They were starting the countdown. As the world turned, the ten launch sites came into view. Four were in the United States, two in Japan, and four on sea-launch platforms in the South Pacific. Collectively, those in the room held their breath as the countdown reached zero. "We have liftoff," a voice came over the speakers. The room erupted in cheers.

President Tindall, who was present on a secure video feed, watched in silence. He knew the next few hours would change the course of history.

Beijing, China, FRC Space Center

China's Space Minister, Youngsim Wu, watched as the lights from the Jinping Moon Rover carved a path through the darkness on the back side of the moon. The digital images had traveled from the moon rover cameras to a communication satellite orbiting the moon before being beamed back to earth, a feat that no country had ever accomplished before.

Youngsim Wu watched with pride. China's dominance of space was well within the grasp of his generation and with it would come great wealth and prestige for China. He struggled to hold back his glee as he looked around the room. The members of the Moon Exploration Team were laughing and smiling and celebrating, yet he doubted any of them realized the full potential of their feat. From the remote station on the moon, China controlled the ultimate upper ground. Hidden on the back side of the moon, China could develop military and peaceful exploration of space.

The celebration was interrupted when a member of China's Intelligence entered the room and whispered in his ear.

"I must go," Wu said to his assistant. "See that they get back to business. We must use our accomplishments to move toward the end goal."

Wu quickly left with the officer. They made the quick trip down a long corridor to the Ministry of Space Military Applications Council Chambers.

"You must see this," Chengfu Yang, the Minister of War said as soon as he saw Wu come through the door. He pointed to a panoramic screen. "Replay," he ordered a young officer sitting at a computer. Immediately the screen showed ten different frames all showing rocket launch sites. Simultaneously the rockets ignited and lifted off.

"Are we under attack?" Wu asked nervously.

"No, we have traced their trajectory and they are all headed to geosynchronous orbit."

"Then they are new satellites," Wu said, rubbing his chin, not sure what to make of the situation. "Maybe they are trying to overwhelm our new satellite defense systems."

"How can that be? They must know we have their Paradox system and it cannot be defeated," Yang said.

Youngsim Wu sighed. "It was only a matter of time. Our Russian partners failed us when they didn't stop the new satellite development. They were to destroy the Paradox facility, but now the Americans, in a final battle, have sent up enough Paradox satellites to destroy every one of ours." He paused for a moment deep in thought. "They know if we activate our defenses, all geosynchronous orbits will be destroyed."

"That is what's troubling me," Yang said, pinching his lips as he often did when perplexed. "How far are we from having our moon base established?"

"My program is long range. We are years from replacing our satellites with a moon-based system."

Yang nodded and pinched his lips again. "Then we must wait and see what the Americans are doing."

"If you activate our defenses, you risk wiping out our satellite orbits with the debris it will create," Wu was deeply troubled.

"That is what they are expecting," Yang said angrily. "They overwhelm our satellites and we do nothing. My mission is to stop the American domination of space and the threat we face from their nuclear weapons. I cannot wait until they catch up with your long range program."

"Then I suggest you give me a greater part of the space budget. I cannot do miracles with only the left overs you throw to the dogs."

"Careful with your tongue, Youngsim Wu. Your father can no longer protect you."

"My sincere apology. I will be honored to speed up my program if you can see that I get a greater part of the budget. In the meantime, we must learn what the latest move by the Americans means. Surely they do not intend to destroy our satellites, for in doing so, they destroy theirs."

"I accept your apology," Yang said. "Return to your celebration. I will deal with the American aggression."

Pentagon Air Force Space Command Situation Room

"You're certain we want to do this?" General Cramer asked watching the first of the Paradox 221 satellites position itself in orbit.

"The President gave the go-ahead when he authorized the launch. Everything is preprogrammed to start as soon as the last satellite reaches orbit," General Mellon said.

"Most of the world will not even notice a change," Nendel said, somberly. He checked the time. In twenty seconds the free world would switch from Geo-satellite communication to High Altitude Platform communication. In the same moment Paradox would deploy. All satellite space-based communication throughout the world would cease to exist.

From the White House Situation Room, Tindall watched what was unfolding in space. It didn't matter that the United States activated the Paradox defense system first; the same end result would have been realized if China or Russia would have used their defense systems to try and destroy Paradox. Complete annihilation of space based platforms would happen no matter, but now the United States and its allies were the only ones prepared for the chaos descending on the world. *Operation Oracle* was in its final stages. He stared at the screen holding his breath as the final satellite reached orbit, knowing every country that considered the United States its enemy would view the coming disaster an act of war.

"Get ready," General Mitchel said.

General Cramer held his breath. The lights flickered and went out. The screen went dark as the system rebooted. In less than a second the screen was up again, showing the latest version of Paradox satellites doing what they were programmed to do, but this time the pictures were relayed from a HAP telescope through a ground station to the Pentagon.

The room remained silent as they watched the split screen showing Paradox sending out micro satellite swarms with only one mission, destroy everything in its path. The micro satellites drifted like a cloud blocking all ground signals from reaching nearby satellites. As the tiny satellites sensed proximity to a larger satellite, they exploded creating a larger cloud of debris. Suddenly the screen lit up as a US communication satellite traveling at sixty-eight miles per second came in contact with the cloud. The screen went dark and came up again.

"This view is from one of the HAPs over Hawaii," Mitchel said. "In a few more minutes there won't be any deep space eyes in the sky, so to speak. Our only view of space will be from earth based telescopes, HAPs, or low earth orbiting platforms like Hubble or the International Space Station."

The debris from the satellite hitting the cloud of tiny exploding satellites unfolded on the screen like a plague of locusts destroying everything in its path, only to grow larger with every collision, becoming an ever larger monster.

"Jesus," Cramer said, watching the chaos. "The computer simulations were tame compared to what's actually going on up there."

"It'll all be over in a few minutes," Mitchel said.

"We may have started World War Three," Nendel said. "The fallout from this preemptive strike will likely piss off a good part of the world."

"At least it will be a conventional war," Cramer said.

Nendel knew that statement was mistaken. His sources told him Russia may still have the capability of sending any number of ICBMs into major US cities.

Chapter 19

Portland, Oregon

Patricia Westland stood in the darkened studio and waited for the back-up generators to kick in. She had never experienced a complete blackout before. Outside the KPDX studio, the entire city appeared to be without power. The emergency lights came on and then flickered out again. The power came back up and she along with everyone in the studio, wondered what had just happened. Her producer pointed her finger at Patricia indicating she would have to adlib. They were still in the middle of a live broadcast.

"We're not certain what just happened," Patricia said, "but you can be sure the KPDX team will look into why we had a brief interruption in our broadcast, and I will report it to you. Thanks for staying with us." She looked down at her computer screen.

"This has just come into our news feed. It is reported that the power outage was not localized. At the same moment the power went out across the nation. It lasted exactly thirty-seven seconds. The cause is unknown, but several un-named sources are saying it was a cyberattack on our electrical grid. I've come to take early reports in situations like this with a grain of salt." Her computer let out an audible beep and she glanced down again.

"This is incredible, and it just came in, so bear with me while I try to verify this. It seems the power was disrupted around the world. Sources in Europe and Asia have reported a similar outage." She turned and looked down placing one hand over her right ear as one of her assistants talked into her earpiece. She nodded.

"I just learned the White House Press Secretary has released a statement." She read it from the screen. "The brief power outage the American people experienced was widespread.

NOAA, that's the National Oceanic and Atmospheric Administration has just reported it was a large solar flare that disrupted our power. It was a temporary glitch and our back-up systems kicked in to shorten the duration of the problem. Not all countries have the same ability to rapidly respond to such emergencies and may take days or weeks to bring their systems back up. We should expect to experience difficulty in communicating with foreign countries, especially China and Russia as all satellite communication systems appear to be down." Patricia looked back up at the camera. "So there you have it, nothing to be worried about. A few phone calls with Russia or China may not be possible for a sometime. This is Patricia Westland reporting live from our studio in beautiful Portland, Oregon." She smiled as the station went to commercial.

North Star Industries

"That was it," David said to his team. He looked at Scott, who seemed to be puzzled. "What's on your mind, Scott? I know that look."

"It's too late to do anything about it," Scott said, looking at the anxious faces in the room. "I guess our job is finished, here."

"We're going to miss working with you," Charlene Wilson said. "There's a team from General Cramer's office arriving tomorrow to shut down North Star. For some of us, it was our life." Her lips started to tremble. "China and Russia aren't going to stand by and let us destroy their countries."

"How can you have any sympathy for them? It's clear they were about to do the same thing to us," Gil Thompson said. "If they wouldn't have stolen the Paradox plans, none of this would have happened."

"It is what it is," David said, "but I don't think your job here is done yet. I got word from DARPA that they want both of you working on a new system. There's a company in Colorado that's developing a communication system that bounces signals off the moon. Loss of geosynchronous space is only going to be a temporary problem. You'll have a job if you want it and Scott and I will be around until North Star closes its doors for good."

"How long will that be?" Charlene asked.

David looked at Scott and William Peck, one of the executives at North Star who had passed the security checks and been allowed to kept his job.

Peck removed his glasses and pinched the bridge of his nose. "I expect it to take a few weeks to mothball the place. Once all the critical information is collected and removed, then it's only a matter of auctioning off the assets. I've engaged a firm to take care of that. The rest of it will be tied up in courts for years."

"I guess that's it," Scott said. "I enjoyed working with all of you. I wish it could have been under different circumstances."

"Mr. Tanner," the receptionist at the front desk leaned through the door. "Director Nendel is on the line for you. Do you want me to transfer the call from your office?"

"I'll take it in my office," Scott said getting up. "We're finished here. Thanks everybody."

Back in his office, he picked up the phone. "Richard, what's up?"

"You know that Russian connection with the bike gang you found?"

"Technically it was David who found it, but go ahead."

"The FBI got one of them to talk. He was pretty low level, but he gave us a name that was important."

"Where is this going?" Scott asked. "I'm about to wrap things up here and get back to my operation at the coast."

"Bear with me. We were able to tap in on some conversations between the guy behind the North Star attack and a contact in Moscow. The long and short of it is Russia was scamming China. Russia has concentrated all its resources the past ten years in low earth maneuverable orbital devices. They wanted the US and China out of the deep space game. They are way ahead in low earth orbiting systems."

"Admiral, correct me if I'm wrong, but you are saying Russia wasn't shut down by Paradox."

"It means our HAPs are vulnerable to attack from above. While we've been putting our resources into geosynchronous satellites, they have been doing the same thing in low earth orbit. We thought we were in trouble with China, but now Russia controls low earth orbit."

"We're talking about the area in space where the International Space Station orbits?" Scott asked, already knowing the answer.

"Russia has enough maneuverable satellites in low earth orbit to direct their arsenal of ICBMs. China has been effectively neutralized as a nuclear threat, but Russia is now the Alpha Male."

"Richard, it sounds serious, but how does it affect me?"

"Russia just moved one of its satellites next to China's space station. It's synched its orbit with the station. We think Russia is making a move on China."

"Richard, this is way above my pay grade. I'm out here trying to close down North Star and you're telling me there's another war starting."

"Think of it as a continuation. I know you don't want to hear this, but you need to keep North Star open and keep your team together. We want to put Paradox in low earth orbit."

"I'm not even sure that can be done. The plant is already going up for auction. You said this was going to be a two-week assignment."

"I'm on my way out there. Arrange a meeting with David Stafford and his team. I'll have General Cramer and General Mitchel with me, maybe even President Tindall. We've got to nip this one in the bud."

"Okay, Richard, but David isn't going to like it."

"That's why you're going to talk to him. I didn't want to get hung up on."

South China Sea

Admiral Bohai Lang had served aboard the aircraft carrier *Liánoning Jiàn* as a training officer when it was still the Kuznetsov-class aircraft cruiser *Riga*. All through the First and Second World Wars, China had lagged behind the rest of the nations in advanced weaponry. It had only been in the last twenty years that it had started to modernize its fleet of battleships and aircraft, and now, much of the weapons had been made worthless by the destruction of their communication satellites.

As it left the South China Sea, Admiral Lang's flagship was accompanied by seven destroyers and a dozen cruisers and support vessels. In the waters beneath the fleet were seven submarines, all equipped with medium range ballistic missiles, capable of delivering a nuclear warhead up to 5500 km or 3400 miles. Their destination was Hawaii still some 5,000 miles from their current position. At a top speed of 27 knots, the journey to the minimum launch range would take another three days. If they could remain undetected until then, the United States would pay for the destruction of China's satellites. Admiral Lang's orders were to impart maximum damage on the Hawaiian Islands in retribution for the act of war the US had taken. The armada would then travel to within range of the western coast of the United States and lay waste to any and all cities for as far as its missiles would reach.

Lang stood on the deck outside the bridge and let the cool salt sea air flow over his face. He considered his mission and the impact it would make on the world. His children and grandchildren had embraced western technology. They played with their electronic devices and were first in line to upgrade when new versions became available, but that had all come to an abrupt halt when the satellites were destroyed.

Strange, he thought. He had never considered the United States his enemy until now. He had seen the old ways of the Communist Party and the struggle of his people under Communism, but in the past twenty years life had gradually improved. China had prospered. He had imagined a world where his children would live without struggle.

Had his leaders thrown all that away? What made a country that depended on China attack it? Was it true it was unprovoked? I will never know, he thought. *I will follow orders like I always have and trust that our leaders will not destroy us.*

North Star Industries

David Stafford broke the news to his team. He wished he could have been as excited as they were when he told them North Star would be staying open with a new mission. After the meeting he made his way along the hallway to Scott's office.

"I told them," David said, taking a seat in the corner of the room. "So you want to clue me in? We're letting our own business go down the tubes while we start World War Three because our Government screwed up?"

"Russia was developing low orbit weapon systems while we were busy worrying about China and geosynchronous space."

"I'm still trying to figure how this has become our problem." David was clearly not happy. "Other than your father working here, we don't have a connection with North Star. Anyone with a business degree and a little manufacturing experience could run this place, especially with the level of engineering and research personnel they have working here."

"You're right. If my father hadn't been killed, then we wouldn't be in the middle of this, but Nendel doesn't seem to trust anybody he doesn't know personally, and we are where we are."

"So I take it I have to be on my best behavior when the big guns show up in the morning?"

Scott smiled. "As impossible as it seems, that would be good. General Cramer thought you did a good job with the team getting Paradox ready to launch."

"Banjo Eyes said that?"

"Not to me. Nendel told me."

"Well, if he really thinks that, I'll try to negotiate a better salary."

"Better? We aren't being payed anything."

"My point. How long are we going to carry the Government?"

"Okay," Scott said. "I know it's not about money. What's the rub?"

"I want to get back to developing my own things."

"Okay. Find a way to defeat the Russians at their own game. Their satellites are moving around and threatening the low earth orbiting satellites. Nendel said they might be taking over China's space station and making it look like we did it."

"Nendel thought the HAPs were going to solve the problem. How many more things are going on we don't know about. You'd think that information collection system he's running would know everything by now."

"Too much information," Scott said. "It's all there, but getting it to the right people is a problem. Right now I'm not sure where this is going. If we haven't already started a war, we're about to. We can't let Russia screw around with us."

"Jesus, Scott. Can't you see this kind of stuff has been going on for years? I can't figure out why we're in the middle of this right now!"

Scott couldn't remember seeing David so upset. Having attended college in the ultra-liberal Hippy environment of USC Berkeley, he knew David's politics didn't line up with his, but his Country needed him now. He didn't want to see David blow it.

"Just promise me you'll hear Nendel out before you go off on him. He wouldn't be asking for our help unless he needed it."

A thousand National Guard troops still roamed the campus of North Star. When Nendel arrived by helicopter, three armed soldiers escorted him to the Executive Building auditorium. It was a small theater-like setting with a stage and rows of seats set in a semi-circle that rose from the stage like the inside of a shallow bowl. A digital screen dominated the back of the stage.

From the stage Scott looked around the room to make certain everyone was present. In addition to David's team, members of production management were attending. The twenty or so people scattered about the room made it appear nearly empty. Nendel entered through a door at the back of the room, leaving his escorts and walking down the sloped aisle alone. He climbed the steps to the stage where Scott and David greeted him.

Scott stretched out his hand. "Everyone is here."

"Did you establish a secure link with the Pentagon?"

"All set," David said. "We're ready to go."

"We've got a few more coming," Nendel said. "Could you get all the North Star people together? The President will want to meet them personally."

"Tindall is here?" Scott asked.

"He will be along with his staff, the head of the Joint Chiefs, and their staffs." Nendel looked around the room. "I hope this place is large enough to hold all of them."

Scott punched a button on a remote control and a podium with a microphone rose from the stage. He stepped up to it and tapped the microphone. "Attention, everyone, I need all the North Star personnel in the front row. There are a number of other guests coming and you need to be front and center."

As a few grumbling people in the back got up and made their way to the front, a commotion in the back of the theater caused everyone to turn and watch as a dozen men dressed in black came through the doors and stationed themselves around the room.

"If those are ours, this could be the safest place in the world," David quipped.

"Or the hottest target," Scott said, nervously. He leaned into the mike. "Come on, North Star employees. This isn't church. It's okay if you sit in front."

Another commotion in the back and three generals walked in. Scott and David had met Cramer, but the other two would need introduction. As the North Star managers were assembling in front, Charlene Wilson called up to David standing just above her on stage. "David, what's going on?"

David leaned down. "We're all going to find out together."

Several National Guard members came from behind the stage and set up a line of chairs at the back of the stage.

"This reminds me of Crater Lake," David said, tapping Scott on the shoulder. "We all know how that turned out."

Scott shook his head. "You promised to be on your best behavior."

David eyed him saying, "this is my best, believe me."

Members of the President's staff, military aides, and personnel started streaming in and filling seats.

Nendel grabbed the mike from the podium and walked to the front of the stage. "Ladies and gentlemen, I just got word President Tindall has landed and is on the campus. Please find a seat and the President will be joining us momentarily."

David looked at Scott. "We're in real trouble if all the President's men are here at North Star."

"You're probably right," Scott said. "There's no way this could all be done off the radar. I wonder what the news is going to say about this much brass and the President showing up here."

David didn't have time to answer. Nendel announced the President's arrival and everyone stood and clapped to greet him.

Tindall walked down the aisle shaking hands with a few people as he passed. Accompanied by two Secret Service members, he made his way onstage.

"Ladies and Gentlemen, the President of the United States, Geoffrey Tindall," Nendel said. He returned the mike to the podium and stepped aside for the President.

Tindall adjusted the mike down a bit and gazed out over the small group of people. It reminded him of the early days of his political career. He was running for a state office, which he ended up losing. His campaign had started in a movie theater about the same size as the auditorium he was standing in now. He swallowed hard, hoping this campaign wouldn't end as disastrously as that one. He took a drink from the bottle of water provided for him and said, "I'm going to skip the introductions, but as you can see there are a number of our top military and political leaders with me today.

"Fifteen years ago North Star Industries came to our Government with a bold new idea to protect the sovereignty of space. Sadly, all of that technology has been lost to China and any country they shared it with. You at North Star were part of an aggressive response to the stealing of our technology. The launch of the latest Paradox satellites was successful in dealing a decisive blow to China for their illegal and subversive actions. The power blip you all experienced was part of that response. I can now share with you what I didn't with the rest of the Country, because you are the real heroes of this episode in our history.

With the launching of Paradox, much of the world's communications was destroyed. China is no longer able to communicate through their satellite systems. To protect our citizens, we have put in place a new global communication system relying on an array of thousands of high altitude platforms. The short blackout we experienced was caused as the new system was brought up to power and the old system was destroyed. We believe the new system will be more difficult for our enemies to attack, in that there are thousands of relay stations, as opposed to the few satellites in geosynchronous orbit. Unfortunately,... "

David nudged Scott, "Here it comes. Any time the word unfortunately is used in a sentence it means someone screwed up."

The President paused, glancing back at David.

"Sorry," David said. "Go ahead."

"Unfortunately, we were concerned about China and the aggressive actions they were taking, and not watching Russia as closely as we should have been.

"The rioting in the streets and the recent attack on North Star, while being carried out in concert with China, was a diversion. We know now that Russia used our preoccupation with China to launch a number of low earth orbit maneuverable platforms, which we believe are capable of launching nuclear weapons from space. They have already demonstrated the ability to move these platforms around changing the height and shape of their orbit, an ability required to launch weapons from low earth orbit."

Tindall cleared his throat and took another drink of water.

"I didn't want to be a wartime president. Frankly, I've done everything in my power to avoid conflict, but it appears war is unavoidable. We have nothing in our arsenal to combat a Russian attack from space. As I am telling this to you, China has directed their Navy Fleet into the Pacific. All indications are they will attack Hawaii and possibly, if they can get close enough, the mainland of the United States. We cannot let that happen.

"Ladies and gentlemen, you will read about it in the papers tomorrow morning. China has announced it is at war with the United States. Russia is their ally. I've asked Congress and received authority through a new War Powers Act to engage China in a conventional war, but if Russia decides to engage us, we will most certainly be in a nuclear war. This is why I am here with some of the brightest minds on the planet. We need a way to stop this. I am asking that the creative minds that developed Paradox put their collective ideas together and find a way to neutralize any attack from space. We will win a conventional war with China, but there is no certainty of the outcome of a war with Russia. With that I'll turn it over to General Mellon, the Chairman of the Joint Chiefs." He turned to Mellon who was sitting in one of the chairs behind him.

Mellon stood a good four inches above the President. His full head of white hair and weathered face, not only showed his age of 73, but also hinted to the hardships he had suffered through those years. He had started his career in Viet Nam as a young lieutenant, seeing war in its worst form. He was a career soldier with frontline experience, but was known to hate war. Throughout his military career he had brokered more peace talks than he had fought wars. That was why Tindall had chosen him to lead the Armed Forces. In contrast to his propensity to extend an olive branch to the enemy, he was known as a no nonsense leader and a fierce fighter if he was cornered, making him comfortable on the battlefield and in front of a congressional committee.

General Mellon paused for a moment looking at his audience. He saw youth in its purest form: Young men and women in uniform who had served their Country in battle sitting alongside young men and women who were serving in a different way. These had been chosen to save the Nation. They would come through. They had to.

"It wasn't your fault," General Mellon said. "No one in this room bares the responsibility for the mess we are in. Assignment of fault will no doubt be debated for years to come, but there is no time for that now. Like it or not, the burden now rests on the people in this room. Look around you. You will see a hundred or so of our finest military service members, engineers, physicists, munitions, electronics and battlefield specialists. They are here to work alongside the North Star team to solve a problem we don't even know how to define at the moment. Look around you. Look to the person on your left and on your right. This is the new team at North Star."

While General Mellon introduced the members of the Armed Forces in the audience, Scott looked at the faces on his team. Clearly they were concerned. The military personnel outnumbered them, two-to-one. He leaned over to David. "How do you think they will accept military working beside them?"

"Have them dress in civilian clothes and work alongside them, not look over their shoulder. You do that, then I can handle them."

"I think I can get them to agree to that," Scott said.

Mellon finished the introductions and turned to Scott. "Director Nendel says you were one of the best men who ever served under him. I'm proud to have you leading the North Star team."

Scott shook General Mellon's hand and grabbed the mike from the podium. He walked to the front of the stage. "I'm going to introduce the North Star personnel and then I understand we have some footage to show you before we break for lunch. I'm told the new North Star team will be sequestered on campus until we have a solution. Your families will be notified and any pressing problems resolved. If you have any special needs or concerns, please see me in my office."

The room erupted in chatter, most of them wondering what sequester would mean.

"They are holding us hostage," David said.

"I thought of it as a kidnapping," Scott said, "but either way it's in our best interest to cooperate."

*****

Cheyenne Mountain Complex, Colorado Springs, Colorado

Traffic backed up five miles from the main entrance to the underground chamber 2,000 feet below the east side of the granite mountain. A roadblock had been set up to turn away traffic from the complex and make the arrival of President Tindall as secret as possible.

Neighboring Petersen Airforce Base had put the Country on alert. The Country was officially at war. The Sixth Fleet had left Pearl Harbor to engage the fleet from China that was steaming toward Hawaii. No one knew what to expect. The precaution to move the President and members of Congress to the secure location was hotly debated, but in the end, the Presidency and Government had to remain intact after a nuclear attack.

The *New York Times* headline read *Nuclear War Imminent.*

From the Cheyenne Mountain Complex, President Tindall addressed a nation in fear.

"Fellow citizens, my message to you is one of grave importance. China has notified me by special currier that they have declared war against the United States.

"You have heard news reports that Russian mercenaries attacked a defense satellite facility in Oregon. We know now that the mercenaries were part of a coordinated effort between Russia and China to destroy our satellite capability. We responded to the threat by launching a group of defense satellites designed to remove deep space as a possibility for launching an attack on our Nation. China no longer can use deep space to threaten our Nation, but Russia remains a threat. I'm asking all citizens to go about your daily routine as best you can. Do not be alarmed by the recent correction in the stock market. As soon as things settle down, the markets will recover. I am putting the Country under martial law to protect citizens from the widespread looting and attacks on our businesses. I am also imposing a curfew in the larger cities. Tune your TV and radios to this channel for daily briefings at 8:00 p.m. Eastern Time. Obey the soldiers and government personnel in your states and cities and hopefully this threat will be over soon. God bless each and every one of you and God bless America."

North Star Industries

Scott handed David a fresh cup of coffee. "How'd it go on the first day with the new team?"

David took the cup and sat on the bar stool in the hotel suite they were now sharing to make room for the military guests. In addition to the ones who had attended the meeting, hundreds of North Star employees were being housed in government prefab housing dropped on campus from heavy-lift helicopters. The campus had been turned into a city overnight. The perimeter fencing had been heightened and a row of razor wire added. Remote controlled drones constantly patrolled overhead.

"I'm amazed at the resiliency of the team. They were able to grasp the problem and come up with a few scenarios that just might work," David said.

Scott stood on the other side of the bar facing David. He tested the temperature of the steaming cup of coffee he held before taking a sip. "You didn't mention the military personnel assigned to you."

"Thanks for taking my advice and having them dress as civilians," David said. "They are some sharp cookies. One of them suggested something the entire team thought might work."

"Are you running with it? Time is running out."

"You don't even want to hear what it is?"

"What I think doesn't matter. Will it meet the objective?"

"No," David said. "I had to play devil's advocate. The whole team was arguing with me, but I couldn't let them go with something that would only solve half of the problem."

"Now you've got my interest. What did they propose?"

"Sending up more HAPs with the capability of looking up toward the LOE satellites and taking out targets in orbit."

"You mean, take out the Russian missiles when they drop out of orbit. It sounds like a good idea. Can we do it?"

"Sure, and pretty quickly, but destroying Russian weapons isn't going to win the war."

"Why not?"

David tasted his coffee and poured it in the sink. "The only way we've been able to keep the peace throughout the Cold War is through mutual assured destruction. Russia has enough warheads on ICBMs, they could overwhelm us if they launched them all at once. The purpose of their orbiting weapons was meant to upset that balance and it has. We need something that will make the Russians fear us as much as we do them. Shooting their nukes out of the sky is only going to piss them off and we'll be right back where we started."

"Right now I think the free world would welcome that reset," Scott said, "but I know you well enough, you have something else in mind. What is it?"

"Now you're interested," David said. "I don't know why I bounce my ideas off of you, you never think they will work."

Scott looked at the clock on the stove. "I'm going to be late for a meeting. Promise me you won't piss off any generals today."

"I was about to tell you my idea," David protested.

"Later," Scott said, heading toward the door. "Just make sure it will work."

Scott jogged across the campus toward the executive offices. It had been a full day since the President had left North Star and departed for his bunker in Cheyenne Mountain. A lot had happened in a short time. He half expected to see bombs going off and smoke in the sky, but the sky was crystal clear and the campus was quiet. He stopped long enough to watch a robin looking at him curiously as it tugged a night crawler from the wet grass. "That's it, little fella," he said. "The early bird gets the worm."

Charlene Wilson was standing outside David's apartment building when he descended the stairs ready to start the day.

"Good morning, Charlene, is something wrong?" David asked.

"The team asked me to pitch the HAP idea to you again once you had a chance to sleep on it. Some feel pretty strongly that it's our best option."

"They didn't hear me when I said it would only solve half the problem?"

"They did, but unless you have something better, you're going to be facing a mutiny."

"Believe me, I know that. Let's take a minute," he motioned toward a park bench along the paved path leading to Research, "I want to run something by you."

They sat on the bench and David thought for a moment. Charlene was a scientist and would want to have details that he hadn't worked out. "I want you to imagine something," David began. "Imagine you are a Russian general in charge of the nuclear missile program."

"There are dozens of generals," Charlene interrupted.

"Okay, imagine you are one of hundreds of generals overseeing the nuclear missile sites on ground, at sea and in submarines under the sea. When we destroy their space based weapon, they will have thousands of warheads at their disposal to retaliate. What is keeping them from launching the first volley of missiles at us?"

"They fear we will do the same. Our missiles will pass each other on the way to mutual assured destruction. If we have enough warning, we will launch our own attack."

"You said, *if*." David emphasized the word.

"In a worst case scenario we wouldn't detect the threat until it was too late and we wouldn't have time to respond."

"But they can't surprise us with ground launched missiles. We have too many safeguards in place. A surprise attack would have to come from space."

"Which they can do," Charlene added. "That's why the team wants to eliminate that possibility and put us back on Cold War footing."

David grinned. "What if we didn't destroy anything? What if we made the weapons inoperable?"

"You mean the space weapons? That's what Paradox did. Without GPS, China's missiles are not much more effective than long range SCUD missiles at this point."

David nodded; she was buying into his point. "But they still have nuclear warheads and they can still do a great deal of damage, if they are launched. Taking away the guidance system makes them like a blind suicide bomber. You've heard the term, 'even a blind squirrel finds a nut once in a while;' well, in addition to cutting off his sight, we need to cut off the squirrel's legs."

"But we're talking about missiles, not squirrels," Charlene said. "How do you cut off a missile's legs?"

"Semantics," David said. "Get the team together. I want to address them in the Research conference room as soon as possible." He got up and started back toward his apartment.

"Where are you going?" Charlene asked.

"I'll catch up with you in ten minutes." He ran back toward his apartment. He had been working on something unrelated to North Star and needed it for show and tell.

David gave a sloppy solute to General Cramer as he entered the conference room. He noted Scott had made it to the meeting and handed a USB drive to Charlene. He stood by Gil, who was talking to General Mellon near the center of the room. Also in the room were about twenty military engineers in civilian clothes. David knew only a few of them by name.

"You were the designer of the Paradox micro-sats weren't you?" David asked Gil.

"Yeah, but it was a joint effort. Charlene's idea; I just made it functional."

David moved to the front of the room and addressed his team. "Please take a seat. "I understand there are some who think we should deploy the anti-missile system that was proposed yesterday. You might remember, I was opposed to that."

The discussion the day before had become quite heated. David's playing it down resulted in mild laughter from those who were in attendance.

"Watch very closely and see if you think you can make this work." He asked Charlene to turn down the lights and play the video he had given her.

"In its simplest form we have two problems in combating space launched Russian nuclear weapons. The first is how to prevent them from being sent into orbit and the second is preventing them from being sent back down. I believe we have most of the pieces in place to do both of those things. The thousands of HAPs in place for communication can easily be modified to detect missile launches from either ground or space, but that won't stop them from doing harm. Our current missile defense system is only fifty percent effective against ICBMs and zero percent against space launched weapons. We can detect them but we can't shoot them down.

"Take a close look at a device I've been developing. I call it Light-Speed." He brought up a picture of a small device and clicked through a number of frames which showed an array of lasers detecting a target and tracking it, relaying the information to another laser that sent out a flash from a hundred laser beams instantly destroying the target.

"This device is already in production in a different form," David said. "The complete system can be supported by High

Altitude Platforms and the system works for devices launched from earth or from low earth orbits in space."

"Let me see that again in slow motion," Cramer said.

David talked the team through the animation step by step, explaining how he had come up with the concept. "I'm simply adapting a targeting system I developed for pinpointing objects at the bottom of the sea and pairing it with the laser system used on the SGTRV developed for DARPA. Both systems are in production and have been proven. We only need to reprogram and repurpose them to detect and destroy missiles.

"As you can see in the animation, I've adapted the swarm technology used in Paradox satellites to a high altitude platform. Instead of sending out separate lasers, these are placed in a cluster, but each laser can hone in and track the path of a missile or bomb to within a few millionths of an inch, sending the information to a second set of high power lasers that can pierce through the missile casing.

"Before you point it out, I know there is a flaw in the design. If the lasers don't destroy the warheads, there is still the danger that one will fall on a populated area. While the likelihood of a nuclear explosion is remote, it could still happen. I have some ideas I want to run past the team I'm hoping will solve that problem. We need to find some serious computing power for the lightning fast response. We'll need the military's help in obtaining an eight-teraflop computer for each platform."

"How many of these Light-Speed things do we have to send up to protect us and our allies?" General Mellon asked.

"About two hundred," David said. "In theory that would protect North America and Europe from land, sea, or space launched weapons. It isn't fail safe, but it is as near as we can come to it on short notice."

"How long to get a system together?" Cramer asked. "Right now we are sitting ducks."

David looked at Gil, who was hiding his eyes. He figured Gil wouldn't want to commit to a tight timeline, but he had to ask. "Gil, the package has to be designed and the codes need to be written. We have to contact the people who make the HAPs. What do you think?"

"Maybe a year," Gil said. He looked at Charlene. "What kind of testing will you need?"

"We can do most of it with simulations, assuming the laser devices already exist." She eyed David. "How soon can you get me two hundred lasers? That's what we need for the first prototype, right?"

"General Cramer, you will need to persuade someone at DARPA to release the lasers I have stocked for the Subglacial Transport and Reconnaissance Vehicle." David said. "You make that happen and I can have them up here in a day."

General Mellon spoke up. "This takes priority over everything right now. If anyone gets on your ass about diverting the lasers, send them to me."

David locked eyes with those in the room. "So what do you think?" David asked, "is this something we can do?"

Scott had watched and listened without comment. He remembered several occasions when he had doubted David's ability to deliver on one of his crazy ideas and had always been proven wrong. He stood up.

"David, I'm guessing the generals need this device much sooner than six months let alone a year. What can you do to speed up the timeframe?"

"Give me the full resources of North Star Industries. Get me those computers and we'll shoot for six months," David said.

Mellon didn't wait for the rest of the military to comment. He got up and said, "Tell Cramer what you need and by when, he'll get it done."

Gil grabbed David by the sleeve. "I said a year, you cut it down to six months, I hope you know what you're doing."

"We haven't got a year," Scott said. "We may not have six-months"

Gil thought it over, seeing the serious expression on Scott's face. "Let's do it for your dad. You have my full support."

"I'm in," Charlene said.

Scott surveyed the room. "Everyone agreed, this is the new plan? I'm honored to be part of the team."

David hung up the phone from the *Sub Zero* assembly plant in San Diego. "The lasers will arrive around midnight by private jet," he said to Scott.

"I like your plan," Scott said. "If you are going to hunt deer, you do it with a rifle. If you're going bird hunting, do it with a shotgun. I want to know the hidden risks you failed to tell your team and the generals."

"What makes you think there are hidden risks?"

"Because, there always are."

"Weight," David said. "We need to keep the package below two hundred pounds so the HAP can support it."

"Well, you have a dedicated facility and all the resources you need. It better weigh less than two hundred pounds."

Chapter 20

Pacific Ocean, Flagship of the Seventh Fleet

The Admiral's flag ship *USS Mount Rainier* was a *Blue Ridge* class command ship named after the high peak in Washington State located about fifty miles south-south east of Seattle. At an elevation of 14, 411 feet, it stands fourth highest in the continental United States, but is believed to be the most dangerous mountain in the Cascade Range, being an active volcano near a densely populated area. Even though *Mount Rainier* was the most sophisticated Command, Control, Communications, Computer, and Intelligence ship ever commissioned, it had only defensive armament. Any command Admiral Rahm gave would be carried out by the other ships in his fleet.

Admiral Nelson Rahm picked up the phone and called the flagship of the Seventh Fleet which had been diverted from its route to New Zealand on a northwestern heading that would intercept the threat from China. There was no mistaking China's intentions and the earlier order to engage only if fired upon, were now being rescinded. The new orders were to prevent the launching of any missiles by a foreign power, by any means necessary. The new orders gave the commanders broad authority to assess a threat and act on it immediately. Both China and Russia had been warned that any launch of a missile from land, sea, or space would be considered an attack against the United States and its allies and would be dealt with swiftly.

China had responded, "What the PRC does on its soil or in international waters is no concern of the United States." It was a political snubbing of the nose, but an expected response from a nation that had announced it was at war with the United States.

Russia ignored the warning from the United States, failing to respond. Intel, in the form of digital pictures, relayed from dozens of military designated HAPs to USPACOM, showed a Russian force steaming toward the Chinese armada from the north, a thousand miles east of Japan. The ship movement was relayed with pinpoint accuracy from several HAP radar systems triangulating the location of each vessel. The US was tracking the exact coordinates of the Chinese and Russian ships in real time and they were converging at a point in the Pacific where Admiral Rahm had to stop them. He knew he couldn't let China get within range of US soil to launch their MRBMs. He needed to buy time for the proposed North Star system to be put in place, but had little hope he could accomplish that. The showdown was certain to happen before fall.

Admiral Rahm pointed to a grid on a monitor and commented to his XO, "We have to stop them before they reach this point."

"The Fleet's Fire Control Officers are preparing to launch surface-to-surface cruise missiles," the XO said to Admiral Rahm. "How many, sir?"

"All of them. If we don't stop them in their tracks, we won't live through the counterattack." He turned back to the screen.

"We've got subs, too," the XO said.

"I want every sub spotter we have cruising in a hundred mile radius. The last thing we need is for one of them to slip through."

He watched on his control room screen as volley after volley of cruise missiles rose from the decks of his destroyers. In seconds they disappeared over the horizon.

"We have a submarine!" The voice came over the intercom and didn't identify itself.

"Is it ours?" Rahm asked.

"Commander Trent, sir. She's surfaced in the middle of the fleet. I've never seen anything like this. Underwater drones deployed."

Rahm felt his stomach lurch. It had happened once before in the middle of a Navy exercise and had been considered a stunt. There were really no countermeasures the ships could take without endangering other ships in the fleet. Deck guns, torpedoes and depth charges were not capable of distinguishing the submarine from the dozens of ships in the fleet.

When China had started increasing the size of their navy, they had built hundreds of diesel powered submarines that were almost undetectable. They had managed to make them stealthier than the nuclear powered submarines of the United States Navy.

The order from Commander Trent was seconds old when the first torpedo from the submarine hit.

The torpedo attack came from such a short distance there wasn't time for evasive maneuvers. Rahm watched in horror as one after another of his prized ships exploded from direct underwater hits. They didn't even have time to turn the deck guns on the surfaced submarine and the drones hadn't left the deck. *They must have launched the entire submarine fleet against us*, Rahm thought as he watched much of the Seventh Fleet burning around him.

"Sir, we have wiped out the attacking fleet," his XO said.

Both of them knew it was a tradeoff. The Chinese armada had been a diversion for the submarines. Most likely, at this very moment, other submarines armed with nuclear missiles were slipping past the wreckage of the Seventh Fleet and headed toward Hawaii.

He updated USPACOM on the situation. His last thought before a torpedo hit *Mount Rainier* mid-ship below decks was that he would never see his wife and daughter again. Like the mighty volcano it was named after the *USS Mount Rainier* erupted in a violent explosion.

*****

Cheyenne Mountain Complex, President Tindall's War Room

Tindall had gathered his generals back in the safety of the war room below Cheyenne Mountain. They watched in real time as the Seventh Fleet went down, one ship after the other until *Mount Rainier* was the only ship left. And then, it exploded in a violent eruption.

Speechless, President Tindall looked at General Mellon. "What the hell just happened?" Tindall finally asked. "Didn't we see this coming?"

"I'd call it a draw," General Mellon said, trying to put the best spin on it he could think of. "We took out their surface ships and they took out ours."

"We have a thousand men in the water. What are we doing to save them?"

"We held back our aircraft carriers. We can send out search planes. We've got a dozen sub destroyers on the way. If they have their underwater navy together down there we'll find them and stop them."

"Too damn little, too damn late," Tindall said gruffly. "Why didn't we see this coming?"

Mellon knew better than to respond. They had screwed up: Underestimated the power of the conventional strike force: Underestimated the resolve of China to neutralize the United States as an adversary. "Maybe they are ready to talk," Mellon said.

"I'll bet," Tindall said angrily. "They seem to be holding all the cards, why wouldn't they be willing to talk. I want a plan to keep them from attacking our mainland, General. What are you going to do to keep our people safe?"

"We've already set up an iron fence around the Hawaiian islands. Not all of their *Jin* class subs have been equipped with the quiet engines. They may have surprised us once, but they won't again."

"I wish I could believe you."

Mellon knew the *Jin* class submarines were capable of launching twelve nuclear missiles each. If any of them got closer to the mainland than Hawaii, any city in the western two-thirds of the United States could become a target. If they penetrated the territorial waters of the United States or Canada, the entire Eastern Seaboard of the United States was at risk.

"You might want to get some sleep," General Mellon suggested. "I think the big battle is over. From here on out it's going to be a battle here and there as our sub chasers find and take out the subs."

Tindall felt tired. He wasn't sure if it was from stress or fatigue, either way he knew he would have to be thinking clearly in the hours ahead. If a nuclear missile was fired at the United States, he would have to respond in kind. With less than six months left in office, he was leaving a mess for the next president.

"Wake me if anything happens," Tindall said. "I mean it. Anything!"

North Star Industries, two weeks later

"Do you know how difficult it was for me to get hold of you?" Patricia asked.

She was upset. He didn't have a chance to tell her he was being locked inside the complex until the new system was completed. Communications in and out of the complex went through a special station that scrambled the calls.

"All the calls coming in and out of here are monitored," Scott said. "I can't tell you much about what's going on."

"Let me tell you," Patricia said. "There was a report that came out of Japan that the Seventh Fleet was nearly destroyed by Chinese submarines."

"We're at war. I'm sure it wasn't that bad," Scott tried to reassure her. In fact it was the first he had heard about the battle in the Pacific. News to the North Star facility was being blacked out.

"We're not getting any news we can trust. While you are locked in your own private world, people are panicking out here. They are afraid the West Coast will be attacked by China. If I can believe the reports out of Europe, that's exactly what is going to happen."

"Can you do me a favor and call my mom and sister. Tell them I'm okay, you spoke to me and I'll contact them as soon as I can."

"Scott, I don't understand what's going on. I'm scared."

"I know it's tough, but you have to hang in there for a few more weeks. As soon as I can get out of here, we'll have a drink and relax."

"A few weeks. Does that mean this will be over in just a few weeks?"

"It means, after this is over, we can discuss it. Don't read anything into it. I love you. I've gotta go."

"I love you, too," Patricia said. She held on to her phone until it went dark. *Did he really mean a few weeks, or was he trying to make me feel better?*

"How'd she get through to you?" David asked, looking up from the couch where he sat with a pad and pen in hand.

"Who knows, she's a reporter. She knows how to get into places she isn't supposed to."

"I miss Fay," David said. "I'd give anything to hear her voice right now."

Scott didn't answer. He stared out across the campus. A least a hundred soldiers were roaming about with their automatic weapons strapped across their fronts.

"Did she give you any news from the outside?" David asked.

"We lost a battle in the Pacific. She didn't know if it was real news or internet babble. She seemed pretty upset."

"She should be. The more I think about it, new weapons never stop war; they just change the nature of it. The one with the biggest gun rules, until the next guy develops a bigger one."

"You're being clinical. You don't really think that's what we're doing?"

David sounded frustrated. "I don't know what to think anymore. If we can stop this madness for a little while, I'll take it as a win."

"How soon are we going to be ready to go?"

"Another two months, maybe. Everything is going smoothly. My crew wants to get the job done and get on with their lives, so I know as soon as it can happen it will."

"I'll second that. You know, I'm proud of you," Scott said. "Seriously."

David stood and walked over to him. "We make a good team. Let's get this done and take some serious downtime. I'll fly us all to a tropical paradise that never heard of China or Russia."

Scott smiled. "You are a dreamer. Give me a day on the beach with the wind and rain hitting my face and I'll be fine."

Scott's phone rang. "Scott Tanner."

"Hold for General Mellon."

Scott turned away from the phone. "General Mellon," he said to David.

"General," Scott said.

"Scott, I suppose you heard about the battle in the Pacific?"

"I have David Stafford here. Is it all right for him to listen in?"

"Sure. He should hear this."

General Mellon filled them in on what had happened. Thirty of our best ships sunk and nearly a thousand lives lost. "But that's not why I'm calling. Is there anyway of adapting our submarine detection devices to our HAPs? We've been encountering submarines here and there and I'm telling you they are all headed our way."

"It can be done," David answered, "but we're loading the HAPs pretty heavy with the *Light-Speed* technology. I doubt they can handle the additional weight."

"What I need at this moment is a line of defense along the western coastline from Alaska to South America. About seven-thousand miles long. We have electronic listening devices in place off the coast, but China has found a way to sneak past them. Our devices are not sensitive enough to catch the new *Jin* class submarines."

David said, "I'm thinking you need to go with an improvement over our current underwater detection devices."

"You know of something that can detect one of the Chinese *Jin* class super quiet subs, I'm listening?"

"Ultra Low Frequency sonar coupled with a super computer will work," David said.

"We already have that," Mellon said. "It isn't effective against this threat."

"What you have is Extreme Low Frequency communication. To make it work for detection you need the power of the super computer with some algorithms to paint pictures with sound. The Navy already owns the patent. If you want I'll get you in touch with my contact at DARPA."

"No need. Sometimes I think the right hand doesn't know what the left hand is working on. You keep focused on what you're doing. I'll checkout ULF. "

"No problem, General. You probably need to redirect the DARPA program for your immediate need. It's all there, just needs to be repackaged, like we did *Light-Speed*."

"Keep up the good work," General Mellon said, "We're depending on you both."

"Holy shit," David said. "Look at the time. We're supposed to be at the *Light-Speed* simulation in the R&D conference room."

They arrived to a dozen befuddled individuals milling around the conference room table. "What's happening?" David asked Charlene.

"We can't seem to get the computer powered up," Gil said. "It was working when we left Engineering, but it's dead in here. We thought it was a low battery and we plugged it in."

David looked at the laptop. He saw it was plugged into an outlet that was affixed to the top of the table. He reached under the table and flipped a switch and the computer started to boot up.

Charlene gave him an embarrassed look and shook her head.

"That's why he's making the big bucks," Scott said.

The simulation showed a high altitude platform shaped like a giant doughnut the size of a football stadium. In the doughnut hole, a long tube was suspended. It was the size of two oil drums stacked together. On the top and bottom was a dome that appeared to have dozens of holes looking much like the eye of a giant fly. Charlene started to narrate the demonstration.

"This tube houses the *Light-Speed* lasers," She pointed to the dome on either end. "Fifty lasers face up at space and fifty are facing down toward the earth. Each laser is fitted with a tracking motor attached to a gimbal, allowing complete maneuverability. Each laser can hone in on a separate target or, using swarm algorithms, attack a single target. When one locks on a target the rest aim at it and determine if it's the only threat or if there are others and fire accordingly. This is why we need the big computing power. It all happens in a fraction of a second, at the speed of light. The range of a single array of lasers is two hundred fifty miles in any direction. The doughnut shaped wing is made from carbon fiber reinforced Mylar and filled with helium. It can stand the frigid upper atmosphere and the pressure from the helium inside. The top surface of the doughnut wing is coated with flexible solar cells which keep the batteries charged while they in turn recharge the capacitors.

"A single blast from the lasers is up to fifty-thousand kilowatts, enough to destroy a missile by burning holes through its guidance system incapacitating it. We suspect if it hit in the right spot it could cut a missile in two."

As she spoke, the simulation showed a nuclear bomb dropping out of orbit and heading toward earth. The lasers detected it and fired in the blink of an eye, causing a massive fireball.

"Let me show you that in slow motion," Charlene said, proudly.

The sequence started with a small burst of gas slowing the weapon's speed until it started dropping out of orbit. As it approached within 250 miles of a platform the lasers started tracking it. The lasers fired burning holes through the casing. As the warhead continued to fall it tumbled through the atmosphere catching fire and breaking apart. In another simulation the earth facing lasers continued to fire at the falling bomb, causing it to explode in the upper atmosphere.

"The nice thing about nuclear warheads is they are not armed in space. They have several fail-safe mechanisms, such as pressure activated triggers, that do not allow the missile to be armed until it is in the vicinity of the target, usually a mile or less from ground. If any of the safety mechanisms is compromised, the bomb will not explode. Without its guidance system, most of the warheads will burn up as it falls through the atmosphere. Our calculus gives us a ninety-nine percent probability of destroying a missile, if it is in the range of the platform."

"Great computer model," Scott said. "Will it really work that well, I mean 99%?"

"Our data says it will," Gil said. "We already have the first prototype ready to deliver to Marin Aerospace to be attached to the HAP. We could have the first one up in a few days."

"Wow," Scott said. "You guys are so far ahead of schedule, the generals are going to think you padded the timeline."

"We can drag it out another month if you want," Gil said, joking.

"Nendel and the generals will be back tonight. Maybe you can show this to them. It's sure to put a smile on their faces."

"We wanted you to see it first," Gil said. "We needed someone to show us how to power up the computer." He laughed. "My team says they are ready for production, but want to wait until the first one is up."

"We can't wait," Scott said. He was thinking about the loss of the ships in the Pacific and the conversation he and David had

had with General Mellon. "We need as many of these things up as soon as possible. I know General Cramer has already developed a launch grid to cover as many populated areas as possible. The first one will go up off the coast of Los Angeles."

"We better be sure it works," David said. "Is there anything I can do to help speed things up? I mean other than flipping the power switch." He was glad to see them smile. Like him, they were tired and a little humor helped their spirits.

Chapter 21

South Pacific Ocean

A thousand miles south of Hawaii, edging along the Kingman Reef, five *Jin* class submarines glided along the ocean floor, taking cover in the acoustic shadow of the reef. Using their latest communication technology, the submarines sent messages using ULF radios with super computer algorithms to separate the signals from the background noise of the sea. In addition to messaging the super computing power allowed them to send out signals mimicking marine wildlife, masking the signature of their engines. The technology made them nearly undetectable. Using this technology they could travel in packs, much like the wolf packs the Nazis used in World War II.

The five submarines had traveled undetected, from Liaoning, Xiaopingdao Submarine Base at the north tip of the Yellow Sea, to their present position over a two-week period and, had used the battle in the Pacific as a diversion to avoid detection. Instead of traveling to Hawaii, like the Americans expected, they had moved south giving Hawaii a wide berth.

China wanted to attack the United States not a tiny cluster of islands thousands of miles from the mainland. They had already destroyed the heart of the Seventh Fleet and wanted to get within striking distance of the United States before the Six Fleet completed the long journey from the Atlantic and the Middle East to join up with the remainder of the Seventh Fleet.

China knew they would not be able to survive another naval battle, at least not a conventional one against the far superior United States Navy.

China planned to position their submarines 200 miles off the West Coast of the United States and strike every major metropolitan area, causing unimaginable loses of life and property. Only then did they believe the United States would surrender.

Hauxin Lin, the Communist Party representative aboard the flagship for the Submarine Fleet, told Fleet Commander Hai Qingdao: "We have not made the same mistake Japan made when they attacked Pearl Harbor,"

Commander Qingdao looked down at the overweight bureaucrat. It was no secret that he despised the Communist Party politician assigned to his boat. The crew referred to Hauxin Lin as "Fat Cat". Like a cat, he silently showed up when you least expected him, and he never passed up a meal. Some had joked they should shower him with treats until he collapsed from a heart attack, or he could no longer fit through the narrow bulkhead doors. Inwardly, Commander Qingdao chuckled at the possibility.

"But like Japan, we may have underestimated our enemy," Commander Qingdao said. "Let me ask you, what will happen to our land if we succeed in attacking the United States?"

Hauxin Lin frowned. "You do not believe in the mission, Commander?"

"I believe the Americans will not be bombed into obscurity. We will defeat them, only temporarily. Their resolve will be hardened by our attack. Are we really prepared to take on such a military giant?"

"Ah, that is where your thinking is wrong. Our little fleet has sixty nuclear warheads, each one capable of wiping out a major city. Our guidance systems no longer rely on satellites, but on celestial navigation. That is why we will attack at night, when it will put the most fear into the heart of our enemy. You see, the giant, as you like to describe our enemy, will fall hard. Our leaders have made the calculation. It is certain."

Qingdao was getting tired of the conversation. There was nothing he could say that would make the party leader understand. He could carry out the mission and hope he was wrong for the sake of his family living in Beijing. There was little doubt that Beijing would be the first target the Americans would strike in retaliation.

"Don't you have anything better to do?" Qingdao asked.

Lin smiled, showing yellow, tobacco-stained teeth.

"Careful, Commander. You are on the edge of thin ice. You don't want to fall in the icy water."

"You think I'm afraid of the Party? I only tolerate you, because you have a part of the launch code needed for me to fulfill my mission."

"You spent some time in America," Lin said. "How did you find the Americans?"

"I found them arrogant, wasteful, and self-absorbed, just like much of our youth. They forget the mistakes of the past quickly so they continue making new ones."

"As our leaders have long espoused," Lin said. "Americans are weakened by their overindulgence. Take away their toys and they will run home crying."

"You are wrong. Take away their toys and they will fight like hell to get them back. They are an impatient race. They look only at tomorrow. That is what we should fear."

"Fear. You fear that they don't have patience?"

"I fear that they will want to win the war quickly. To do that, they will have to take great risks. They may act impulsively and unpredictably."

"With what? We have dealt them a major blow. We are sneaking up on them from the depths of the sea. They will not have time to act impulsively. After our attack, the focus of the Americans will only be on survival. They will not have the will for a counterattack."

"Hauxin Lin, you look like you are hungry. I heard the cook has prepared a fresh batch of won ton for the evening meal. He may need someone to taste it to make certain it is fit for my crew."

"Commander, it seems you are trying to get rid of me by bribing me with food?"

Commander Qingdao shrugged. "I'm just telling you what the cook said. Tell him to give you the special treat he has prepared."

"Perhaps I should give it a try. We wouldn't want your crew to be poisoned, would we?"

"I assure you it is not poison."

"Let me be the judge of that," Lin said, squeezing between the sonar operator's station and a stack of electronic instruments.

The commander watched him make his way through the bulkhead door. *Maybe he will eat too much and die of a heart attack,* he thought. He smiled. *Such good fortune will not likely be mine.*

*****

Portland, Oregon

The public was not yet aware of the destruction of the satellite systems. With the switch from satellites to HAPs, nothing in the normal day-to-day lives of Americans had changed. Their GPS system had been switched over to a low elevation navigation tracking system code named LENT. It worked similar to GPS, but was much more precise, using several HAPs to pinpoint a vehicle's position.

The lack of a satellite link between the United States, China, and Russia had been explained as a wartime restriction. Landlines were still capable of getting calls across the Atlantic, but to get a call patched through to China or Russia was nearly impossible and certain to be monitored if it could be done. Patricia, like millions of Americans, was not aware that the enemy no longer had GPS capability.

The city had been under blackout rules and a curfew for two weeks. Nearly every night, because of the late hour of her newscast, Patricia had been stopped and questioned by soldiers. She let everyone know how stupid she thought the rule was. And at the Starbucks near her studio she mentioned it to a woman she had seen often and visited with when she was enjoying her favorite summer drink, a caramel Frappe. The woman ordered the same thing and followed her to a table.

"Do you mind if I join you?" the woman asked.

"Please sit," Patricia said. "This is the only indulgence I allow myself since the war started. Who knows how long it will be before coffee is rationed?"

"You think there is a danger of that?" the woman asked.

"I was joking," Patricia said. "But it makes about as much sense as the blackout. What good is a blackout?" Patricia complained. "We are surely not afraid of an air raid. Besides, everybody uses GPS to navigate now days. Even if the city is dark, they can pinpoint us to within a few feet. If we are going to be attacked, I guarantee a blackout is not going to prevent it. They are doing it as a punishment," Patricia continued. "If they could target our cities during the Cold War they surely have better capability today. Our Government is imposing a blackout just to trick us into feeling safer."

"You must lay awake thinking about these things," the woman said.

"I'll bet it's a holdover from the last big war. It wouldn't be the first time there was some kind of outdated law used to put restrictions on the public."

The woman put her hand on Patricia's arm. "A beautiful girl like you should have other things to think about than blackouts and curfews. I'll bet you have a nice young man to share the dark nights with."

Patricia shook her head. "I can't believe I'm telling you this, but I've got nothing better to do. My bed is pretty empty these days."

"I remember you saying your man was not around."

Patricia shook her head, affirmatively. "I prefer to think he is doing his part to get the war over quickly. He says it won't be much longer."

"He's working on something special?" her friend asked.

Patricia shrugged. "He can't tell me anything. I have no idea what he's doing."

"Still he wouldn't tell you it would be over soon if he wasn't certain what he was working on might shorten the war?"

"Don't go putting too much in what I said. Scott really doesn't tell me much. He just seemed to be a little more upbeat when I talked to him last. I read it as they might have something that will defeat China."

"Well, let's hope he's right." Her friend checked her watch. "I need to run and buy groceries before the lights go out."

"I will be doing the Eleven O'clock News as usual," Patricia said. "Finding answers for the public is like pulling teeth these days."

The woman stood by the table. "Anything new you can tell me?"

"Tune in at eleven," Patricia said, standing and walking out with the woman. She waived as they went separate ways and walked the short distance to the KPDX studio.

The woman entered her apartment on the fourth story of a sprawling apartment complex on the East Side. She had chosen the top floor even though there was no elevator. She liked being above most of the trees on the manicured grounds.

She wrote a message on her computer and saved it to a SanDisk, a tiny storage device about the size of a postage stamp, removed it from her computer, and slipped it into a special slot in a tiny homing drone. The drone was preprogrammed to fly across town, deliver the tiny chip and return to her apartment. She would leave the window open and the lights off until it completed its mission. For this simple act, a payment would be wired to an offshore bank. She hoped the tiny piece of news would be considered significant enough for the payment.

She held the drone out the window and watched it quickly disappear into the darkness. As soon as it was out of sight she attached a piece of netting over the open window to catch it when it returned.

An hour later the tiny drone crashed into the net. She picked it up, removed the message attached and closed the window. Now she could turn on the eleven o'clock news.

"Good evening," Patricia greeted the camera. "I'm Patricia Westland and it's time for news and commentary. We are in day thirteen of a war with Russia and China and we are still being kept in the dark." She smiled. "Pardon the pun, but this isn't World War II, is it?

"This is the twenty-first Century. If we are attacked, it will be by missiles launched a continent away. They don't need to see our lights to know where to drop the bomb."

Across town, FBI Agent Reese was watching the eleven o'clock news. She picked up the phone and called her partner. "Hey, Gordy, are you watching KPDX?"

"No, I was sleeping. What's up?"

"Patricia Westland is at it again. She's calling for the people to rise up against a black-out."

"I thought she was reporting news. What's she doing?"

"I guess there isn't enough news to keep her busy, so she's started her own rebellion."

"What do you think we should do?"

"Shut her down."

"It's news; First Amendment, and all that stuff. No way are we going to be able to do that."

"She has to be spoken to," Reese said. "She's going to have this city lit up like a search light if she has her way."

Gordon agreed, but he wasn't certain how to approach her. He couldn't just come out and say he expected our enemy would use conventional targeting techniques because we had destroyed all of their satellites. They no longer had GPS to guide their missiles, that information was still classified.

"What do you think we can say to quiet her?" Gordon asked, then added, "without giving away classified information."

"We should just bring her in and tell her she's on the verge of inciting a riot. She keeps it up we will charge her with treason."

"You can try it, but she's an educated woman. She will claim she has the right to say anything she thinks and hide behind the First Amendment."

"So we do nothing?"

"I didn't say that. Maybe we can reason with her. Call on her patriotic duty in time of war. She's engaged to a former Navy SEAL; she ought to understand duty and Country come first."

Patricia exited the elevator leading to the parking garage and looked out into what appeared to be a black hole. She hated the blackout. She reached in her purse and removed a pair of miniature night vision glasses and scanned the garage for her car. She carefully walked toward it. She used her remote key to actuate the lock and climbed inside. The dome light had been taken out according to blackout instructions, but she knew her car well enough to find the starter button, even without the aid of the cumbersome visual aide, so she placed the goggles on the center console and reached for the starter button.

"Don't start it yet," Agent Reese said from the cramped back seat.

"Jesus, you scared me!" Patricia said. "If I didn't recognize your voice, you'd be dead meat. Breaking and entering, that's a crime."

"So report me," Reese said. "I'm here to ask a favor. "

"You aren't likely to get me to do anything by scaring me half to death."

"I'm sorry. I thought you would see me with the night vision glasses. I apologize."

"What do you want?"

"For the sake of national security, you need to lay off the banter about the blackout. We have reason to believe any attack on our cities will not use satellite navigation. We believe the blackout is necessary to protect our cities."

"Don't pull that crap with me. The town is deserted at night, soldiers are roaming the streets and the citizens are scared to death. Keeping them in the dark isn't helping."

"Look, I don't disagree with you. I wouldn't put up with it either if I didn't believe it was to keep us safe."

"I can't believe you've got nothing better to do than keep me from talking. First you threaten me with the Russian connection. I went along with you there. All it accomplished was a delay in the truth getting out. The people are going to find the truth, if not from me, then from someone else. What's next? Are you going to arrest me?"

"I could arrest you for treason." Reese said calmly.

Patricia was quiet for a long moment. "Get out of my car, and quit threatening me!"

Gordon was listening in on the conversation through his earpiece. When Reese returned he said, "That went well, but you forgot to mention her boyfriend."

"You want me to go back?" Reese asked.

Gordon chuckled. "No, I think you did enough damage for today."

Scott checked the clock. The phone on his nightstand was ringing. He picked it up.

"Tanner here."

"Scott, you need to tell me what's going on. The FBI contacted me after my last newscast. I need some answers."

Patricia sounded hysterical.

Scott had caught her news broadcast and had thought about calling her, but knew where that would go, so put it out of his mind. He was concerned that Patricia was getting herself in hot water, but didn't figure it was bad enough to get the FBI involved.

There had been a tremendous clampdown on the press. So called "fake news" seemed to dominate the airwaves and in these uneasy times much of it was believed. If Patricia, in her job as a broadcast journalist, participated in the half truths, she would be taken seriously. Satellite communications with China and Russia had been stopped, but the internet seemed to be unaffected. Information, like water finding the path of least resistance, always found a way to get out, true or not. China was using rumors and false reporting to fight their battles. In past wars, it had been called propaganda, but in today's world it was given equal weight to real news. Much of it was a bit of truth slanted to give the reader a one-sided opinion. Algorithms had been written for computers that could spit out a fake news story by simply reading and rewriting an actual event. Patricia was in the wrong place at the wrong time. She was as much the enemy as China and Russia. Patricia was on the verge of falling into the trap of mixing fact with fiction, but Scott wasn't going to be the one to tell her. He couldn't do it with any credibility without divulging classified information.

"Patricia, I'm sorry, but I can't talk," Scott said. "Listen to me. You need to drop the news commentary." He hung up. It was the only thing he could do under the circumstances. He knew his hanging up would infuriate her and he would face the consequences later, but it was the only thing he could think of that could let her know the gravity of the situation they were all facing. We were at war and that called for different rules. Everyone was called to sacrifice individual rights for the benefit of the Country. He had been in the service, he understood. *Why didn't Patricia get it?*

Santa Catalina Island, California

Located about twenty-six miles south south-west of Los Angeles; Santa Catalina Island hosts over a million tourists a year. The island is 22 miles long, has a population of just over 4,000, most residing in the largest city, Avalon. In the early 1900s, Wrigley, the chewing gum giant, owned most of the island. Now it was going through another chapter in its history. It had been two weeks since President Tindall had signed a document allowing the Air Force to evacuate the 4,000 or so citizens and set up the island as a military base.

A small van pulled up to the dock at Avalon, opened its rear doors, and accepted a package from a small lift truck. This was the day everyone at North Star had been waiting for. The team back home was watching via a secure feed from the island to the North Star conference room. Especially exciting was this day had come much earlier than they had expected.

Scott Tanner and David Stafford had arrived on the island by helicopter in the early morning hours along with Chief Engineer Gil Thompson and Research Director Charlene Wilson. They were there to observe the launching of *Paradox X*, the designation given to the new type of high altitude missile defense platform. The rumors of submarines off the coast was not good and the launching couldn't happen soon enough. Nearly twenty million people along California's coastal cities were depending on it for the protection it promised.

The van with the package climbed a freshly graveled road up the mountain to the highest point on the island. Behind the van was a string of vehicles carrying brass from every branch of the service, and in the rear vehicle, four from North Star Industries.

They jostled back and forth in the hard seats of the Hummer as it made the slow trip up the mountain.

"You look nervous," Scott said to Charlene, who was buckled in next to him.

"A little," Charlene said. "I've never been invited to a launch before."

"Just routine," David said. "The generals want to have somebody present to blame if something goes wrong."

"He's kidding," Scott said, seeing Charlene's facial expression. "They want you and Gil to be here to give it the once over before it goes up."

Chapter 22

Pacific Ocean, two-hundred miles west of San Francisco, California

Admiral Hai Qingdao didn't like formalities and inside the kill zone, 200 feet below the surface, he had insisted there be no celebration. He had successfully brought his fleet of five submarines inside the territorial waters of the United States. Any noise his crew made would almost certainly be picked up by one of the hundreds of acoustical sensors planted along the sea floor. It was early morning. He would have to remain silent until darkness set in.

What a surprise will awaken you, he mused. He had sent his last message 600 miles back as his small fleet paralleled the coastline of the United States. By now the other four submarines would be positioned with their missiles ready to target every major city in the United States. It was a sobering thought to hold the destruction of an entire nation in your hands. *It is an honor that my Country has chosen me for a mission that will change world history*, Qingdao thought.

Cheyenne Mountain Complex

President Tindall grew uneasy the longer he was trapped underground. "I should have stayed in the White House, that's what the people expect their leaders to do, war or no war," he said to his National Security Advisor, Biggs.

Biggs removed his glasses and ran a hand over his thinning hair. "The people understand, sir."

"Understand?" Tindall tossed the report he'd been reading on his desk. "Understand what? That I can't protect them? That we can't defeat an enemy, that ten years ago they wouldn't have dared attack us. What they understand is, I'm inside a granite mountain protected from what we think might be a nuclear attack, and they are being left outside. What kind of leadership is that?"

"Sir, Washington DC is certain to be one of the first targets. You will be no good to the Nation if you are vaporized."

"Thank you for that," Tindall huffed. "And you think I'll be able to face them after a good portion of our cities are vaporized?"

Biggs was at a loss for words. He knew how important a president's legacy was to him, but there wouldn't be anything for the historians to write about if Tindall became a victim of his own ego.

"We think the threat will be short lived, Mr. President. I received word they are launching the new Paradox X defense shield as we speak."

"Then it will be safe for me to go back?" Tindall asked.

"It's only the first step in a two hundred-piece puzzle," Biggs said. "We need another couple hundred X platforms in the air before we can safely return."

"Bullshit. I want to return today. How can the American people put their trust in me if I'm hiding in a cave? It's time for me to get out there and reassure the people."

"Sir, you may not think that once you've read this morning's intel." He handed a thin folder to the President.

Tindall looked up from the report. "They don't know how many got through? I was told the HAPs were going to provide reliable data on submarine movement. We can't even keep track of a few hundred submarines."

He tossed the report on his desk, scattering a dozen pieces of paper to the floor. "Where's the rest of my Intel committee?"

"They are in California at the launching of Paradox X."

"We have submarines off our coast and the heads of Intel are celebrating the launch of a new platform?" He shook his head. "I guess it should make sense. Get a message to them. I want them back here immediately."

Biggs normally would have balked at being treated like Tindall's aide, but right now he was happy to get out of the line of fire. "I'll call them right away, sir. Anything else?"

"Find out where my wife is. It's our thirty-fifth anniversary."

"Congratulations, sir." Biggs headed for the steel door leading to one of the tunnels in the complex. *Kudos to her for putting up with you that long,* he thought.

Santa Catalina Island

"I thought they said this thing could be launched in fifteen minutes," Scott said, noting the time.

"This being the first one," David said, "they are double checking all the systems. It may be another hour before they start filling the balloon." David hoisted himself up on the hood of the Humvee and lay back in the sun. "Don't get this kind of sun in Oregon," he said, adjusting his dark glasses.

"I'm glad you can enjoy it. Did you tell the team to keep cranking these things out?"

"That's the plan," David said, nonchalantly.

Scott watched Charlene and Gil go through the diagnostic tests one last time. He saw a General pick up his cell phone. He tapped David. "General Mellon just got a call. Looks like the ceremony is about to be cut short."

David lifted himself up by his elbows. Mellon was pointing to Cramer and Nendel. "We may be the only dignitaries left," David said grinning.

"Why are you grinning?" Scott asked.

"Now that I'm out of the complex, I thought I might call Fay and meet up with her, before returning to North Star. It will only be for the weekend."

"And you think you'll be able to get away once the brass leaves?"

"Hey, she's less than four hundred miles north of here. She'll be glad to hear from me. My crew knows what to do."

"She's still in the Bay Area? I thought you would have told her to go inland someplace, like Wyoming or Montana. Someplace safe."

"Like you told Patricia?"

"Portland isn't a prime target like San Francisco."

"It is if they want to destroy North Star," David said. "No place on the West Coast is safe."

"I suppose you're right. Just how are you going to go AWOL without getting caught?"

"I may need your help for that," David said, jumping down from the hood of the vehicle. "Be right back, I'm going to wish the brass a safe journey."

Cheyenne Mountain Complex

Director Nendel got the information first and relayed it to President Tindall, who immediately handed it to Biggs. They had all been whisked to an isolated bunker in the mountain complex where they could watch what had been unfolding for the better part of an hour off the coast of Washington.

"That's our sub destroyer," Nendel said.

"Where are they?"

"Two hundred miles due west of Seattle. Our new sensors detected it. Unfortunately it's the only one in existence."

"And they think it's one of the *Jin* class subs?" the President asked.

"It has to be. We know the signature of their boomers and this was completely different. Sounded like some kind of a marine mammal. A seal or sea lion."

"I'm surprised we detected it," Tindall said.

"One of our sonar operators was on the ball, that's all I can say. He knew where the sensor was placed and knew seals wouldn't be that far out to sea."

"Remind me to give that man a medal," Tindall said.

"Woman, sir. Lt. JG Marcia Nichols."

"What's she doing now," Tindall asked, looking back at the screen.

"Nichols, sir?"

"The sub chaser. It's just sitting there."

"I suspect its using laser penetrators to pinpoint the target along with magnetometer equipped and underwater robots. Now that we know she's down there, we'll find her and flush her out."

"There are bound to be others," Tindall said gravely, looking at Nendel for confirmation.

Nendel nodded and remained silent.

Portland, Oregon

Patricia sipped a caramel Frappe and looked out into the streets. The sunshine, clear sky, and warm breeze made it a perfect day for shopping, but the streets of downtown Portland had nearly as many soldiers roaming around as shoppers.

She checked her most reliable European news sources on her tablet and stopped on a report out of Canada. A Canadian journalist stationed in British Columbia was reporting a US ship had intercepted a Chinese submarine off the coast of Washington and was dropping depth charges. She knew that couldn't be true. The Navy didn't use the highly ineffective depth charges anymore. It had to be a Canadian ship or the report was inaccurate. She contacted one of her reporter friends who worked for the

Vancouver Star, the largest newspaper in Western Canada. She was talking to her, when her coffee friend showed up and slid out a chair next to her.

"...okay, you'll call me back, then. Fifteen minutes. I'm counting on you."

"What was that all about?" the woman asked.

"Probably another false news report," Patricia said. "Someone reported one of our ships was dropping depth charges. We don't use those anymore. We use missiles and underwater robots now."

"Oh," the woman slid her coffee to the center of the small table and leaned in toward Patricia, "sometimes there's a kernel of truth in the biggest of lies. Just because they are not dropping depth charges doesn't mean they aren't chasing a submarine."

Patricia sipped her coffee and smiled. She didn't even know the name of the woman, but it seemed like they were old friends. She couldn't remember seeing her until a few weeks ago and she seemed to be in the coffee shop every time Patricia was. "You must live around here," Patricia said.

"Why do you say that?"

"I don't know." Patricia shrugged. "I come here a lot and you're here about the same times I am."

"I work around the corner; one of the attorneys who charge their clients too much and brags about it."

"Which one?" Patricia asked.

"You wouldn't know him," the woman said, getting up. "I need to be going." She needed a moment to think.

"Wait," Patricia said. "We've been sharing coffee breaks for weeks and I don't know your name."

"Nancy Downing," the woman said. "I work at Kenmore and Davis." It was a lie, she hoped Patricia wouldn't bother to check out. She picked up her coffee and remained standing.

"I'm sorry, Nancy," Patricia said. "I'm a reporter. I'm just naturally inquisitive. I didn't mean to pry."

Nancy smiled. "I guess I can spare a few more minutes. What's the latest in fake news?"

Patricia laughed. It was a joke she used to explain all the rumors going around. Some of them were outright outlandish. "Some kind of new sub detecting technology deployed off our coast," Patricia said. "We supposedly have found a Chinese sub trying to penetrate our boundary. If it's true, it won't last long against our defenses. That might have spawned the story about the depth charges."

"Interesting," Nancy said. "What makes you think it isn't true?"

"The reporter said we were dropping depth charges. Acoustic listening devices on the sea floor are public information. Anyone can find it."

"You seem to have a pretty good grasp on this stuff," Nancy said.

"My fiancé is a Navy SEAL, or I should say a former SEAL. He knows all about this stuff," she bragged.

Nancy tightened her lips to keep from smiling. "Assuming the submarine really did make it inside our territorial waters, what technology should the reporter have said was being used against it?"

"Underwater drones. They're the latest thing. They can be deployed like a torpedo, swim around until they find an enemy submarine and boom. All gone."

"Sounds effective," Nancy said. "Now I really do have to go. My boss will kill me." She got up and hurried out.

North Star Industries

Jack Forester had been with North Star from the beginning. At fifty, he was older than many of the production crew and had been around long enough to know when things weren't moving as smoothly as he was being told. He was a family man with three children, two in high school and the youngest, a surprise only in the third grade. He was a proud parent and proud American. He took the war personally.

He listened to the excuses from his crew for not making the goal they had set two days ago and was disappointed. He was in danger of not having the second Paradox X completed by the time David and Scott returned. They were expected back later that evening.

"I don't want to hear any more excuses," Jack finally said. "You have the tools, you have the brainpower, you don't seem to have the will."

"We're tired," one of his crew said.

"All right," Jack said. "Get this bird finished by five this evening and I'll see if I can get you all the weekend off."

That seemed to have the desired effect, Jack thought, watching his crew get back to work. *I hope I can deliver.*

Chapter 23

Cheyenne Mountain Complex

A cheer went up in the room when three underwater drones honed in on the submarine, ignoring the defensive measures the commander of the submarine had deployed. The explosion left no doubt to the destiny of the submarine and its crew. The submarine broke completely in half and looked like a bomb had gone off in its hold. The cheering stopped when those in the room saw President Tindall was hanging his head.

"What's the matter, Mr. President?" General Mellon asked.

"There are others out there. We don't know how many got through or where they are."

"I can tell you Los Angeles is safe. With Paradox X fifteen miles up nothing within five-hundred miles of her will get past," Mellon said in a reassuring tone.

Tindall shook his head. "We know each submarine carries at least twelve missiles. Say there are another ten out there. That's a hundred-twenty missiles. One Paradox X platform doesn't sound like much against those odds. What can we do? We have to think they will deploy everything they have the first chance they get. Tell me I'm wrong."

"We have every aircraft available flying nonstop along the coast looking for any submarines that may be out there." Cramer joined the conversation.

"It's not a matter of resources," Tindall said. "It's a matter of technology. Isn't there any way we can get more of those acoustical sensors in the water?"

Mellon shook his head. "We didn't even know this one would work. We've dumped all of our Big Computing power into the Paradox X program. It was a tough choice. We bet on stopping the missiles over stopping the submarines. We had to make a choice."

Tindall massaged his forehead with his right hand, slowly shaking his head back and forth.

"Are you all right, Mr. President?" Mellon asked.

Tindall let out a long sigh. "No, I'm not all right, General. Our Nation is about to be destroyed and we don't have any way of stopping it."

Portland, Oregon

The tiny drone raced across the sky dodging the taller buildings and following the pre-programmed flightpath until it ran headlong into a badminton net staked in the backyard of one of the multimillion dollar homes in the West Hills of the city.

The ingenious plan had first been proposed by a member of the PRC Embassy in San Francisco and approved by Xi Wuhan himself. The West Hills mansion was purchased by a local business man using money funneled from Beijing through a Cayman Island bank. Robert Wang used the secluded property for every kind of activity from lucrative import deals with China to human trafficking. The spy game was new to him, but it had proved more profitable than his import business now that the embargo set by President Tindall was in effect.

China had anticipated their embassies would be closed, the diplomats would be deported, and another source of information gathering would need to take over. Now that system was in full swing.

The drones were modified, off the shelf toys equipped with state-of-the-art lithium-ion batteries, giving them up to an hour of flight without recharging. Wang was proud that he had modified the *pigeons,* as he called them, himself. The guidance system triangulated from the many cell towers in the city allowing pinpoint accuracy. Wang had often mused that his *pigeon* would make a perfect terror weapon if equipped with a tiny explosive instead of the high-energy battery, but for now the delivery of messages was the primary goal. A single one of his *pigeon* drones could carry the information of the entire Portland City Library, if necessary.

He smiled as he watched the drone crash into the netting and break apart, just as it was designed to do. He picked up the pieces and placed them in a container and took them inside where he retrieved the tiny chip, reassembled the drone and sent it on its way again.

PRC Embassy, San Francisco, California

Three FBI agents seated in the communications room of the Chinese Embassy waited as the message from Robert Wang appeared on the screen. The closing of the Embassy had gone unreported on the news and the evacuation delayed until an FBI surveillance team was in place. When it did happen, a FBI SWAT team stormed the facility, deploying skilled Special Forces from the sky and the ground without warning, in the middle of the afternoon. Their objective was to take over the embassy before all the equipment and documents were destroyed. This had been accomplished with inside help from Sue Ling, a Chinese National from Taiwan, who had been in the Embassy at the prescribed time. Sue Ling had been on the FBI payroll for over a year. She would help secure the facility.

Portland, Oregon

From the embassy in San Francisco, the information was traced back to the West Hills address in Portland and a team from the Portland FBI field office converged on the property by helicopter and three ground vehicles. Robert Wang was taken into custody. Moments later Marie Porter, the woman who Patricia knew as Nancy, was in handcuffs.

Patricia Westland watched as the breaking news came into the studio. When the friend from the coffee house was identified, her stomach lurched. "Oh, my God!" She shouted, catching the attention of several in the room.

"What's the matter?" Jim Doyle, her boss's boss asked.

Patricia went pale. She didn't know whether to respond or try to hide the truth, but it wasn't something that she could keep quiet about. At any minute she could be fingered as a spy. She had provided information to Marie Porter, although the woman had identified herself under another name.

Patricia looked at Doyle, her hand over her mouth as if to keep the words she was about to say from coming out. "I know that woman. Well, I don't know her as Marie Porter. She told me her name was Nancy Downing."

"Go on," Doyle encouraged. "You know her, so what?"

"I might have given her some information," Patricia said.

Jim furrowed his brow and narrowed his eyes. "What kind of information?"

"It was innocent. I didn't know she was a spy. We were having coffee."

"What kind of information?"

Patricia removed a napkin from a holder on a nearby counter near the coffee dispenser and dabbed the tears from her eyes. "We talked about submarine detecting equipment."

"How do you know anything about submarines?" Doyle was shaking his head, wondering how he was going to deal with one of his reporters making the headlines.

"I picked it up from a report from a British source," Patricia said. "I was joking that I thought it might be fake news."

"You need to report it to the FBI," Jim said. "Give me your phone."

She reluctantly handed it to him. "What are you doing?"

He dialed the local FBI office. "This is the agent who has been asking about you." He handed the phone back to her. "Talk to him. You have to get ahead of this."

"And if I don't?" Patricia felt betrayed. She eyed her boss who was standing behind Doyle. She was shaking her head. Her own boss wasn't standing up for her.

"If you can't get a handle on this, you're fired," Doyle said.

She could see he was serious. She slowly raised the phone to her ear.

"Agent Gordon," a voice answered.

North Star Industries

Scott Tanner arrived back at his office and checked in with Jack Forester, the Assembly supervisor. It was three in the afternoon. He had left California three hours earlier. David had rented a small plane and left the Orange County Airport for Oakland. The last thing he had said was, "hold down the fort, I'll be back tomorrow."

Scott hated that David had decided to take a detour in the middle of their push to get the Paradox X in production, but the launch of the platform from Santa Catalina Island had gone without a hitch and David's team had assured him they had everything under control. David deserved a visit to his friend since she was only a few hours away by airplane.

Scott reflected on the short conversation. David had obviously set him up. Charlene and Gil both had argued David's point. The truth was, Scott could not come up with an argument of how it would be detrimental to the program if David went missing for a day, so he ignored his gut, and agreed. Now, he was back at North Star and David was with Fay in San Francisco. If there were any technical glitches with production, he would have to handle them.

Scott's secretary interrupted his thoughts. "General Mellon is on the line and he says it's urgent."

"Thanks," Scott said. He picked up the phone. "General Mellon, Tanner here, what can I do for you?"

"I just left the President," Mellon said. "Have you heard about the submarine we intercepted off the Washington Coast?"

"No," Scott said, "I just got back."

"We have reason to believe a number of China's subs have slipped through our defenses and are off the West Coast. We intercepted one off Washington using the ULF technology David Stafford suggested, but that's the only sensor of that type in place and we haven't got the means to detect any along the rest of the coast. Frankly we dumped all our marbles into Paradox X. We moved all our Big Computer technology your way at the expense of the offshore submarine detecting ULF microphones. Now that we know the listening device works, I hope that wasn't a mistake."

"Where are you going with this, General?" Scott asked.

"We need another bird in the air right away. We believe an attack is imminent, we only have one Paradox X platform in place and that isn't enough."

Mellon sounded desperate, but Scott didn't have the answer he wanted. "I just talked with Assembly and we're not due to have another platform completed until next week," Scott said.

"We need another platform up today. Scott, you have to do something, anything. The Country is in real trouble."

Scott was quiet as he thought about a response he knew the general wouldn't like. "General, I'll do everything I can to get the next platform in the air, but today is out of the question. Diagnostics take the better part of two days."

"You mean you have a bird ready, but it hasn't been inspected?" Mellon asked.

"One is due to be finished late today. I just got back, so I can't tell you if it's on schedule or not."

"Scott, consider this as coming straight from President Tindall himself. Forget the diagnostics. Get that bird up today.

Launch it from the grounds at North Star if you have to, but get it up. Call me back when you have a time."

"I'll do my best," Scott said.

"Goddamn it, son," General Mellon said. "Every Chinese sub off our coast carries at least a dozen mid-range nuclear missiles. The one we blew up off the coast of Seattle was close enough to hit targets on the Eastern Seaboard. Do you understand what I'm saying? Every major city in the country is at risk of being destroyed and we haven't got a way to stop it."

"I understand, General. I'll call you back." Scott hung up and ran out the door. "I'm headed to the Assembly Building," Scott yelled as he ran past his secretary. He ran down the path passing several soldiers who were caught by surprise. By the time he reached the Assembly Building, the guard at the door had been notified and stopped him. Scott flashed his credentials and was allowed to pass. As soon as he was in the building he called Jack Forester on the inside line and had him meet him at the entrance to the cleanroom.

"What's up, Scott?" Jack asked. "You look out of breath."

Scott smiled. "I guess civilian life is catching up with me."

"What can I do for you?" Jack asked.

"We need to launch a bird today," Scott said.

"We've got one nearly ready, but we haven't run it through diagnostics."

"You know the one we sent up in California went off without a hitch," Scott said. "Your people are doing a first class job, and you can tell them that. This one is going up without testing, so it better be good."

"I know it's important," Jack said. "We were a little behind schedule this morning and I told my crew they could have the weekend off, if they caught back up and had the bird finished by shift end today."

"You told them what?"

"I needed to get them motivated. If you say it isn't possible, then I understand, but these people have made a big sacrifice agreeing to be sequestered here. They were told it would be until the first two Paradox platforms were finished. This is number two. They all know that, and I said you would be keeping your promise."

Scott thought about what Mellon had said. If they didn't get this one finished and launched, it would not matter. If there were submarines off the coast ready to attack, none of them would survive to see their families again. "Okay," Scott said. "If I get Gil and Charlene on the line to do a spot inspection, how long before we can get it ready to launch?"

"Honestly, my people know what they are doing. Gil and Charlene will only be a distraction."

"Okay, without testing. For all our sakes, we need to trust your people take their jobs seriously." Scott hoped he wasn't making the biggest mistake in his life.

"I know my people. They are dedicated. We are just wrapping up things now. Give me an hour and I'll have it on the shipping dock."

"No, take it to the hill outside the Executive Building."
"Pardon?"
"We're going to launch it from here."
"Does Engineering know about this?" Jack asked.
"You're the first to know. Now get it ready. We need to get it up before nightfall."
"And my people can take the weekend off?"
"They can watch the launch if they want, but yes. They will be free to take the weekend off."

*****

Oakland, California

David Stafford landed the Twin Apache he had rented at the John Wayne Airport in Southern California three hours earlier. Throughout much of the flight he had mused about the how surprised Fay would be when she arrived home and he was sitting on her deck.

"Friday afternoon traffic is crazy," the taxi driver said to David. "I will have you there in less than an hour."

David checked his cell phone for the time. It was a few minutes after four. "That will be great," he said. "Can we make a short stop at a market, maybe when we get out of the worst of it?"

"I know of a place where you can buy anything. You got a girl and want to party, I can get you anything, you know what I mean?"

"Just a market will do. I need a bottle of wine and some flowers."

"Okay. You didn't look like the wild type," the driver said, glancing back at him and smiling. "If she doesn't work out, call me. I'll find you some fun." He winked at David.

"I'll be fine. Just get me there before five."

Two-hundred miles west of San Francisco

"Silence is the most difficult part of warfare," Commander Qingdao said in a low voice to Communist Party Associate Lin. "Some think of war as being all guns and bombs, but silence is also an important aspect."

"But you don't even know the rest of your command is in place. Are you going to contact them before the attack?"

"At the last moment. We will wait until most of the cities are asleep. It will have the greatest psychological impact if the citizens are shaken from their slumber." He was standing before a video monitor with an outline of the United States. Thirty-six cities were represented by pulsing pinpoints of light. "These are the targets," Qingdao said. "Each will have two missiles strike from two different directions."

Hauxin Lin studied the map. "Ah, this is Washington DC," he said putting his fat finger on the screen. "I think you should use four missiles, just for effect."

"It is a ghost town," the commander said. "Our intelligence found out the President and all of his Cabinet, as well as Congress evacuated the city a week ago."

"Then what is the point. We kill a town occupied by lawyers and bureaucrats. No one will miss them. The American people will think we have done them a favor."

Qingdao smiled. He despised the overweight bureaucrat, but he had made a good joke. "The Americans might well think the same thing if they had the upper hand and were targeting Beijing."

"You are certain they have no defense?" The man asked, removing his finger from Washington DC and placing it on New York City. He then touched Boston and Philadelphia.

"We have taken out all of their satellites. They have responded by putting communication platforms fifteen miles up. They call them HAP, high altitude platforms. Our intelligence tells us they are only communication and surveillance platforms, but they are working on a new defense system they call Paradox X. That is why we must act tonight. They falsely believe we have no means of hitting their targets, but our celestial navigation system, while not being as accurate as GPS can hit major targets. We don't have to have pinpoint accuracy when we target a major city. The people will panic and destroy themselves if a nuclear bomb even comes close. I almost feel sorry for the politicians hiding beneath the mountain in Colorado. They will survive the attack only to be slaughtered when their people find out about their cowardice. But that is good. They will still be alive to sign the surrender to our Government. The world order will be uniquely different tomorrow morning."

A broad grin covered Hauxin Lin's face. "The cook said he is baking pastries for the celebration once this is over," Lin said. "I think I should go and test them."

"You may want to catch some sleep. I will need to have your code to launch the missiles."

The pudgy man subconsciously wrapped his fingers around the plastic card hanging around his neck. It had several columns of numbers printed on it. Only he knew which column would complete the launch code for the nuclear warheads. It made him feel powerful. Without him, there would be no attack. It was also his assurance that he would make it through the voyage alive. "Don't worry about me, Commander. I know you won't start without me."

Chapter 24

Oakland, California

David checked his cell phone. It was 8:57 p.m. and Fay had not arrived at her apartment. *Maybe I should call her*, he thought. The truth was he had fallen asleep on the balcony while waiting and nearly panicked when he heard a car door shut. He heard footsteps on the stairs and abruptly stood, nearly stumbling reaching for the flowers. It was still daylight, but the sun was low in the sky and long shadows covered the apartment.

Fay shook her head and grinned. "David, what on earth are you doing here?"

He opened his arms and they embraced. "I couldn't live another moment without you. I thought I'd surprise you and take you to dinner, but it looks like you might have already eaten." He handed her the flowers. "I'm afraid they have gone a bit too long without water. They badly need a drink, as do I."

Fay took the flowers and kissed him on the cheek. "I did have dinner, but if that bottle of Champagne is for us, then I'd better put it on ice."

She opened the door and they entered her apartment.

"It looks different," David said.

Fay went in the kitchen and ran some ice from the dispenser into a container and placed the bottle in it. "What's the occasion?"

"Does there have to be an occasion for me to see my significant other?"

Fay shrugged. "It's just you were so tied up the last time we spoke. I didn't expect to see you for at least two more weeks."

"We were doing some work down in L A and I was so close, I didn't want to pass up the opportunity. I could have gone the other direction and checked out my company in San Diego."

She smiled. "Come here, handsome. I missed you."

They hugged again and this time David kissed her long and passionately.

"I swear," Fay said, leaning back to catch her breath. "You really did miss me. I was beginning to wonder if I'd ever see you again."

"In case you hadn't heard, I'm fighting it on the home front. I went AWOL just to see you."

"Then let's celebrate," Fay said. "We have exactly seventeen minutes until all the lights go out."

David looked around. "You don't have blackout curtains."

"An unnecessary expense," Fay said. "I've adjusted my routine to fit the demands of our Government. I go to bed earlier. Daylight arrives at just before six in the morning. I get up and it's been working just fine."

"I hope you like warm Champagne," David said. "You don't happen to have some food around. I missed dinner."

"That's what you get for not calling. I would have told you where I was and we could have eaten together." She pulled a box of crackers from the cupboard and handed them to him with a jar of peanut butter. "I was going to go shopping in the morning. I hope you don't have a peanut allergy."

"It'll do. Since I've been at North Star I've been eating in the cafeteria. Great food. I don't have a thing in my cupboard."

David spread some peanut butter on a cracker and offered it to her.

"No thanks." She tested the Champagne. "This is still too warm." She took a bottle of Riesling from the refrigerator. "It's a Napa Valley vineyard. Not Dom Perignon, but it's pretty good."

"I hear Riesling goes perfect with peanut butter and crackers," David said.

The night was warm and they took the bottle out on the balcony. One by one they watched the lights go out over the city. It was as if a black cloth had fallen over the city. Just as gradually the stars began to appear.

"You know," Fay said, looking up at the night sky, "until the war, I never saw the stars over the city. Aren't they magnificent?"

David wrapped an arm around her, his wine glass in his other hand. "I guess there is a good side to everything. You get to see the night sky and get a full eight hours sleep."

"What do you get out of it?" Fay asked, still looking up.

"One of my inventions is up there somewhere," he said.

"Let's go inside," Fay said, "in ten minutes we won't be able to see enough to find the bedroom." She looked at David's overnight bag. "You sure travel light,"

"I packed for one day. This is day two, but I have my toothbrush and an extra pair of sox, what else do I need?"

"Clothes are so overrated," Fay said, removing her blouse.

Two hours earlier, North Star Industries

A cheer went up as two dozen North Star employees watched the balloon rise from the knoll outside the Executive Building.

"That's it," Jack Forester said to one of his supervisors. "Your people did a good job. Make sure they are back here Monday morning. We have another dozen to assemble next week."

"I don't think that will be a problem," his supervisor said.

"Mr. Tanner, I'm going now. There's nothing more I or my crew can do."

Scott was still watching the silver object drift up. It was nearly out of sight. He turned to Forester. "It's okay, Jack, go home and give your wife and kids a hug."

"What about you? You have a weekend lined up?"

"Maybe," Scott said. "I wanted to wait to see if we actually pulled this thing off. I have a very pretty lady I'm thinking of calling."

"You better call her," Gil said. "I overheard the Assembly crew is getting the weekend off, what about us?"

"Go ahead," Scott said. "I need to make a few calls and I'm going AWOL with everybody else."

Gil laughed. "I'll see you on Monday, then."

Scott watched as the North Star employees drifted off. All that was left were a dozen soldiers standing near a Humvee. He walked back to his office and picked up the phone.

"It's in the air, General," he said to General Mellon. "It will take another two hours to be fully functional."

"I'll tell the President. Scott, tell your team the Country is grateful for their effort."

"I would, but they all went home for the weekend."

"What the hell, man, we're in the middle of a war."

"I seem to recall a certain General telling the North Star employees they would only be sequestered until the first two birds are launched. They all watched the second one hit the sky."

"Jesus Christ, you put me in a bind. I'm supposed to tell the President we sent the people home before we even got into production."

"With all due respect, sir, you made the agreement. I didn't."

"You knew it was just to appease the dissenters. We need them back on site now!"

"Sorry, sir. It's too late. There is nothing more we can do to prevent an attack. They should be home with their families. With all due respect, sir, I think this would be a good time for all of you huddled inside Cheyenne Mountain to do the same."

Mellon was quiet. Scott knew anyone with the command of Mellon wasn't used to being spoken to so bluntly. It was one time he was thankful he wasn't still in uniform.

"Scott," Mellon, finally spoke, "if you have someone you need to be with, I understand."

Scott disconnected and called Patricia.

Patricia took a sip of water from a bottle given to her by Agent Gordon. She looked down at her phone vibrating across the conference room table. "Can I answer this?" she asked reaching for it.

"Go ahead," Agent Gordon said. "I want to know who it is."

"It's Scott," Patricia said, answering it. "Scott, I can't talk right now, I'm at FBI headquarters and they are interrogating me."

"What?"

Patricia looked at Gordon, who was giving her a disgusted look and shaking his head. "You know that woman spy they busted?" Patricia asked.

"What spy? Listen. I know the last time we spoke I cut you off short. I'm sorry but I want to make it up to you. I have the weekend off if you want to get together."

Patricia looked at Gordon. "Am I under arrest?"

"No."

"They said I wasn't under arrest, so, can you make it into town?"

"I thought we could go to my place."

Patricia looked at Gordon again, this time putting her hand over the phone. "Are we done? Can I go?"

"Give me the phone," Gordon said reaching out his hand.

Patricia handed it to him, eying him curiously.

"Scott, this is Special Agent Gordon. In case you haven't kept up with the news, your girl is in trouble. She got tangled up with a spy. If I didn't have such a full plate, I'd keep her here over the weekend, but it's a madhouse around here. If I let you have her for the weekend, can you promise to have her back on Monday?"

"Uh, yeah," Scott replied. "It sounds like a lot more is happening than I'm aware of."

"She can fill you in. How long before you can pick her up?"

It took Scott thirty minutes to make it from Hillsboro to the Portland Airport by company helicopter. He arrived at 8:03 Pacific Daylight Time.

"I hope you don't mind the helicopter," Scott said. "I only have the weekend and I want to make the most of it."

"But I need to get my things," Patricia protested.

"We can pick up what you need at the Coast. I want to get there before dark."

"No!" Patricia said. "If I'm going to your place, I want to go by my place and pick up some of my things."

"Patricia," Scott said, looking into her eyes. "It's important we go now. You'll have to trust me on this."

She looked at him incredulously. "Okay. I can see you're serious. What are you not telling me?"

The helicopter landed on the wet packed sand left by the low tide. They held hands and watched it lift off.

"He'll return Monday morning," Scott said, "so enjoy your freedom while you can."

"I remember the last time we spent the night here," Patricia said. "I hope this night turns out better."

Scott squeezed her hand looking down at her and smiling. "As I recall, the night turned out just fine. It was the next morning that was all screwed up."

"Yeah, I guess it was the next morning. Have you been back since?"

"First time," Scott said, looking up the path to the house.

"It's a good thing I cleaned out the fridge and took out the garbage before I left," Patricia said.

"Thanks for that. You must have suspected I'd be gone for awhile."

"It's a girl thing. Fish doesn't keep very well."

"The house is still here, and if I recall correctly, there is a bottle of Merlot in the wine rack that is begging to be opened."

They settled on the deck watching the sun filter through fluffy clouds casting a pink glow over the water.

"This place is heaven," Patricia said. "Why don't we ditch the authorities and spend the rest of our lives right here."

"I need to talk to you about that," Scott said.

Pacific Ocean, two hundred miles west of San Francisco

Commander Qingdao looked down on the sleeping Hauxin Lin. The fat man was snoring loudly, snorting like a pig taking a nap after a big meal. If he could, he would rip the code from around the man's neck and launche the missiles himself, but protocol called for the commanding officer to have only a part of the code, and the politician to have the other. Neither knew what the other person's code was. If a code was entered incorrectly the missile could not be armed. Each card contained nine columns of figures mixed with numbers. Only the person carrying the card knew which column was the correct one. It was meant to prevent the very act the commander was contemplating. But, alas, he needed the fat bastard, and the fat bastard needed him. If they screwed up, they would both be convicted of treason.

"Wake up, Hauxin Lin. Your Country needs you." Commander Qingdao shook the man until he stirred back to reality.

"You know, I was dreaming about a beautiful woman," Lin said, struggling to sit up and put his feet on the deck. "She had big brown eyes and hair as black as a raven's back."

"Enough with your stories. We have exactly four minutes to prepare the missiles for launch."

"Have you checked the position of the others?" Lin inquired, referring to the rest of the submarine fleet.

"That is the next step. Come on, put on your shoes."

In the control room, Commander Qingdao paired his part of the arming code with Lin's by entering the characters from his card. Once the missiles were ready for launch, he went to the safe and pulled out an envelope. It was only then that he knew his targets. He then used his ultra-low frequency hydrophone to contact the other submarines in his fleet. His first attempt was to the submarine off the Seattle Coast. When there was no response, he looked at Lin.

"What is it, Commander?" Lin asked.

"He does not respond."

"What does that mean?"

"It means we are twelve missiles short of completing our mission."

"What cities will be spared?"

"I do not know. Every submarine has sealed orders in the safe. Only the Captain knows what his targets are."

"You must make the calls to the others," Lin encouraged.

Commander Qingdao contacted the submarine off the Oregon coast. The response was an affirmation, "ready to launch."

The message was the same for the submarines off the coast of Los Angeles and San Diego. "We have four of our five boats," Commander Qingdao said. "We can still destroy many of the major industrial cities of the US."

He sent out one final message. "Mark time, countdown one minute to launch. Mark." He pressed the digital timer and electronic numbers started scrolling past on a large digital clock in the control room. "At zero, launch tubes one through twelve without further orders."

The crew knew what the clock meant. They had held their collective breath in anticipation for the past thirty minutes as the submarine rose to missile launch depth.

Chapter 25

Oakland, California

The sky lit up like a bolt of lightning had struck. It was so bright it lit up the bedroom where David and Fay had just finished making love and startled them from a lovers embrace.

"What the hell was that?" David asked.

"Maybe a transformer blew," Fay said.

David got up and pulled on his pants. He made his way to the glass door and out to the balcony. Another blinding flash and Fay was beside him, her naked body trembling. She grabbed his hand and held on tight.

"What do you think is happening?" Fay asked.

David didn't answer. His mind was racing. If nuclear bombs had gone off it would be seconds before they would be vaporized. There was absolutely nothing he could do about it.

"We're under attack," he said.

"What should we do?"

"There isn't anything we can do," David said. "We didn't get our defense system in place soon enough." He stared out the window wondering if this was the last view he would ever see. Far in the distance another flash of lightning. He braced himself, but the nuclear wind never arrived. "We may have escaped the holocaust," he finally said, pulling Fay closer to him.

"David, you're scaring me. What is happening?"

"The reason I was in California was to launch the first operational prototype of Paradox X, a missile defense system my team at North Star put together. We were hoping China wouldn't attack so quickly. Their submarines must have breached our underwater detection systems. I have no doubt we are being attacked."

Fay was astounded. "Your Paradox X is stopping it, right?"

"We put our only system in place off the coast of Los Angeles. It has an effective range of five hundred miles, but that's only two hundred fifty miles from its center. The fact it's working up this far is a miracle. We're a good fifty miles past its design range."

Another flash, this one even farther from them. By now lights were coming on around the city. "Turn on the TV," David said, flipping the light switch.

"Are you sure?"

"They know where we are." David said. "Let's see if anyone knows what's going on."

The news broadcaster was clearly shaken by the events that were taking place outside. She was a young woman who looked like she must have been the only newscaster in the building at the time of the first explosion. This could be her fifteen minutes of fame. She looked terrified.

"…we have received hundreds of calls over the past few minutes and we don't know for certain what the flashes of lights are in the sky. Some have speculated it is a meteor shower. Others say we are under attack. I'm not sure what to believe. If anyone out there knows what is happening, call the number at the bottom of the screen. Please, this is serious. Only those who are knowledgeable should call. We don't want the line tied up…"

"Are you going to call," Fay asked.

"It's better they don't know the truth," David said. "Some of those missiles are headed inland. Chicago, New York, Washington DC. Paradox X doesn't have the power to stop all of them."

*****

Waldport, Oregon

"I need something stronger than this," Scott said, setting the bottle of Merlot aside without opening it. "You want a Scotch on the rocks?"

"I'm fine with the wine," Patricia said.

Scott opened the bottle and poured a glass for her.

Scott was filling a short glass with ice, when the sky over the ocean lit up in a flash so bright he nearly dropped the glass.

Patricia ran to the glass doors that looked out over the ocean. In a few seconds, no longer than the time it took to reach the deck, everything had gone dark again. Then like a clap of thunder they were both shaken and nearly knocked off their feet.

Before he could respond, another flash of light over the ocean caused them to shield their eyes.

"What is it?" Patricia asked.

"Paradox X," Scott said, pulling her close to him. He didn't know if the system would be 100% successful but from what he could see it was working as advertised. "I'm worried about David. He took a side trip to San Francisco to visit Fay. We haven't deployed a system in that area."

Suddenly a flash of light directly overhead, high in the sky caused them to duck for cover. Several seconds later a sonic boom shook the house. From their vantage point they could see a ball of fire cutting an erratic path through the sky. Patricia held on to him tightly.

"That must have been a long range missile," Scott said. "It was pretty high."

A loud thumping noise caused them to turn as several Coast Guard helicopters raced out to sea. Seconds later a low flying turbine powered aircraft seemed to skim the water as it headed west, its wing lights twinkling in the night. "There must be a sub out there," Scott said, stating the obvious.

Whatever they were after, it was too far out and too dark for them to follow. The helicopters and plane soon disappeared over the horizon. It was quiet for a few minutes.

"I'm going to call David," Scott said, going inside to get his cell phone. He quick dialed the number and walked outside again. The irritating computer generated voice on the phone informed him that all circuits were busy and he should try again later. "The lines are jammed," he said.

"I need to call Dad and see if he and Billy are okay," Patricia said.

She got the same message. "They'll be okay," Scott assured her. "He lives in the mountains. They will target the big cities."

"Billy's in Portland," she said. "You knew this would happen and you got me out and left my brother!"

Scott grabbed her arms and held her. "I thought something might happen, but had no idea. How do you know he didn't go home for the weekend?"

Patricia took a deep breath to calm herself. "I'm okay. You can let go of me."

Scott pulled her to him and hugged her. "I'm sorry. So much has been going on. We're just going to have to wait this out."

"I should be back at the station. This is big news."

"You're in my custody until Monday. You are staying right here."

Pacific Ocean, two hundred miles west of Los Angeles

The papers had reported thirty-two Coast Guard vessels patrolled the coastline of California along with hundreds of aircraft.

When missiles started breaking the water, Captain Roberto Garcia, piloting the Cutter 798, was nearly on top of it and directed an anti-submarine aircraft to the exact coordinates. Within minutes three aircraft appeared and fired missiles causing the midnight-black water to erupt in a geyser that nearly capsized the cutter nearly a mile away.

Garcia directed his helmsman to steer a course for the area where the explosion had occurred to search for survivors. The size of the explosion made the likelihood of finding anybody alive unlikely, but he needed to confirm the kill and finish the job with torpedoes if necessary.

Three hundred miles north, Commander Hai Qingdao having launched his supply of ballistic missiles, gave the order to dive, and set a course due west of his position off the coast of San Francisco. "We have escaped the worst of it for now," he said to Hauxin Lin.

Cheyenne Mountain, Colorado

President Tindall watched several monitors showing activity off the West Coast.

"We have another submarine kill off Los Angeles," his National Security Advisor said.

"Any word of how many more there are?" Tindall asked.

"No way of knowing, sir," Biggs said. "For what it's worth, Paradox X is working. We have more than two dozen missiles intercepted so far."

"General Cramer!" Tindall called over the din in the room.

Cramer turned toward the President. "Yes, sir."

"Have any missiles made it inland?"

"We have no reports of any making it more than a few hundred miles inland. I just picked up a report of debris falling along the Oregon-Idaho border. Apparently a missile casing fell on a house in Boise and killed two of the occupants."

"Keep me informed," Tindall said. "How much time do the people in Washington DC have if we can't stop them?"

"An hour at most, sir. About the same for anywhere on the East Coast."

"If one gets through, I want to know where it will hit and when. The least we can do is let the people know they are about to be hit."

"Will do, Mr. President."

"Sir," Admiral Nendel said.

Tindall was watching a monitor showing missiles streaming from a submarine. "Where the hell is that?" he asked. "If we have pictures of it why isn't it at the bottom of the ocean by now?"

"That's cell phone video off San Francisco. It was taken by a Japanese super tanker that just happened to be in the area. The Coast Guard has dispatched aircraft to the site, but the sub had already struck and disappeared by the time we got there."

"You mean this is old data?" Tindall was about to explode.

"Ten minutes ago," Nendel said. "Sir, I wanted to bring your attention to an event that is unfolding off the southern coast of California. One of our subs has encountered a Chinese submarine heading out to sea. We believe it already fired its payload. Our sub is tracking the *Jin* class sub and is requesting permission to engage."

"What the hell, Richard. We're in a war. He doesn't need permission."

"The submarine doesn't appear to be a threat anymore," Nendel said. "The Captain seemed uncertain of the protocol for a situation like that."

"Jesus Christ, where has that man been," Tindall was irate.

"It's the Roosevelt, sir."

Tindall didn't breath for a full minute. "You're sure?"

"The fleet Commander told him to engage," Nendel said, "but his hesitation may have cost him."

Tindall's youngest son was a lieutenant commander on the *Roosevelt* a *Sea Wolf* class nuclear sub which was part of the Pacific Fleet.

Tindall pursed his lips. "How bad is it?"

"We have a report of an explosion. Communication is down at the moment. We have ships in the area trying to verify."

"Keep me informed," Tindall said.

"Of course, sir. I thought you would want to know."

"Thanks, Richard." Tindall turned to Cramer again. "Do we have any news from the East Coast?"

"Sir, all the communications are jammed, even the military system. We don't know if it's because of system overload or intentional."

Oakland, California

It had been five minutes since the last flash of light in the sky. It seemed that the city had woken up and every house was lit up.

"It's over," Fay said.

"Maybe," David said.

"You think there's more?"

"Paradox gets its energy from solar cells," he said. "It's running on battery power. I doubt it would be effective if there is another attack before the batteries have a chance to recharge."

"But there won't be another attack," Fay said.

"I don't know. I doubt they would make the same mistake Japan made." He took her in his arms. "We've done everything we can. Nothing to do but wait." His phone buzzed and he answered.

"Scott, is everything okay where you are?"

"I was going to ask you the same thing. From what I can tell, Paradox did what it was supposed to do."

"We had some fireworks down here," David said, "but the system we put in place over Los Angeles seemed to cover us up here. You sound good. Everything all right in Portland?"

"I'm not in Portland. Patricia and I took the weekend off and are at my place."

"You took a vacation and all hell broke out. Are you sure everything is okay up there?"

"We got the second bird up about five last night."

"How did you manage that? It wasn't due for another week."

"We skipped the diagnostics."

"Damn, Scott, that was risky."

"It wasn't my call. Mellon seemed to know something was in the works and demanded we put it up the second it was assembled. Your team did a great job. It seemed to function perfectly, if the lightning strikes in the sky are any indication."

"Fay and I were just talking about that. If there is a subsequent attack, Paradox will be ineffective."

Scott was silent as he thought about it. Of course there would be a second attack. China wouldn't make the same mistake Japan made.

"You think China knows?" Scott asked.

"I hope not." David was thinking. "I'm not sure Nendel or Cramer know it. They may be relying on Paradox to do something it's not capable of doing."

"You want me to break the news or do you want me to be the messenger who gets killed?"

"You're the President of North Star. That's why they pay you the big bucks."

"Sometimes your humor escapes me," Scott quipped. "Keep your head down, I'll see if I can reach Nendel."

Scott tried for an hour to reach Nendel, but the circuits were busy. The sun came over the hills to the east of his house before he was finally connected on Nendel's private number.

"Scott, what a relief to hear from you," Nendel said. "That second bird you got up kept the Northwest clear of any hits."

"How about the rest of the country?" Scott asked.

"Not a single hit. We dodged a bullet. I hope we can do it again."

"That's why I'm calling," Scott said. "If there is another attack before Paradox X recharges the batteries, it's all over."

"How long does that take?" Nendel asked.

"We're not certain, but we know it's not going to be fully charged tonight. I thought you might want to tell the President."

Nendel looked across the room and saw the President smiling. *His son must be okay*, he thought pushing himself through a room full of military. He reached the President.

"Richard. My son sunk the bastard. There's one less sub to worry about today," he said proudly.

"General Mellon and General Cramer, you're going to want to hear this."

Both men joined Nendel and the President. "We know China isn't going to let history repeat itself," Nendel said. "China is certain to have another attack planned. Any idea of when it will occur?"

"Why?" Cramer asked.

"Paradox X is solar powered. It needs time to recharge the batteries."

"Good God," Tindall said. "They could launch another attack any minute."

General Mellon looked at Nendel. "How long to recharge?"

General Mellon, Cramer, and the President were all staring at Nendel. "Too long," Nendel said. "Our model called for a lot more platforms to be in position before an attack."

Cramer looked across the room. "General Mitchel, come over here."

Mitchel joined them.

"If China launches another missile attack, Paradox X can't defend us," Cramer said gravely. "At least, if it happens before the solar batteries are recharged."

"How long is that?" Mitchel asked. He looked at the blank faces and knew the answer.

Nendel threw up his hands. "We've got every piece of hardware that will float combing the waters along the West Coast. There isn't a plane or helicopter in the Coast Guard that isn't looking for submarines right now. If they can't stop a second attack, we're screwed."

"What do we do now?" Tindall asked.

"We wait," Mellon said. "And pray, if you're so inclined."

Chapter 26

Pacific Ocean, seven hundred miles west of Los Angeles

Commander Qingdao slowed his submarine to a crawl and pinged the submarine heading in his direction. He had identified it as one of his. At this moment he would have liked to surface and exchange stories and well wishes, but the sun was high and they dared not expose their whereabouts to the aircraft circling overhead. He knew some of the aircraft were equipped with metal detecting hardware, gravimeters, and sensitive underwater radar. His mission was now to draw the sub-spotter's attention out to sea providing a diversion for the inbound submarine to slip through the defenses.

"You shouldn't be so happy," Commander Qingdao said to Lin. "We have completed the first part of our mission and now we enter the most dangerous part. We must make our position known to the enemy."

"You are not going to expose us like a sitting duck," Lin protested.

"Periscope depth," Qingdao told his XO.

Silently the submarine rose.

"Commander, we have contact, eighteen-hundred meters," the sonar man said.

"Let the race begin. All ahead full."

"Deploy countermeasures."

"Countermeasures deployed."

"Left full rudder."

The explosion off the port bow shook the submarine. Another explosion shook them again and the Commander's cup of tea shattered on the deck.

"Dive six hundred meters," Qingdao said.

Lin stared wide-eyed at the digital depth meter as the numbers rapidly blinked by. He was aware of every creak and growl the hull made as the sea threatened to crush it. Sometimes it sounded like it was alive, in pain like a woman giving birth.

"Six hundred meters," his dive officer said.

"We are safe!" Lin exclaimed. "We have escaped. Good job, Commander Qingdao."

"Quiet, you pig," Qingdao said. "Take it down to 700 meters."

The submarine continued to descend.

Hauxin Lin held his breath as the digital numbers went from green to red. He started to sweat profusely.

The submarine settled. "Steady at 700 meters."

"Have we lost him?" Qingdao asked his sonar operator.

"No contact, sir."

"Good."

"You see we sometimes have to sacrifice so that others can succeed," he said to Lin. "XO, set a course for Haiphong."

Six hundred feet above the water the Boeing P-8A Poseidon banked and made another pass over the rolling sea. There was no indication that the two torpedoes they had dropped had hit their mark. No debris field was evident. "We have to go in," the copilot said, checking the fuel gauge. They had been on the hunt for fourteen hours and their fuel was running low. "That son of a bitch got away from us. Are there any surface ships in the area?" the pilot asked.

"Negative. Most of the ships are patrolling closer to shore."

"All right, we're heading in."

*****

Cheyenne Mountain Complex

"What the hell is happening?" Tindall asked Biggs.

Biggs rushed over to the President. "Sir?"

Tindall tossed his hands in the air. "I can't stand the waiting. It's too quiet. The second attack should have come by now." His staff had told him China wouldn't make the same mistake Japan had made in attacking Pearl Harbor. A second attack was a certainty. "What are they waiting for?"

Biggs moved his glasses up and rested them on his bald head giving him the look of a four-eyed frog. "I don't know, sir." He wanted to say something, but he wasn't sure what. It was quiet and he thought that was a good thing.

"Something the matter, Mr. President?" General Cramer asked.

"We don't have any pictures. Is anything happening out there? Are we preparing a counter attack? I need to know what we are doing to protect the Country."

"We are using all our resources protecting the homeland at the moment. General Mellon has convened a meeting of the Joint Chiefs. They should have something to present to you by eighteen hundred hours."

"So for now we're just waiting. I want to launch an all-out attack against China. They need to pay for attacking us. I want a missile with Chairman Wuhan's name on it dropped down his smokestack in Beijing."

"I'll tell General Mellon," General Cramer said. He saw General Mitchel and made a bee- line for him. "Something's gotten to the President. He's ready to throw the works at China."

"It's about time," Mitchel said. "He's paying for eight years of military budget cuts."

"Don't give me that political bullshit," Cramer said. "No amount of preparation could have prevented this, let alone predicted we'd be fighting a country that ten years ago wasn't even considered a threat."

Mitchel could have argued with him. The Joint Chiefs had covered this scenario, or at least a similar one. Cramer had diverted anti-submarine funds to shore up funding for the Paradox program. It wasn't anyone's fault, but it was always a juggling act to put the resources in the right place.

"What happens if they launch another attack?" General Mitchel asked. "I've got family in St. Paul!"

"I honestly don't know," Cramer admitted. "When we had the birds in the sky we could point them anywhere on earth and know what was going on. Today we're lucky to get our commanders in on a conference call. If they let loose with another volley of missiles, it may be all over.

"You don't think Mellon will be considering surrender as an option?"

Cramer couldn't keep himself from laughing. "The President is finally ready to fight a war and you're talking about surrender."

"There are millions of lives at stake. Chin's had a shot at us. We dodged a bullet. Now, let's go to the bargaining table."

"I'm sure you have a point." Cramer checked his watch. "Meeting time. I hope Mellon doesn't invite the President."

Mitchel shook his head. "The day Tindall was sworn into office, he told me he was going to let the generals fight the wars. He was going to keep the peace."

"It almost worked," Cramer said. "Walk with me. It sounds like we are on the same page. We may be the only voice of reason in the room."

Oakland, California

The events from the night before were the only thing on the local news channels in Washington, Oregon, and California, but for the rest of the United States, it was reported as a West Coast phenomenon. Some stations in the Midwest and East didn't even cover it as an attack. China was mentioned only once on CNN in connection with the submarine that was sunk off of Washington State. Fox News reported a major lightning storm over the Pacific. Reporters embedded with the President in Cheyenne Mountain Complex were unaware there had been an attack. Whether by design or accident, the American public was mostly unaware of the attack.

"Flipping through the channels isn't going to change anything," Fay said, handing David a glass of ice tea.

"I can't believe there isn't more on what happened last night," David said, turning back to the TV.

"We know more than most," Fay said. "There isn't any way for the rest of the country to know."

"But we were under attack and it is bound to happen again. Are we going to live our lives like nothing is happening, right up to —"

"The end," Fay finished his sentence. "I, for one, am willing to do that. I'd rather not know the end is coming."

"You say that because you know," David said, taking a sip of tea. "I still have a plane at the airport. We can go there and fly someplace less populated."

"We'd just get caught in traffic," Fay said. "I'd rather take my chances here where I'm comfortable. The anticipation is killing me." She wasn't as positive as she was only moments earlier.

"That's got me puzzled," David said. "Maybe we are putting too much pressure on them."

"What do you mean?"

"There was a picture of San Francisco showing dozens of ships in the water. The skies are filled with airplanes. They must be looking for submarines."

"What if they attack by air?" Fay asked.

"We have a lot better defense against an attack from the air. No…I think they are worried more submarines are positioned off our shore and the only way to prevent an attack is to keep enough pressure on them, preventing them from rising to launch depth."

"You're no fun when you are this way," Fay said turning off the TV. "I think you're obsessing about this too much. Maybe there won't be another attack."

"Maybe," David agreed. He turned the TV back on.

"Fine," Fay said. "You sit here and obsess over something you can't do anything about. I'm going to go to the store and get something for dinner tonight."

*****

Waldport, Oregon

Patricia set her glass of wine on the small table next to her chair on Scott's deck. She had been watching unusual activity a few miles out to sea. Scott had fallen asleep on the couch and she didn't want to wake him. Neither of them had slept the night before. She lifted a pair of binoculars and focused in on some boats and an airplane circling overhead. A Coast Guard cutter was circling in the water. Men on the deck were scurrying about. They were close enough in, the water couldn't have been that deep. She remembered fishing boats dropping crab nets about the same distance out. A few minutes passed and a helicopter joined the cutter and hovered overhead. She went in to wake Scott.

Scott removed a telescope from the hall closet and set it up on the deck. As he was focused on the scene another ship appeared on the horizon.

"What's that?" Patricia asked.

"It's a fishing trawler. I'm not sure what it's doing, it's not Coast Guard." He adjusted the telescope and read the name. "I know that ship. It's docked right beside mine in Coos Bay. *Sugar Time,*" he said. "The captain's name is Ginger Sugar."

"You're kidding," Patricia said, hitting him on the shoulder. "She sounds like a stripper."

"The captain is a he. Reddest hair I ever saw on anyone. He has a bright red beard. Looks like a Viking." He peered through the telescope. "They are going to use it to raise something from the ocean."

Patricia was watching through the binoculars. "You don't think it's one of those missiles?"

"Could be," Scott said. "I hope the hell they know what they are doing." Scott picked up his phone and called the Commander at the North Bend Coast Guard Station. "Hey, Paul, you've got some activity a couple clicks off my property. What's going on."

"Scott, where the hell you been?"

"I took a job in the big city for a few weeks. You want to tell me if I should be concerned?"

"Well, maybe," Lieutenant Commander Paul Phillips said.

Scott could almost hear him chuckling.

"I can hear you laughing. What's so funny?"

"One of our anti-sub spotters caught an anomaly on his mag. Probably nothing. We asked *Sugar Time* to pull it up. They were in the area."

"So you don't think it could be a missile?"

"Hadn't thought of it. Nice talking to you, Scott. I'll call the cutter and let them know to leave it be if it's a nuke."

"He doesn't think it's anything," Scott said.

"There is a lot of excitement over nothing, then," Patricia said, still watching the activity through the binoculars.

Scott put his eye to the telescope again. "Ginger, you stupid ass," he said.

"What?" Patricia asked.

"He's going to try and hook onto whatever it is with a grappling hook on his winch. I hope it's not a live round."

"I thought you said it was nothing."

"I said Paul didn't think it was anything."

As they watched, two men dressed in scuba gear dropped, feet first, into the water.

"They could have asked and I would have loaned them the underwater robot," Scott said.

The divers disappeared and in a few minutes one of them surfaced and made a circular motion with his hand. They started the winch and the trawler leaned to one side as the cable tightened.

"Whatever it is, it's heavy," Scott said. "That's about as much weight as that ship can handle."

"It looks pretty long," Patricia said.

"Jesus," Scott said as the nose of the object broke the surface. He could see the Chinese characters written in black on a white background on the side of what was obviously an unexploded missile. "Drop it," he shouted, as if they could hear him.

Scott turned to Patricia, feeling helpless. "I can't believe I'm watching this."

"Wait! Something's happening," Patricia said. Scott put his eye to the telescope again. "They're putting it back."

"They're leaving it here!" Patricia said incredulously. "That's practically in your back yard."

"Good thing I'm not planning on selling the house," Scott said.

Patricia gave him a confused look.

"A nuke in my back yard doesn't help property value," Scott said.

Cheyenne Mountain Complex

Against many of the generals' hopes, President Tindall entered the large conference room and took his seat at the head of the table. When Tindall was present the atmosphere in the room changed. Mellon knew it and so did the other generals. War with a politician questioning every action slowed the process. Most of the highest ranking members in the room already knew what they wanted to do and now they would have to explain their actions in detail.

Tindall leaned back in his chair and looked around the room. He honed in on Admiral Joan Dorsey, the only woman in the room with the rank of General or above. She had two stars on her shoulders and a splash of medals covering the left side of her uniform. He had only spoken to her once before, but found her to be levelheaded and a clear thinker. He could almost guess where the others would be, but wanted to hear her take on the situation.

"Joan, why don't you start us off; we all know why we are here."

Admiral Dorsey leaned into the microphone in front of her. "I would like to start off by saying I just learned an unexploded nuclear missile was found in the water off the coast of Oregon. This leaves no doubt that we were under a nuclear attack last night."

"Excuse me, Doris," the President interrupted. "You're sure it was a nuke?"

"Positive. We got a radiation signature. The missile was a JL-2 with a range of 3,500 nautical miles. It could have easily reached Washington DC, or any number of Eastern cities."

"Do we know what brought it down?" Tindall asked.

"A three-foot section of the nozzle was missing. The motor flamed out. The only reason it didn't explode is that it didn't reach a high enough altitude to arm. May I continue?"

"Sorry," Tindall said. He waved her on.

"In the event of a nuclear attack we have several options, the most severe is an attack in kind. The international courts would support a full and complete attack on China's mainland. We have five *Los Angeles* class fast attack submarines two thousand miles off the coast of China. They have more than enough power and range to hit every major population area in China. But I'm not recommending that…not unless they launch another attack against us." She paused and gauged the look on the faces of her peers.

"A second option would be to launch several hundred Tomahawk cruise missiles at the man-made island bases in the

South China Sea. It would let China know we mean business without causing any civilian casualties.

"A third option would be to launch Tomahawk missiles at their major cities starting with Beijing."

"If I may interrupt, Admiral," General Mellon leaned into his microphone. "A retaliatory strike with Tomahawk missiles is like bringing a water pistol to a gun fight. Unless we put some serious hurt on their people, they won't learn a lesson. They will see an attack like that as a weakness."

"Admiral Dorsey, do you have more?" President Tindall asked.

She glared at General Mellon. "I just think a nuclear missile strike is premature at this time."

"Why?" Tindall demanded. "The bastards were willing to use them on us."

"We don't have a navigation system in that part of the world. A surgical strike with ICBMs isn't possible since out satellite navigation system went down."

Tindall leaned into his microphone. "Come on Generals, I need you all to weigh in on this. Do you agree with her, General Mellon?"

Mellon cleared his throat and looked around the room before coming back to the President. "Mostly true, Mr. President. We can launch nuclear warheads, but they would have to be manually programmed, much like we did back in the Sixties. We don't have any manual coordinates for China."

"Why not?" Tindall demanded.

"Because, in the Sixties, China wasn't considered a threat. All the launch codes are for cities in Russia,"

"Sir, if I might interject something," Nendel said. "I'm no longer a part of the Navy, but if I'm not mistaken, a ballistic missile launched from one of our subs could be programmed accurately enough to destroy a heavily populated area such as Beijing. We're talking about a nuclear bomb, not a cruise missile. How accurate do we have to be? We wouldn't need more than one for them to get the message."

"And what message would that be?" Mellon asked.

"Back the fuck off," Admiral Dorsey said. The statement was out of character for her and Mellon wasn't sure whether it was meant for him or was an answer to his question.

Cramer had listened long enough. "Mr. President, China has thrown everything they have at us and not done a single bit of damage. Now would be a good time to approach them and strike a deal."

"Two of our senior citizens, a husband and his wife were killed last night when one of the missiles we shot down crashed into their house. He was a Viet Nam veteran and a decorated war hero. I doubt their children would agree no damage was done."

"Mr. President," General Mitchel spoke up. "Everyone seems to agree that China must pay for attacking us. Hell, they wiped out half of the Pacific Fleet. We can't let them get away with that, but dropping a nuclear weapon in the middle of Beijing is going to play havoc in China for years to come. I think I have another option that could satisfy everyone."

"Let's hear it," Tindall said.

"China has been expanding its reach by making military installations in the South China Sea. We could easily lob a nuclear warhead in the center of each of those islands, and at the same time send a hundred Tomahawks right down the PRC's throat in Beijing. We don't kill as many people, but we still make a statement loud and clear." Mitchel glanced around the room. He was expecting opposition.

"I'll go along with that," General Mellon said. "But only if they don't launch a second attack. If one of their nukes explodes on American soil, I go back to manually aiming the missiles and dropping as many as we can on their cities. We have to bring them to their knees."

Tindall said. "Can anyone tell me why they haven't launched a second attack?"

Nendel spoke up. "Mr. President, we were able to intercept a ULF message an hour ago. We believe China has had a problem getting their submarines in position to launch their IRBMs."

"English," Tindall said.

"Intermediate-range ballistic missiles," Nendel said. "They have to get within six hundred miles of our shore to hit Chicago. If they want to hit Washington DC or New York they need to be within two hundred miles. Of course they could take out Los Angeles, Seattle and San Francisco from pretty far out."

"So what are you saying?"

"I can't say for certain. For some reason they were not in position to launch an attack immediately after their first attempt. Maybe we scared them off when they weren't able to get any missiles past Paradox X."

"I have a theory on that," Admiral Dorsey said.

All eyes turned to her. "When we lost the ability to guide our missiles by satellite, China lost the same capability. An early version of their missiles had a celestial navigation system. They were able to triangulate off the stars. Of course the system only works at night."

"You think that's why they launched a night attack?" Tindall asked.

"And why the second attack won't come until after dark on the Pacific Coast."

"If you are correct, our citizens are in for another scary night," Tindall said. "Anyone else want to add to the discussion?"

"Sir," Nendel spoke up. "Relying on Paradox X to perform as well as it did last night is a monumental risk. We were lucky. We only have two platforms up. Our plan calls for two hundred. We only have one percent of our shield in place. We need to do everything in our power to prevent another attack."

"I'll take that as a push for a peaceful solution," Tindall said, "but right now I'm not betting on it." He waited a long minute. "If there is no further discussion, I'd like a plan on my desk with two options. One, an immediate response to the attack last night and two, what we do if they launch another attack."

Chapter 27

Oakland, California

David disconnected from his chief scientist, Charlene Wilson. He had been trying to get through to her at her home for hours, wanting the answer to a question that was bugging him. How long would it take the Paradox X batteries to fully recharge? How long before the Country could withstand another full-scale attack? It seemed everyone assumed a few hours of recharging would be enough time, but it was really a more complex problem. How low were the batteries to begin with and how much energy was required for each laser that was fired? What Charlene told him made him uneasy.

David hung up the phone for the fifth time. He had been trying to reach the Cheyenne Mountain Complex to let Cramer and Nendel know that Paradox X could not withstand another attack like the night before. The batteries would only be at 20 percent power. Finally, he gave up and got through to Scott.

Fay came back from shopping and David raised a finger to let her know he was on the phone.

"That's right," David said, "the information we've been using was calculated under the assumption the entire system was up and running. We only have one percent of it in place."

Scott muted the TV. He checked his watch. Nightfall would arrive in less than two hours. He was still looking at the TV when a picture of a submarine came on the screen. "Just a minute," he said to David.

"Turn on Fox News channel," he said. "I think there's been another submarine detected off the coast of Washington."

"Turn on Fox News," David said to Fay. "There's been

another submarine incident."

David and Scott were silent for a few minutes watching footage from one of the 117 Boeing P8A Anti-Submarine aircraft flying along the Pacific shoreline.

"It's a different one from the day before," Scott announced. "We need to call Nendel." Without saying it, both knew this meant another attack was no longer a probability, but a certainty. There were still submarines off the coast.

"I already tried to get through to the Cheyenne Mountain Complex," David said.

"I have Nendel's private number," Scott said. "It's the only way I've been able to get through."

"He isn't going to want to hear what I have to tell him," David said.

"Hang on the line," Scott said, "I'll see if we can make this a conference call."

David was about to explain how Scott could connect the three of them when the line went dead. In a few moments he heard Nendel on the line.

"Scott is that you?" he heard Nendel's voice.

"Yeah, David should also be on the line. We have some news that may change the calculus of the situation."

"Just a minute, I'm going to patch you into the speaker system."

After a moment they heard Nendel's voice. "Scott, you caught us in a meeting with the Joint Chiefs and President Tindall. I think we are all interested in what you have to say."

"I'm going to let David Stafford give you the latest information," Scott said.

David felt his throat tighten. He reached for what was left of a glass of ice tea and took a gulp. "Mr. President and the rest of you, I have some bad news. As of ten p.m., ninety minutes from now, the sun will be going down out here and Paradox X will have only twenty percent power."

"I think I know what that means," President Tindall said, "but would you expand on it a bit, so we are all on the same page."

"The Country cannot survive another attack like we had last night."

"But we can stop some of them," Nendel said, trying to get something positive out of the discussion.

"A few... maybe," David said. "Sir, we've never had this scenario in our test model. We assumed all the system would be in place."

"Scott and David, this is General Cramer. What is your best assumption?'

There was silence as David and Scott both considered the ramifications of their response. Individually, they came up with the same conclusion.

Scott spoke first. "David, correct me if you disagree. Twenty percent power will give us some limited ability, but the limited power will result in eighty percent fewer kills."

"Actually it's worse than that," David said. "The system uses power to locate and lock onto the targets. My guess is we're looking at fifteen percent of the kills, as you call it."

There was silence on the other end.

"This is General Mellon. Thank you for being so blunt. We have some work to do on this end."

"Are you still there?" David asked after it was obvious the connection to the Cheyenne Complex had been broken.

"Yeah," Scott said. "I'm feeling kind of helpless, right now."

"Me too," David said. "I'll call if we survive the night."

"Yeah," Scott said. "Tell Fay we're thinking of you guys. I wish you would have headed inland."

"We considered it," David said. "Prevailing winds and fallout, we decided to stay put."

David knew what Scott was saying. Scott and Patricia were away from any big city and had a much better chance of survival should Portland take a direct hit.

*****

Cheyenne Mountain Complex

"This doesn't change our options," Admiral Dorsey said.

"No, but it sure as hell changes the one we should pick," General Mellon said. "I go back to launching an attack against Beijing and not waiting for another attack on us."

"We no longer have a probability of an attack," Nendel said. "An attack is a certainty and it's also a certainty the Country will not survive it."

General Cramer and Mitchel were having a private conversation near one end of the conference table. The President cleared his throat. "General Cramer, do you have something to add to the discussion?"

"Sorry, sir," Cramer said. "In light of the latest information, General Mitchel and I think the original plan is the best, but we should launch it immediately and not wait for casualties from a second attack."

"He's right, sir," Admiral Dorsey said. "If we attack right away there is still a chance they will call off their attack. They don't know our system isn't fully functional."

"What if they do know?" Mellon questioned her.

"We don't have time for another debate," Tindall said. "I'm going with the original plan and am launching the attack immediately. As a backup, if we sustain an attack, that is if China does not call off their attack, then we will also send a nuclear missile into Beijing."

"And if they don't call it off then what?" Mellon asked.

Tindall pursed his lips. "God help us all, if that doesn't work."

Waldport, Oregon

"The president is on TV," Patricia said.

Scott couldn't help but to check his watch every few minutes. The sun was starting to set and in another thirty minutes it would be dark outside.

Patricia turned up the volume.

"...thirty minutes ago I authorized a nuclear attack against the Peoples Republic of China in retaliation for the attack they made against the United States nearly twenty hours ago. The decision was not made lightly. Today a second *Jin* class nuclear submarine was torpedoed off the coast of Washington State. This second incidence is proof China was considering another attack against the American people. Sadly, the citizens of the United States need to brace for another attack, which we believe could occur at any moment. Find your loved ones and hold them close. God bless you all, and God bless our Nation."

Patricia stared at the screen. She could see the tears streaming from President Tindall's eyes and she started to cry.

Scott wrapped his arms around her and held her close.

Chapter 28

Beijing, China

Deep in an underground bunker, Chairman Xi Wuhan watched the destruction of his man-made islands in the South China Sea. He had watched on a large screen with many of his generals and top advisors. They had expected a response, but what had caught them by surprise were the targets. As he watched the first island vaporize, he felt sadness for the men and women, soldiers, sailors and airmen, who occupied the newly established military bases. When the cloud had settled there was nothing left; not a single identifiable object. The small fleet was no longer there. The years of construction had all vanished. In place of the island was a deep hole in the ocean, steaming like the caldera of a giant underwater volcano.

On another screen the same scene seemed to play over again, but it was another of his man-made island military bases.

"Sir," one of his generals interrupted the chairman's muse. "Beijing is under attack."

"What is next?" the Chairman asked. He could barely contain his anger.

"Sir?"

"We launched a full scale attack against the United States last night. You said President Tindall would surrender, but not a single American city was hit with our warheads. I am demanding to know, what is next? Are they going to destroy our missiles again, and then start destroying our cities one by one!"

Chairman Wuhan stood up and grabbed the teapot from a tray in front of him. He tossed it the length of the room. It crashed against the giant monitor at the end of the room shattering the screen and sending up a shower of sparks. "You have completely underestimated the resolve of the United States. Call off the attack."

"Mr. Chairman," the head of the Peoples Liberation Army/Navy said, standing up, "I disagree. We need to see how this plays out?"

"Plays out? Is this a game? You have all failed your Country." He turned to several soldiers who were guarding the door. "Take them all into custody. I will deal with them later."

The soldiers chambered shells in their automatic weapons and pointed them at the members in the room. "All of them," Wuhan repeated to the armed soldier next to him. "Get Chang Yao." Chang Yao was one of his personal aides.

"Mr. Chairman," the young man said, squeezing by the generals who were being escorted from the room.

Wuhan looked at his aide. The man was barely in his twenties. "I have failed your generation. Get President Tindall on the phone."

"But sir, all communication with America has been cut off for weeks now."

"Get the Embassy in Paris," Wuhan said. "They will patch me through."

"Yes, sir."

It took ten minutes, but the connections were made and President Tindall answered.

"I have ordered all my submarines back to port. There is no longer a need for hostilities between our two countries," Wuhan said.

Tindall had to stop himself from letting out a sigh of relief over the phone. "I will do the same as soon as I verify your submarines are all leaving the waters off our coast," Tindall said, choking back tears of relief. He put his hand over the phone and waved the people from the room.

"Chairman Wuhan," Tindal said into the phone. "You did the right thing."

There was no response on the other end. After a few

minutes Tindall hung up. He looked at the bank of clocks on the wall; it was exactly ten o'clock in Washington, Oregon and California. He started to cry.

Oakland, California

David and Fay sat on the balcony in each other's arms looking at the night sky. It was curious how the city reacted to the news of an impending nuclear attack. No longer did it look like a blacked out void.

"Strange reaction to the end of the world," Fay whispered in David's ear.

"I am happy I'm with the person I love," he said to her. He looked up as a flash of light lit up the entire city.

Fay grabbed David and pulled him closer to her. The blast from the explosion knocked them to the floor.

Waldport, Oregon

"I don't want to stay out here and watch it happen," Patricia said.

Scott held up his finger. "I'm talking to Mom." He had finally caught up with her at his sister's house.

"I love you, Mom. Find someplace to hide. A basement, anyplace with some concrete between you and…"

"Scott, honey," his mother stopped him. "I have had a good life. Tell Patricia we love her."

Scott watched a streak of fire cross the sky. It seemed to go a long way inland, before he saw a flash of light. Seconds later he heard what sounded like thunder.

Patricia saw it, too. She grabbed Scott and pulled him

inside.

The phone went dead and Scott set it on the table.

"We'll get through this," Patricia said putting her head on his chest and holding him tightly.

"You know, they arrested Wilkes and charged him with the death of my father," Scott said. "After this ends, if we are still here, I hope he gets the death penalty."

"But he's committed treason, too," Patricia said. "If he's tried in Federal Court, the most he will get is life without parole."

"Then I want to see that he gets that. Do you want a drink?"

"I don't need one," she said softly. "Hold me until this is all over."

He was amazed at how well she was handling the uncertainty. He was also relieved. He was dealing with his own fear of impending doom.

Scott led her to the couch where they reclined in each other's arms. They fell asleep.

When the phone on the table buzzed, Scott woke with a terrible ache in his arm. It had been wrapped around Patricia all night. He slowly slipped it out from under her and made his way to the kitchen. It was still dark outside. He could see the moon hanging over the ocean. He picked up his phone and didn't recognize the number that was calling. Under any other circumstances he might have declined the call, but he answered.

"Scott, that was a hell of a night."

"David. You're all right?"

"Some war we fought," David said.

"You think it's over?"

"Hey, buddy. Everybody is celebrating. Where have you been?"

"The war is over?"

David's voice was being drowned out by the background noise.

"What's going on? It sounds like you are having a party."

"Hell yeah," David said. "We're all having a party."

Scott heard someone blow a horn over the phone. Patricia got up and came over.

"Turn on the TV," Scott said.

Patricia turned on to Fox News, the last channel they had been watching.

"… there hasn't been this much excitement since the end of World War II. We are at the White House waiting for President Tindall's helicopter to arrive…I think I see it…yes there it is Marine One, the President is about to return to the White House…"

"I've got to go," Scott said to David. "I'm glad you and Fay are okay."

"Are you hearing this?" Patricia said, fighting back tears.

Scott grabbed her and spun her around. "Marry me," he said. He kissed her before she could answer.

"Wow," Patricia said. "I wasn't expecting that."

"You're not ready yet," Scott said hesitantly.

"Yes, you fool. I've been ready ever since you asked me the last time, I just didn't realize it until…until things got put into perspective." She looked at him through blurry green eyes. "I love you, Scott Tanner."

"Let's do it soon," Scott said.

Scott's phone started buzzing again. "Forget it," Scott said.

It continued to buzz and Patricia caught it before it fell to the floor. She handed it to him, "It's David."

Scott took it. "Honestly, your call woke up Patricia and me and we hadn't heard the news. What happened?"

"Fay and I have decided to get married."

Scott was silent. "Uh, congratulations."

"You don't sound very happy for me."

"You keep surprising me."

"I want you to be my best man."

"I just asked Patricia again and she said yes. We want to do it soon. I want you to be my best man."

"A double wedding. I like that."

"Wait, I didn't say anything about…"

"What was that all about?" Patricia asked.

"He hung up on me. He wants a double wedding."

"David and Fay?"

"I didn't agree," Scott said looking at her.

"I like it," Patricia said, "as long as they are not willing to wait."

Chapter 28

Moscow, Russia

Russian President Mordashov took the message from one of his aides and read it. It was lacking in details. "Find General Timchenko and tell him to come to my office."

General Timchenko had been on the job as Commander of the Joint Russian Armed Forces for six weeks. He was young and ambitious, not to mention the son of a billionaire oligarch and one of Mordashov's greatest supporters. He had a unique way of looking at war. For him it was not only about power, but also about the accumulation of wealth. More precisely power through wealth.

"Oleg," Mordashov said, using the young man's given name. He grabbed General Timchenko and hugged him in a very unprofessional manner. "I can do that, because I have known you since you were in diapers and your father and I have been good friends from our youth."

General Oleg Timchenko, looking a little embarrassed, straightened his uniform and glanced at the others in the room. "I think he is going to ask a favor of me, no?"

The Cabinet members standing by a large wooden conference table laughed. They knew how close the President and Timchenko were, otherwise the young general would not be in power.

"Russia has taken a bit of a beating, from the Chinese-American, war. We have lost several ships in the battle defending the failed Chinese attack on America. China is weakened as a result of poor planning and many military mistakes. China owes us for standing beside her. Find out what they need and sell it to them at an inflated price."

"Mr. President, I already know what they want."

"And is it something we have?"

"It is something we have many of. We were smart not to upgrade our ICBMs when digital and GPS technology came along. Our missiles have the capability of attacking with great accuracy and they do not rely on satellites or celestial navigation. China needs our missiles if she is to defend herself from America."

"And Russia?" Mordashov asked.

"They are our missiles, programmed by our people. We can make certain they do not have the capability of being used against us."

"Very well. See what you can do."

Chapter 29

June, nine months later

David Stafford and Fay Connor were married in a lavish double wedding with Scott Tanner and Patricia Westland. David Stafford and Fay are now living in San Diego. Today was the opening of a new headquarters building dedicated to the men and women working for Stafford-Tanner Enterprise. He watched as Fay cut the tape and opened the tall glass doors and welcomed the employees into the tall gleaming building that appeared to be walled with glass. He wished Scott could be there for the dedication, but he knew the importance of the find his partner had made off the Oregon Coast.

"Tomorrow we leave for Europe on our honeymoon," David announced to the crowd raising Fay's hand. He stood on his toes and kissed her to the excitement and cheering of those in attendance.

Scott Tanner watched the water and seaweed drip from the barnacle encrusted piece of metal his first mate was bringing up from the deep. He was certain it was part of a deck gun from a Japanese submarine thought to have been sunk off the Oregon Coast shortly after the start of World War II.

He couldn't wait to let his wife know he had finally found the submarine he had been searching for over the past year. If he was correct, his discovery would change the writing of World War II history in the waters off the Pacific Northwest.

Patricia Westland-Tanner gave up reporting the news and was now writing a Romantic Suspense novel. She worked from her office on the top floor of the house on the Oregon Coast Scott had built for them.

Richard Nendel returned to his job as Director of the NSA. He has yet to meet the new President.

Geoffrey Tindall, with his hands wrapped around the handle of a shovel, lifted the first scoop of earth at the site of the Geoffrey Tindall Presidential Library. His full time job was now focused on putting his term in office in the most positive light. He had ended a war, but that would not make him the President of Peace he had hoped would be his legacy.

China, under a new trade agreement with the United States was rapidly deploying high altitude communication platforms so it could tap into the world communication network.

Chairman Wuhan continued to lead the country with new PRC Army/Navy leadership.

East of Beijing, missile sites were being prepared for the arrival of a hundred Soviet-era ICBMs targeted at the major cities in the United States. In addition, it was upgrading its nuclear arsenal to include a global positioning system based on HAP technology. China's moon station had been deemed too expensive and the project had been abandoned.

North Star Industries completed the Paradox X missile defense system. The company was now owned by a giant Defense Industry contractor. Only the new president of North Star and a few high government officials knew what they were working on. The employees were still subjected to daily searches as they entered and left the property.

Gilbert Thompson was still the Chief Engineer.

Charlene Wilson retired from North Star and opened a business developing and building micro-robotic surgical equipment.

Russian President Mordashov was elected in another landslide victory. He was rumored to be the richest man in the world, while the crumbling infrastructure of the country continued to suffer and his people struggled to find enough food for their children.

General Cramer, ready for his commencement address, looked out over the sea of young faces, the new protectors of the

Nation. Graduation at the Air Force Academy was two weeks late this due to interruptions from the war. He knew they would be faced with many challenges, but a war in space would not be one of them, at least not in the foreseeable future.

About the Author

Larry LaVoie is the author of more than twenty novels, most of them thrillers set in the Pacific Northwest. He lives with his wife, Anna, in a small coastal town in Oregon.
Check out these thrillers and others by Larry LaVoie:
www.amazon.com/Larry-LaVoie/e/B004KECU14

Caldera, The Yellowstone Brief, Leap of Faith, Lesser of Two Evils, Hot Ashes Cold Granite, Army of the White Horse, Destination Uncertain, The Lightstream Conspiracy, The Kessler Syndrome, Spontaneous Combustion, Fear not Thine Image, Crater, Sub Zero, Paradox, Ghost Flight, Code of Silence, Code of Terror, Code Zero, Code of Deception, Threads of The Shroud.

Made in the USA
Columbia, SC
22 May 2022

60611771R00154